L.O.S.T.

Debbie Tanner Federici was born and raised in rural southeastern Arizona. She and her husband now live with their three sons in a large, metropolitan Sanctuary called Phoenix.

Susan Vaught is a writer and a psychologist in private practice. She lives with her son and daughter in Westmoreland, a small Sanctuary in present-day Tennessee.

L.O.S.T.

DEBBIE FEDERICI
SUSAN VAUGHT

Llewellyn Publications
St. Paul, Minnesota

FIRST EDITION
First Printing, 2004

Book editing and design by Megan Atwood and Andrew Karre
Cover art (texture) © PhotoDisc, Inc.
Cover design by Ellen Dahl

Library of Congress Cataloging-in-Publication Data
Federici, Debbie Tanner, 1965-
    L.O.S.T. / Debbie Tanner Federici & Susan Vaught.— 1st ed.
        p. cm.
    Summary: Pulled from an ordinary life the summer before his senior year in high school, Bren is amazed to learn that the girl who carried him through space and time is the queen of all witches, who believes that he is destined to defeat a terrible evil.
        ISBN: 0-7387-0561-6
    [1. Magic—Fiction. 2. Witches—Fiction. 3. Space and time—Fiction.] I. Title: Live Oak Springs Township. II. Vaught, Susan, 1965- III. Title.

Llewellyn Worldwide does not participate in, endorse, or have any authority or responsibility concerning private business transactions between our authors and the public.

All mail addressed to the author is forwarded but the publisher cannot, unless specifically instructed by the author, give out an address or phone number.

Any Internet references contained in this work are current at publication time, but the publisher cannot guarantee that a specific location will continue to be maintained. Please refer to the publisher's website for links to authors' websites and other sources.

Llewellyn Publications
A Division of Llewellyn Worldwide, Ltd.
P.O. Box 64383, Dept. 0-7387-0561-6
St. Paul, MN 55164-0383, U.S.A.
www.llewellyn.com

Printed in the United States of America

Acknowledgments

Thanks to my mom and dad, Robert and Karen Tanner, for always believing in me; my husband Frank for putting up with me locking myself away for hours on end to write; and my three sons, Tony, Kyle, and Matthew, for being the inspiration for Bren. Thanks to Wendy Eversen HP for help with Asta; Susan for giving Bren his match in Jazz; and most of all, thank you to Jan Gentner for inviting me to San Diego, which started this wild journey to L.O.S.T.

—Debbie

Thanks to my son JB for keeping my love of fantasy alive; my daughter Gynni and my extra son Brandon for teaching this old Catholic a lot about Wicca; and Gisele for always cheering me along. Thanks to my mother for being open-minded; and most of all, thanks to Debbie, who dared me to write a chapter 2 to equal her chapter 1.

—Susan

From both of us, thank you to Sheri Gilbert for being a stalwart critique partner under pressure. Thank you to Megan Atwood for taking a chance on L.O.S.T. and for being so enthusiastic; and Andrew Karre for dreams and all those boyish things.

—Debbie & Susan

Tho Shadowe darkness bynde them,
He shall come to fynde hys power,
Ande yf hys soule be goode,
Ande yf she trayne hym true,
Ande yf theyr hearts be joyned,
Bye hys sworde the Path be freed.

    —Passage MCLXXX
     Wytches Book of Tyme

chapter one

It all happened because I had to pee.

I'm not kidding, and I'm not talking just any old call of nature. I'm talking leg-and-eye-crossing, I'm-going-to-piss-my-shorts pain.

And there I was, driving on Interstate 8, that stretch of freeway between Yuma and San Diego. You know, that section where the signs tell you to turn off your air conditioning because your car will overheat, and it's so long it feels like it'll never end, and there's nowhere for a guy to pull to the side of the road and find a bush.

I was dying.

My mom's purple truck rattled as I drove, making everything worse. It was the first day of June, less than three months before I was supposed to start my senior year at Yuma High. Mom and Dad had flown off to the East Coast with my kid brother Todd, and I was headed to San Diego to stay a week with my best friend, who had just moved away from Yuma. His name's Brandon, and mine's Brenden, so we used to get a lot of mileage out of our names being so close. Friends just call me Bren.

It was amazing that Mom had convinced Dad to let me drive out to San Diego on my own. Dad said he thought I was too impulsive and irresponsible.

"Impulsive and irresponsible." Dad's total opinion of me. "Brenden, you're too impulsive. Brenden, do you always have to be so irresponsible?"

Now Mom, she was great. A little nuts about grammar and not using foul language in front of people, especially girls—but overall, great. She had insisted I should be able to take this trip—told Dad I had to grow up some time, and that he had to let me. She even let me take off without my ADHD meds.

Stupid pills. They made me feel so blah, but I guess they did help me concentrate in school. Well, enough to get by, anyway. School, books, homework . . . not my strong points. I never did well in class. Always one assignment behind, a paper lost, a book I couldn't find—it was hard to keep it all in my head.

Now, I could concentrate on things that interested me a lot. In fact, I could concentrate too much on them sometimes.

"Get your head out of that video game."

"Didn't you notice the trash needed to be taken out, or were you too busy practicing your batting stance?"

That was Dad.

"Leave him alone. You know his ADHD makes him have a one-track mind."

That was Mom. Usually trying to get Dad off my case, which was like scrubbing tar off chrome hubcaps in one-hundred-degree temperatures. And not getting burned in the process.

Dad always said Mom was too "New Age." Mom always said there was a lot in the world my dad didn't under-stand—or wouldn't let himself see. Like my trip, and why I needed to try something on my own, for once. To show myself I could handle it, no matter what Mr. Straight-A Student, History-Professor Dad thought.

"If you don't start to apply yourself, Brenden, you'll always be average. Just plain *average*. Sports won't last for-ever."

Whatever.

I never could please him. Even when I was the varsity baseball team's MVP my junior year—highest batting aver-age of anyone in the past decade—Dad kept harping on how I struck out in the final game of the season.

"You didn't use your head," he said. "Think. Don't let your team down like that again."

"Okay, enough," I muttered to myself. Driving one-handed, I pulled at a loose thread on my T-shirt and sighed. I had to get Dad out of my head and enjoy my vacation away from him.

A whole week.

I couldn't wait to head to the beach with Brandon to check out all the babes in neon orange thongs.

But first I had to take a piss.

Finally, an exit came up with one of those restroom signs, so I turned off the freeway and headed south. Giant trees lined the road, and I was tempted to pull over and hop the fence and just go, but there were homes around and cars whizzing by, and I figured it wouldn't be much farther. Plus, there was this carload of girls behind me, so I was kind of embarrassed to stop.

I swear I had to drive another five miles before I finally made it to a little country convenience store. One of those buildings in the shape of an A. The truck skidded into the parking lot a little too fast, and I applied the brakes, hard. My mom's sunglasses tumbled off the dashboard to my feet, and I stared at them.

Strange.

Why hadn't I noticed them before? Mom never went anywhere without her shades. She'd lay an egg when she realized I took off with them.

Dust swirled around the truck as I hopped out. I rushed into the country store, pushed aside the basket of fruit on the counter. There was a nameplate next to the basket that said "Jasmina."

"Listen, uh, Jazz," I said to the girl. "Where's the restroom?"

"Jasmina," she snapped. She stared at me for a moment, looked me over as if she was checking me out, then pointed up a hill. "The only restroom is in the restaurant," she added in a strange accent.

No kidding. Up a damn hill. Good thing I was too much of a gentleman to let it go right there in that store.

The girl's yellow-brown eyes glittered like she was holding back a laugh. I felt sure she knew I was suffering.

"Thanks," I managed to say before I bolted.

I jogged up the hill, the best a guy can do when dying to go to the bathroom. About a mile of concrete steps led to that restaurant, and I damn near tripped on my way up, which showed it was a good thing I didn't run hurdles in track.

And then, after I tore inside the restaurant and reached the bathroom, the friggin' door was locked. *Locked!* I was going to explode.

I raised my hand to pound on the wood, but the door opened. A weird guy came out. He was a real freak, with straggled blond hair, grungy clothes, and a stubbly face. His odor about knocked me over—alcohol and a woody, perfumy smell. And his eyes—a piercing blue. He pinned me with that electric gaze and grabbed my hand. Before I could even yell at him to get his paws off me, he said in a husky, rumbly voice, "In the cellar. You will find the door in the cellar. Remember that, brother, or you will be sorry."

Chills rolled over me and goose bumps popped out all over my body. The guy weirded me out with his eerie tone and freaky blue eyes. Hell, I was too far gone as it was—I almost wet my pants.

He let go of my hand, turned, and vanished out the door.

And I mean vanished. The guy disappeared. Or at least I thought he did.

For a moment I stood there, blinking, and then I realized the guy had left something in my hand. I couldn't get into the bathroom and lock the door fast enough, so I shoved the thing into my pocket and got down to business.

I thought I'd piss forever. What a relief. Even in a grungy bathroom with toilet paper strewn all over the place, smelling of urine and that gross public-restroom disinfectant. I washed my hands and used the powder soap from the dispenser, but there were no towels and I had to wipe my hands on my jeans. Dad wouldn't have approved. Just like he wouldn't have approved of me stopping at a deserted-looking exit. Dad probably would have gone on to a place he had stopped before, even if it meant a bladder meltdown.

I shook my head, wishing I could get my father out of my brain. It was like he went everywhere with me, watching everything I did and passing judgment on it.

Never in my favor.

I hurried out of the bathroom and trotted into the restaurant, hoping the weirdo wasn't around.

The restaurant was one of those small-town joints with red plastic tumblers and paper mats, and it looked like it had been someone's house at one time. I considered eating there, but decided to grab some fast food once I got back on the freeway. It wasn't that far to San Diego and civilization.

As I headed out the door, I thought about the girl in the store. She had sounded like she was from   or maybe even the real England. She was a b.
Goth. Not total Goth with layers of bag
instead, she had on a snug, black sleevele

black painted nails, dark lips, and long, shiny black hair. Her eyes were like an ancient Egyptian's, only they were pale brown—goldish, really, like a cat's. I couldn't see much of her body because it was hidden behind the checkout counter, but I'd bet she'd look terrific on the beach in San Diego.

Now that I wasn't dying to find a bathroom, I noticed everything around me was kind of interesting. Giant cottonwoods, oaks, and pines crowded around the store, and those bright yellow California poppies were scattered all over the place. Sprinklers chugged on the lawns, making the ch-ch-ch-ch-ch sound that always made it feel even more like summer. I smelled fresh-cut grass and a scent like my mom's rose garden.

All in all, it seemed pretty boring. Except for the bathroom freak. What the hell was he talking about—"the door's in the cellar"? He must have thought I was someone else. That or the guy was wasted. It didn't matter anyway, because I was out of there.

And then I remembered he had put something in my hand. What if it was weed or something? I could get busted for possession, and I'd be in deep shit. I dug into my pocket, pulled the thing out and stopped on the steps to take a look. It was a small figurine, about three inches long and an inch thick. The statue was heavy and solid, and appeared to be carved out of wood. I thought it might be a relic of one of those ancient Aztec gods—it had a headdress, a scepter, and a vicious sneer on its ugly face.

And for a second I swore it wriggled on my palm.

No, of course not. My imagination was running on overdrive.

A creepy feeling skittered over me, like spiders crawling over my skin. I wanted to pitch the thing as far as possible. I leaned back, my arm cocked, pretending I was throwing a baseball from right field to home plate for the last out of the game.

But somehow I couldn't. I just couldn't make myself get rid of it. It sort of stuck in my hand. Like it belonged there. I relaxed my stance and looked at the figurine again, then shoved it into my pocket and hurried down the stairs.

When I reached the grocery store, I stopped dead in my tracks. The parking lot was empty. As in, no cars anywhere.

My mom's truck was gone.

chapter two

The boy was pleasing, if you like that "desperate" look.

Big muscles, golden-brown hair grazing his neck, a day's dark stubble, eyes the color of polished oak, bright and showing a certain . . . *childlike* urgency. He was pleasing, in a rugged sort of way.

Too bad I might have to kill him.

I stretched my fingers and used a cleaning spell to blast away the crumbs and fingerprints the boy had left on the fruit basket. He was messy. Perhaps too messy to save my people.

I sighed.

If Rol, my closest companion, had been there, he would have told me not to be so quick to judge. Rol would have told me the boy had great promise.

9

Well, of course he did. So did everyone born with witching blood, whether they knew it or not. If only we could have recovered all those families forced into hiding by centuries of persecution, our ranks would have been strong indeed.

I studied the "apples" on the counter and couldn't help wondering what would have happened if the boy had seen what those apples really were. It had been my experience that humans had no stomach for spell ingredients. Even those humans with hidden magical blood and talent, nearing the point of conversion to witches. A little training, some belief in their abilities—the conversion was quite easy once it began. Nothing spectacular, and yet miraculous and beautiful, like the blooming of day lilies.

Except when the bloom was putrid, as was the case with Father's former trainee.

"Hurry up," I snapped at Alderon when he walked into the store. The new boy was still up the hill in the bathroom. Brenden, I think his name was. Or Brandon. Or Bren. I saw all three names in his thoughts, and each of them pleased me more than Alderon. "You wanted out, so here's your chance. Take his truck so he can't escape, and go."

Alderon brushed stringy blond hair from his face and glared at me with those eyes. Those hideous neon eyes.

I never trusted men with blue eyes, not after the disaster my father left us when he died. My father's blue eyes had been so good at convincing, at calming. All his promises of how things would be fine, how I'd see him again . . . But enough of that.

Alderon's eyes were nothing like Father's sky-blue windows to his heart. Alderon's were the color of bruises touched with sharp black fire. Seeing that cur leave the Path . . . well, no matter that his magic was so strong that Father had been certain he was the Shadowalker, the one true hero who might save our people from destruction. I believed he betrayed us all.

The blue-eyed piece of scruff in front of me was another one of Father's messes, and I was finally cleaning him up. If I never had to see Alderon's hateful face again, I would count myself blessed. And believe me, blessings were hard to come by in Live Oak Springs Township, at least so far. I had hopes for L.O.S.T. and its future, but they were just that. Hopes.

Alderon interrupted my musings with a hacking cough. I glowered at him, and he grinned, showing his yellowed teeth.

"Without me, you have nothing," he said. "You're only sixteen, Jasmina. How do you expect to save your people from the Shadowmaster with no one to help you?"

"Don't make me forget my own vows." I gripped the cash register with both hands and thought about throwing it at him. It wasn't that heavy, not for me, and what a splendid dent it would have made in Alderon's square head. "I'm preparing to connect L.O.S.T. to the Path. Leave now, or never."

Alderon's mouth became a thin line. His eyes radiated disgust as he spun on his heel and stomped out of the store, the rush of air behind him smelling of potato wine and incense. The man was addled. He spent more time stalking food and spirits than preparing to battle the evil we were facing.

But did Alderon truly have the power to leave the Path? Even at the Path's weakest moment, when I altered the energy it was made of to connect L.O.S.T? Each time Alderon had tried to leave before, he had failed because of the Shadowmaster's wicked spells.

Sweet Goddess, don't let him fail again.

Perhaps the new boy would do better, if he were willing. But willing had never been the issue, not since Nire, the Shadowmaster, had invaded our witches' Sanctuaries. Once I connected L.O.S.T. and took the boy onto the Path, he would have no choice but to stay. Either he would gain the skills necessary to defeat Nire's magic and move between Sanctuaries, or he would be trapped forever in the first Sanctuary we visited.

Rol would not approve of my trickery, of my bringing this boy into our battle without giving him free choice. Of that much, I was certain. But I had nothing left to save my people aside from my tricks. Rol would have to forgive me.

Outside, the boy's truck started. Alderon put the machine in gear and drove away, and if my sensitive ears didn't deceive me, he was cackling like a madman.

May the fates bless the nonwitching world, having to deal with the likes of him.

I thought about the new boy with his polished-oak eyes and his gentle smile, and my gaze dropped to my fingers. Black tint concealed the telltale golden sheen of my nails, but it couldn't coat the sudden golden ache in my heart.

What was I about to do?

"What you have to do," whispered my father's voice, from beyond the Shadows.

"What you must do," insisted all the witches, from all the Sanctuaries.

And that intuition from deep in my gut said Bren was the one who would free the Path from Nire. "If his soul is good. If I train him true." Just like the prophecy foretold.

I covered my face with my cold, cold fingers. Did Father think the same of Alderon? Did he really believe that over-sized oaf was capable of finding Nire and ending the Shadowmaster's hold on the lives and safety of all witches? Was I making the same mistakes Father had made?

Mother's favorite refrain snaked through my thoughts. "Weakness springs from two sources, Jasmina. The mind and the blood. Thanks to your father, you have a liberal amount of both to overcome."

And indeed, I did.

Just the thought of Mother and her constant disapproval—of me, of Father, of everything not clean and perfect—made me shiver. My stomach twisted with guilt. Over Mother's capture. Over Father's death. Over all the other witches who had not survived Nire's attacks.

"Oh, man!"

The new boy's shout brought me to attention.

Outside, he was turning in circles, waving his muscular arms. "My mom's truck!" he yelled. "Where the hell is Mom's truck? I am so dead."

Once more, my heart ached. If I opened the shop door—if I told him to flee before I connected L.O.S.T. to the Path—

this Bren, for that was his name as I saw it in his thoughts, could return to his home. He would be years discovering his witchness—if he ever found it. His life would go on as it should, and he might never know the horrors of the Path.

Goddess, save me. I have to let him go.

Without another moment's hesitation, I hurried to the shop entrance. The boy stopped running and sat heavily on the ground. His longish hair clung to his forehead, hanging close to those fierce, hard eyes. He doubled his fists and looked like he wanted to punch something. In that moment, he seemed even more powerful and pleasing than he had the moment I first saw him. Those hands—so large, so strong . . .

Perfect for swordwork.

And his legs. I felt sure they were muscular beneath his jeans, and his feet more nimble than they first seemed.

Perfect for walking the Path beside me.

"He shall come to find his power . . ." The prophecy from the Witches' Book of Tyme.

It had to be true, or we would all die soon. The Shadow-master would see to that.

I raised my hands and closed my eyes, focusing on the energy around me, before I could change my mind again. A picture of Live Oak Springs Township, the Sanctuary I had created on the boundary between the witching and non-witching worlds, rose in my mind. I imagined L.O.S.T. bathed in bright yellow hues, a bubble floating safely in space, gradually drifting toward the dark ribbon of the Path.

So much preparation. So much energy. No new Sanctuary had been created in the four years since my father's death, because no one besides me had the strength or knowledge to do it. And I wasn't sure I could pull it off. Still, I persevered, practicing, pouring my energy and emotion into building the town, and then hooking it to the Path, to the bridge of energy my father had created.

In my mind, the bubble floated ever closer to the ribbon.

The picture was simple enough, but in truth, very complicated. My father had built a path through time, an energy road, tying together places that had been friendly to witches. He had intended to continue developing it, making it longer and more stable. But, of course, he was killed before he could complete this miracle.

The bubble in my thoughts settled against the ribbon.

A loud snap startled me, and I opened my eyes. The sky had returned to glitter-gold and blue. I had done it. I had successfully connected L.O.S.T. to the Path!

And now I had precious little time. Once in a connected safehaven, the boy and I were on the Path—and L.O.S.T. was now the newest Sanctuary. The Path's energy was still adjusting to L.O.S.T.'s presence, so Nire's interfering spells were weak enough that Bren might successfully travel with me, at least to Shallym. After that, whether he developed the strength to walk the Path beside me, only the fates could decide.

Outside, the boy eased to his feet, obviously surprised by the softer skies now visible even to him. He knew something had changed. He knew something in his world had gone horribly astray. Any moment, he would realize why.

And then he turned and saw me.

His brown eyes narrowed.

I covered my mouth and shivered. The illusions I had cast fell away, and the store reverted to its real appearance, with its real contents. For a moment, for the briefest of moments, Bren seemed to tower above the store. I couldn't tear my gaze from him, or even move my feet to step away.

By the old prophecies . . .

Perhaps this Bren would be our savior after all.

chapter three

My keys—they were gone, and all I had was that figurine in my pocket. Did I leave the keys in the truck? What a stupid, lame-ass thing to do.

Or maybe it was that Goth girl—the one who didn't like it when I called her Jazz. She looked guilty. Maybe she picked my pocket when I was in the store.

"Hey, you!" I yelled at the girl. "Where's my truck?"

The girl dropped her hand from her mouth and stared at me with those witchy gold-brown eyes, as if she was waiting for something. I looked behind her—but the convenience market I'd entered just a few minutes before was gone. A blast of ice-cold air shot through me.

I'd been afraid before, lots of times. But not like this.

What the hell was going on?

The convenience store had turned into something like an enormous roadside market. It was filled with rows of strange-looking fabrics, plants, candles, and things I had no clue as to what they might be. I wasn't even sure I wanted to know. Some of that stuff . . . it looked dangerous. And the smells! So strong, like the onions, garlic, and herbs that my mom cooked with, and the sandalwood incense she burned all the time.

And the sky—it glittered. Like gold dust scattered across a shimmering blue wave. Way too poetic-sounding for me, but that's the only way I could think to describe it. Well, it did also kind of look like that glitter gel toothpaste I used as a kid.

My mouth went dry and I swallowed past the baseball-sized lump in my throat. I turned back to the girl, who seemed as cool and calm as a mannequin. Hell, she would have made a great storefront dummy, as rigid as she stood. Her skin was pale and, well, flawless. Not a strand of hair was out of place, and not a speck of lint or dirt was on her black clothing.

Respond, don't react. Mom's endless preaching echoed in my head. *Think it through.*

Dad's voice came right after that. *You're so impulsive. So irresponsible. Now you've lost your mother's truck and got yourself tangled up with some building-swapping town.*

I clenched and unclenched my fists. Took a deep breath. And strode toward the girl. She stood her ground and raised her chin, as if she might be a queen looking down on some peon.

"Where am I?" I asked through gritted teeth.

"Lost," she replied, her voice soft but clear.

"Do I look stupid? I know I'm lost. Now *where* am I?"

"L-O-S-T." She spelled it out this time, then turned and started toward the building behind her. "It stands for Live Oak Springs Township. And we need to hurry, or you'll be in L.O.S.T. forever."

I reached out, grabbed her upper arm, and pulled her to me. She glanced at my hand and back to my face, and by the look in those wicked eyes, I had the feeling she could easily shove a knife through my heart without a second thought. But for some strange reason, I didn't want to let go, no matter that the girl's weird eyes were spitting fire—a golden sort of fire, a lot like the glitter in the sky.

"Let me go," she demanded, her tone hard. Nothing soft about her now.

I dropped my hand. "I'm not going anywhere until you tell me what's going on."

The girl lifted her chin. "You have no choice, Bren. You have been chosen."

"What do you mean I haven't got a choice? Chosen to do what?" Anger flowed through me in a hot wave. Then it dawned on me that she called me Bren, and I knew I hadn't told her my name. "Wait a minute. How do you know who I am? Who are you?"

"As you well know, my name is Jasmina." She whirled around, and before I had a chance to catch her, she vanished into the spooky shop.

"Wait! Come back." I ran inside, and the first thing I saw was the fruit basket—only all the apples were gone.

Fingers. There were fingers in that basket. Neatly stacked, but definitely fingers.

I blinked and shook my head. Imagining things. I had to be—or this was some big gag. Tearing my eyes away from the shriveled-up thumbs and pinkies, I took off in the direction the girl had disappeared, dodging crates stuffed with . . . dried tarantulas? Toadstools? A foot?

Oh, man.

As I chased after her, I noticed that everything in the shop was arranged neat and orderly. Even the dead spiders were lined up in perfect rows.

"Stop fooling around," I shouted. "I need my truck, and I need to get to San Diego. My friend's waiting for me, and my dad will kill me if I don't find the truck and get my ass—er, butt—out of here." My mom's constant harping about my language rang in my ears even as I dodged something black dangling from the ceiling. I almost fell as my foot slipped on the spotless floor. "Come on, Jazz—Jasmina—whoever you are."

Over stacks of colored cloths, I glimpsed her standing in front of a shimmery wall. She ran one finger down it—and a hole the size of a door appeared in front of her.

"Dammit!" I rounded wooden barrels brimming with grain and saw her dodge through the hole. I charged after her—

Into almost total darkness—a darkness filled with gross smells and screeching noises. The only light filtered in behind me, but as I turned to go back, I saw Jazz run her hand up the hole, and everything went black. It was like she had sealed the entrance shut with her fingers.

I got so dizzy I nearly threw up, and then I felt a hand tug on my arm.

"This way."

Where was she?

Where was I?

I couldn't see a thing. I tried to turn around, but when I looked over my shoulder, everything was dark behind me. And the ground I was standing on seemed to be moving.

"Don't linger." Jazz's voice floated over me like a ghost whisper. "There are things here you don't wish to see."

Cold air chilled my skin, and the darkness smelled of mold and sour dirt. My stomach clenched and it was all I could do to keep from freaking out. Something was . . . bad . . . here. Awful, and dead, and cruel, like the worst evil imaginable.

My knees wobbled because of the sensation of wrongness, and because of the moving ground, but I took a step. And another. It felt like walking on an escalator backward and running away from something horrible, all at once.

Puking was still definitely an option.

"What's going on?" I yelled, trying to keep my balance.

"Hurry! You must follow me."

"I must follow. Yeah." But before I could move, the need to puke overwhelmed me, and I tossed what was left of my breakfast. The wet feel of it on my shirt and the acid taste and smell almost made me sick again.

Jazz tugged at my arm as I swayed and reached for anything to hold me up with my free hand. There was nothing around me but air and the heavy, wrong blackness. Blackness that seemed to move, here and there, just like the floor.

Batting cage, I told myself. Maybe this was like the batting cage. I'd do better with my eyes shut. Just listen for the pitches. Squeezing my eyes closed, I kept walking, allowing Jazz to drag me along. Faster and faster. After a minute, I was almost running. And then I *was* running.

Jazz let go of my arm, and a second later, light hit my eyelids. When I opened them, I could see a doorway. Jazz was heading through it. I ran over that stupid moving floor, through the door, straight into the light.

"You're not getting away." I held my hand up to block the glare as I chased her. And slammed into something hard. Solid.

I stumbled sideways and landed on my ass—and stared up at the most gigantic man I had ever seen. The guy had no shirt on, just a pair of leather pants and boots, and his skin shone like polished ebony. He had awesome muscles. Was he ever buff.

"Who— I mean what—" I stammered. *"Damn.* Who are you?"

Before I knew what was happening, the giant grabbed my wrist and yanked me to my feet. He stepped back, folded his arms, and studied me with his jet-black eyes, like I was a piece of sports equipment he was looking to buy. My puke-soaked shirt felt cold against my chest and the faint stink of it kept me on the edge of sick.

Behind the giant, in the near distance, was a medieval village, like something out of a fantasy movie. Old buildings crammed the street, people rushed around and gabbed with each other, and a horse-drawn cart rattled over the cobblestones. And the smells—you'd think the air would have smelled clean since there didn't seem to be any cars around. But it stunk like manure and rotting fish guts. And something else. Salt. Brine.

Was I near the ocean? But San Diego was still a good hour away. My head swam, and I felt like I'd entered the Twilight Zone or something.

"This pup, is he your choice?" the man asked in an unbelievably deep voice, snatching my attention back to him.

"Yes, Rol, this is the one." Jazz appeared out of nowhere and stood beside me. She had said "the one" as if she was talking about Elvis or the president.

I glared at her. "What the—"

"Did you take him by force?" The giant narrowed his eyes at Jazz.

She looked away from him.

The man she called Rol sighed. Before I could say anything, he grabbed my upper arm and squeezed it half off my body.

"Hey!" I smacked at his hand.

Rol grunted. "For one so young, he is hardy."

He turned me loose, and I rubbed my bruised bicep. "Yeah, well, I play baseball."

Rol and Jazz ignored what I said.

"Left or right-handed?" Jazz asked.

I glared at her. "Left, but I'm a switch-hitter—"

"He'll need a scabbard for his right side," Jazz interrupted. "Do you think his own clothes will do?"

"His tunic—poor workmanship. And the smell, quite foul." Rol grabbed the neck of my T-shirt with both hands and ripped it clean off me.

"What do you think you're doing?" I pushed away from the giant. My whole body started shaking, I was so pissed. "That was my favorite T-shirt. Haven't you ever heard of a washing machine?"

Rol turned to Jazz and continued talking as if I wasn't even there. "His breeches and footwear should do for now. I will get him a proper tunic, leather breeches, and boots."

"Yes, he's fine for the job." Jazz eyed my bare chest and smiled, and I had a sudden urge to cover myself—like no one had ever seen me without a shirt on.

I folded my arms and glared at her. For the first time in my life, I was at a loss for words. It was all so surreal that I knew I had to be dreaming. No way was I standing in some medieval village with a giant and a golden-eyed witch.

chapter four

"Witch."

Bren's thoughts blared like a radio from the non-witching world, hurting my mind's ears. His sculpted body, however, was quite easy on the eyes, and I had to turn my gaze away to keep from staring.

"Yes, I am," I said, sounding softer than intended. I couldn't help it. With his chest bare, his hair loose about his neck, and that damnable stubble of a beard, Bren looked like a wickedly handsome pirate caught between a roar of rage and a moment of embarrassed vulnerability.

Rol frowned. The training master knew me only too well, and disapproval rippled through the iron of his muscles.

"Yes, you are . . . what?" Bren asked.

"I'm a witch." I held up my hands, showing him my dark nails. "Note the paint. The most powerful witches wear such concealment on the nails, eyes, and hair in an attempt to hide themselves when they must mix with unenlightened humans."

"Yeah, right." Bren rolled his eyes. "My mom wears stuff like that all the time. So do half the girls at my school. My brother Todd even got into the act on Halloween. Goth's in. Didn't you know?"

I sighed. "The fact remains, Bren. I'm a witch."

The boy stared at me, splendid in his half-dressed perfection. "Okay," he said. "Pinch me. I'm ready to wake up."

Rol grabbed Bren and nearly squeezed his arm from his body before I could get my hand in the air.

"Cease!" I commanded.

Rol froze. Bren dangled like a doll from Rol's massive hands, kicking and yelling. Nothing moved anywhere around us except Bren. Even the villagers and horses had halted midstep, and the ocean made not a sound. I imagined waves held motionless just before they would crash to sand.

My heart pounded in my throat.

Bren was unaffected by my magic.

Already, he was showing more promise than Alderon ever achieved, even after training. It must be natural for Bren. Something inside of him. Something special. Almost not human.

But how could that be?

All of the oldeFolke were on the Path, in our Sanctuaries. Bren had to be of a human line of witches.

And yet . . .

Bren's inner power coursed within him even as he stopped struggling and climbed out of Rol's statuelike grasp. Energy danced about Bren like a silver light, surprising me to my core. Most of our kind glowed, but more gold or yellow than silver.

What could that mean? Was he some sort of monster in the forming? And yet, I could see concern in Bren's otherwise hardwood eyes. I knew he had no understanding of his own strength. Perhaps I didn't, either. That thought gave me more than a little pause.

Until this moment, I had been assuming Bren was simply talented, yet unaware and unconverted—someone with strong magical potential who didn't yet believe in himself or his ability to tap into the Earth's energy to manage the shape, form, or speed of matter and time.

There was something different about him, though. More different than I had dared to hope for when I sent my magical plea, begging the universe to send me our champion. I would have to discover what that difference was, whether it would help our cause or harm it.

And soon.

"Wh- what did you do to giant-man?" Bren jabbed a finger into Rol's ribs.

"A spell," I replied, doing my best to seem calm. "I asked him to cease before he carried out your ill-conceived order to pinch you. Rol is very loyal."

Bren drew himself up. Gooseflesh spread across his impressive shoulders. "You're not a witch, and this guy's not real. None of this is real. Now tell me how to get back to the store—or horror movie warehouse—or whatever it was."

"The only way you'll get back home is to do what I say." My smile failed me, and the urge to apologize rose like the tide.

For a moment, my father's lopsided smile flashed through my mind. Had Father been this handsome when Mother met him? Is that how he disarmed her constant disapproval? Well, no matter. There was no room in my life for such trivialities.

Straightening, I forced myself to look at Bren. "I need your help. I believe you're the only one who can save us."

Bren's eyes blazed, making him all the more like some god from an ancient tale. Did he have to be so damnably attractive?

At least Alderon was ugly, both in flesh and in spirit. It was easy to hate him, and I wouldn't have cared if he fell from a high cliff. Many times, I would have been pleased to push him.

Bren, though . . . I could feel his kindness even through the growing fire of his anger. And that raw power. It was—he was—intoxicating.

Weakness springs from two sources . . . mind and blood . . . thanks to your father. . .

I closed my eyes for a moment, banishing my mother's voice. Who was she to insult my father constantly? After all, he was of royal birth, not she.

With great concentration, I summoned the image of my father, who always gave me comfort when Mother wasn't confusing me about what a good king he was or wasn't. My father, who laughed when I missed a spell or forgot a potion ingredient. Even when I turned him into a mushroom by mistake.

When I dared to look outside myself again, Bren was frowning at me. If his gaze served as any measure, he would have liked nothing better than to string me from a tree or torch me to cinders. It took all my courage to carry out my bluff of arrogance and unconcern.

When the boy found his voice, he spoke through clenched teeth. "Enough of this bull, Jazz. Take me back to the store—the convenience market, the one I saw when I needed to use the restroom. Take me back now."

He advanced on me, as if to menace—and despite my wishes otherwise, he succeeded.

Why in the name of the fates would I be afraid of this untrained whelp? And yet my breath came shallow, and I raised my hand. "Resume!" I commanded.

Rol and the village snapped to life as if they had never ceased to move.

My training master shot me a perplexed, then angry, frown, and grabbed Bren beneath his arms before the boy could reach me.

"Don't pinch him," I told Rol as he lifted Bren and held him forward like a year-old child. "He spoke in haste."

"Let me go!" Bren shouted, even as he struggled to free himself.

"I apologize," Rol said, "but I cannot comply. Releasing you would jeopardize your safety and our own."

All curiosity had left Bren's sharp eyes. They darted back and forth, taking in his new reality. This ancient place, once carefree, but now just another tense Sanctuary on the Path of Shadows.

L.O.S.T., I reminded myself. There's always L.O.S.T. For hope. For the future.

Live Oak Springs Township could be the Sanctuary Shallym once was. A place attached to the Path, yet still attached to the nonwitching world, where humans and nonhumans wove together like a tapestry. A place where witches and nonwitches lived in peace.

Rol held the boy without flinching, even as Bren demonstrated his impressive natural strength. Punches, kicks—even a few near-lunges—but Rol held him forward and stayed just out of reach. And Bren never offered to strike at me.

"Can't hit a girl," he kept telling himself in his mind.

How sweet. Stupid, perhaps, and a quaint belief he would have to abandon to survive in the witching world—but it was sweet.

"I'd appreciate it if you would calm down and keep your thoughts to yourself." I flicked an annoying piece of lint from my sleeve. "They are terribly distracting."

Bren sputtered, but stopped struggling. I knew he would have sworn, but I caught the strong thought that his mother had chided him for swearing, especially at girls.

My head began to ache with the enormity of the task before us, and I rubbed my temples with two fingers. "Listen carefully, Bren. You aren't dreaming. I am a witch—

though Rol is no giant. He's a training master and a power-ful witch in his own right, savior to thousands and one of our last hopes as a warrior—just as you are. Rol will teach you how to use your . . . um—*muscle.*" I flushed and immediately felt foolish.

Did Bren notice? No hint was forthcoming from his flat expression or his thoughts, which now seemed oddly quiet.

I cleared my throat. "Your magic and your mind, those will be my responsibility."

"Magic? What a pile of sh- crap!" Bren doubled his fists and narrowed his gaze. "You're crazy."

Rol repositioned Bren and stared at him, nose to nose and eye to eye. "Even the would-be Shadowalker may not insult the queen."

"Queen of what?" the boy demanded.

Dread trickled through me. After all, Bren would have to choose of his own free will, at some point. And he had to know, but . . .

But for a moment, I sensed that Bren was the most genuinely good boy I had ever met, and definitely the most handsome.

The Sanctuaries offered pitifully few opportunities for company, and all of my own kind were too frightened to speak to me. Most feared even talking in my presence, preferring instead to leave Shadowhispers or some other form of magical communication. Other than Rol and my sworn servant Acaw, and of course Alderon's incessant grunts and grumbles, and a few of the oldeFolke's mutterings, Bren was one of the few people to talk to me in the four years since my father died. When my mother and the rest of my family were captured by Nire.

I sighed. "Let him go, Rol."

"But, my queen—"

"Let him go!"

Rol snorted and dropped Bren on his backside.

The boy leaped to his feet and towered over me. "Queen of what?" he asked again, each word its own snarl.

I raised my fingers toward the heavens, and with a startled grunt, Rol hid his eyes.

"Truth," I whispered.

All the blackness fell away from my nails, my hair, my eyes—even my clothes. I became my true self, shining like the golden sparkles in the sky. Blinding to nonmagical creatures and magical beings not yet converted, and even to most other witches. More light than substance.

Bren's cough told me that he had seen, and I felt some surprise that he had not cried out in pain. He had been able to look upon me in my real form. Well, no matter. I suspected that now he might believe what I had told him.

"Hide," I said, imagining myself back as I had been, to the form tolerable to most eyes. Black paint again covered the shine of my nails. My eyes were once more robed with deep purple-black powder, and the glow from my hair was snuffed out with modern dyes and concealments.

When Rol dared to look at me again, I faced Bren and took the first step toward putting my life and the lives of my people in Bren's untested hands.

"I am Jasmina Corey," I said. "Queen of the Witches."

chapter five

"Yeah, right. And I'm the King of England." But even as I said it, a chill crept over me. Jazz had turned golden. Even her eyes had damn near glowed.

BREN →

And she had been reading my thoughts. I was sure of it now, and that was enough to give anyone a serious freak-out. It made me feel unclean—violated, even—to know that she had been in my head. And never mind the little King Arthur town in the background. That I couldn't even begin to deal with.

Rol growled and flexed his muscles. Jazz placed her hand on his arm, probably keeping the guy from pounding me into the dirt.

"Listen," I said to Rol, acting as cool and calm as Jazz. Trying to respond instead of react. "It's getting a little chilly out here, and I'm half naked. Think you could find something for me to wear since you shredded my favorite T-shirt?"

The giant dude looked at Jazz. She nodded and seemed to relax—her features softened and her shoulders didn't seem as tense. I hadn't even realized she was keyed-up until that moment. Maybe she wasn't as in control as she made out to be.

"We'll go to Shadowbridge," Jazz said, "where you'll be outfitted and trained." She gestured to the right, which had to be south since the late afternoon sun was behind us.

"Whatever," I grumbled. I just wanted to get a shirt on and get the hell out of there. My dad would really think I was a screw-up now.

Dad's voice echoed in my head. "Can't even drive fifty miles without getting into a mess. You're so irresponsible, Brenden . . ."

The giant led the way down the dusty road, his ebony back gleaming like it was coated in oil. Jazz fell into step beside me, dirt and rocks crunching beneath our shoes, and for a while, neither of us said anything. As we left the weird little village, even weirder villagers scooted out of our way, but they never looked at us. Like we weren't there.

I spat into the bushes to the side of the road to get the acid puke taste out of my mouth. A cool breeze chilled my bare chest while I checked out the sights and tried to figure out where I was. One thing for sure—the ocean was near. I could smell it, and I was positive I could hear waves crashing against the shore.

Maybe I was at a renaissance festival around San Diego. Yeah, like the one that was way east of Phoenix that my mom took me to last February. Of course, that festival was totally lame, nothing like this place, which seemed so real.

"What will it take to convince you?" Jazz murmured. Her shoulder brushed mine and a strange jolt shot through me, like electricity running wild in my body. Even the hair on my arms stood on end. Jazz looked up at me, and for a minute, I thought I might even like her. That she and I could be friends. Maybe more than friends.

No. I scowled and turned away from her. No way. The witch was wrecking my life.

I heard her sigh, but I didn't bother to look at her again. She had a way of taking away my anger, no matter how hard I tried to be ticked. What was it about her, anyway?

My stomach growled so loud that Rol glanced over his shoulder and said, "We shall sup as soon as we arrive."

"Great," I muttered. "She reads my mind and he reads my stomach."

Jazz giggled, and I glanced at her in surprise. She had seemed so serious—so *queenly*—until that silly sound. Her smile lit up her face, and for the first time, I realized how incredibly beautiful she was. And she smelled good. Really good. Like sunshine, cinnamon, and peaches.

"So, how old are you?" I asked without really meaning to.

Her smile widened, and she was beyond beautiful. "Sixteen. And you?"

I raised my eyebrows. "What, you didn't read that in my mind?"

Jazz shook her head, her black hair shimmering in waves over her shoulders. "I can't read your memory. I can hear only what's in your thoughts." She paused and stared at me from beneath her long lashes as we walked. "And your powers are growing. You're already blocking some of those thoughts from me. At least when you consciously wish me out of your mind."

I kicked a rock and watched it bounce off the road and into the bushes before looking back to Jazz. "Then why did you ask what it would take to convince me?"

She shrugged. "I read your expression, not your mind."

"Oh." I found myself smiling, glad I didn't have to worry about her knowing what I was thinking all the time. "Seventeen."

"Perfect," she murmured, and I had the feeling she wasn't talking about my age.

I shoved my hands in my pockets as we walked, and my fingertips brushed the figurine. The one the bathroom-freak crammed into my hand before he disappeared.

"In the cellar. You will find the door in the cellar," the man's scratchy voice said in my mind. "Remember that, brother, or you will be sorry."

I was tempted to pull out the statue and show Jazz, just to see what she thought of it, but something held me back. Like it was my secret, and I didn't want to share it with anyone.

We slowly left the village behind, and soon, we were following Rol up a hill that reminded me of the one leading to the restaurant where I used the restroom. Except this path was made of rocks, not concrete steps, and there was an enormous stone building at the top instead of that lame restaurant that used to be somebody's house.

It seemed like ages since I had stopped at that convenience market, but it had to have been only an hour, tops. I still had time to get a shirt on, eat, and be out of there and on my way to finding my mom's truck. Then I would be off to Brandon's house for a week of sun, surf, and babes. Adios to all this weirdness. But as I glanced at Jazz, I felt as if I might actually miss the chance to get to know her.

I was seriously losing it.

This witch-girl was nothing like the girls I had dated. Hell, she wasn't like any girl I had ever met. At the top of the hill, Jazz opened a wooden box and took out a bunch of notes.

And then the box started whispering.

No kidding. It really did. And Jazz just stood there, listening to it mumble. Sometimes she nodded. Once or twice, she frowned. Rol didn't seem too freaked by the talking box, so I tried to act cool.

When the box stopped mumbling, Jazz glanced at the notes, folded them, and tucked them into her pocket.

Rol came to attention. "Should I take care of anything, Your Highness?"

"Not at the moment. For once, we've had no new disasters." Jazz didn't even look at me as she started walking again, straight toward the big, dark building a few football fields away.

I followed, glancing back at that weird box a few times.

The building they led me to was actually a mansion. The sound of Rol's boots echoed as he jogged up the stone steps to the entrance. Jazz wore a shirt and leggings that clung to her curvy body, and I let her get a little ahead of me so I could watch her walk. Her movements were smooth and graceful, like a dancer's. And yeah, she would look damn good in one of those—

She glanced over her shoulder and narrowed her eyes.

Maybe I still need to be careful with my thoughts. Concentrate. Stay out of my head. Stay out of my head. Stay out . . .

Rol held the door open and motioned us inside the mansion. "Welcome to Shadowbridge Manor."

I had to wait until my eyes adjusted to the dimness for my first glimpse of the place. Mansion, hell! More like a castle. It had massive vaulted ceilings that would put a cathedral to shame. Rose velvet drapes and rich hangings covered the walls.

And everything was spotless. Not a speck of dirt on the floor, no smudges on the walls, no scrapes on the furniture. Nothing like my home—Dad was always yelling at Todd and me to pick up our dirty clothes off the floor and put our stuff away. He complained how nothing stayed nice with kids around. Mom just laughed and said our house had that lived-in look. She actually liked clutter and had all kinds of weird stuff in her backroom, where Todd and I weren't allowed.

My jaw dropped as we were led from one enormous room to another. Finally, we stopped in a dining room with a table long enough to seat twenty people.

Rol glanced at the table, then said to Jazz, "I will see if Acaw might deign to serve our dinner."

"Could you bring back that shirt you promised?" I asked.

Rol nodded, bowed, and turned on his heel.

My mom's voice echoed in my head, telling me not to come to the table without a shirt on, so I decided to remain standing until the giant returned with one. Jazz stood beside me, and the silence between us was stiff and awkward.

I folded my arms across my bare chest and tried not to look at her, studying the room instead. The only light came from floor-to-ceiling windows, and I couldn't see any electric lights or outlets. Candleholders hung on the walls, and a wicked-looking candelabra crouched on the middle of the dining table. Around the table stood chunky straight-backed chairs, but there were only three place settings at one end.

As if they had expected me.

It was so quiet that I could hear Jazz's soft breathing. My gaze seemed drawn to her, and once I looked into those witchy gold eyes, I couldn't look away. Her dark lips parted and I thought about how soft and full they were, but the sound of Rol's boot steps shattered the hold she had on me.

Yep, somehow the witch was getting to me. Getting under my skin. Maybe it was a spell. If I believed in magic, which I didn't.

Rol entered the room and tossed me a light brown shirt that felt like soft leather, like the chamois cloths my dad made me use to clean Mom's truck.

Mom's truck. Shit. I'd be so dead if I didn't find it!

I slid the shirt on, glad not to be walking around half-naked anymore. Out of the corner of my eye, I saw Jazz's face, and I could have sworn she looked disappointed that I wasn't bare-chested any longer.

The shirt was sleeveless, like a muscle shirt. It opened in a V at my neck and had laces I could have drawn tight, but I ignored them.

Rol seated Jazz at the head of the table. The giant put me on one side of her, and he sat on the other side, across from me. In moments, a short guy appeared with platters of roasted chicken, prime rib, potatoes, puddings, and all sorts of things I couldn't identify. My stomach growled as soon as the delicious smells hit my nose, and I ate like it was my last meal. For all I knew, it could be, if I didn't figure out where the hell I was and how I was going to get away.

When I devoured the last apple tart, I pushed my chair away from the table and stood. "Thanks for the shirt and dinner," I said to Rol.

Jazz raised an eyebrow, and Rol stopped in mid-chew.

To Jazz I said, "Maybe I'll see you around."

Before they could reply, I turned and headed out the door.

chapter six

"Do you plan to act?" Rol asked. "I am not certain the streets of Shallym are ready for the likes of him."

I swallowed my last bite of rice pudding, ignoring the flutter of my heart. "Let Bren make his own errors. If he dies by his folly, better sooner than later, so we don't waste time training him."

"You seem too *interested* in this one to take such a casual attitude." Rol emphasized "interested," and I thought about pasting him to Shadowbridge's stone walls. A simple sticky spell would have done it, even for one so large. And Rol would make a fine piece of art—like the time I turned him into a green coat of arms and hung him on Father's wall. Of course, I had been banished to my room for a week for that little prank. And Rol had me run endless laps around

Shadowbridge. To build my stamina, he told Father. Father had only laughed and agreed, saying I would vex my husband sorely one day.

Husband. As if any witch on the Path would give me a second look. With my knowledge and power, I was as attractive to a potential husband as the two-hearted slithers dwelling in the forest. Scales, fangs, fiery breath, and all.

My scowl must have deepened, because the training master glared at me, gripping the table's edge as if to resist anything I tried. Though I was too old to run laps, I was disinclined to try Rol's patience. After all, it was Bren I truly wanted to paste to a wall.

The heavy front door swung open, then closed.

I sighed.

Bren was no doubt making his way into Shallym. Other than my castle grounds and the forbidding woods nearby, there was nowhere else for him to go in this Sanctuary.

I drew a breath and tried to maintain my air of unconcern, but with each passing second, the flutters in my chest increased.

Rol's eyes narrowed as he studied me. Waiting.

Don't be ridiculous, I told myself. Bren was the one. The Shadowwalker. And the Shadowwalker was quite capable of caring for himself. But Bren was untrained, and brimming with a wild, wild energy. And that mouth. What if Bren angered a hag? Woke a slither? Or, fates forbid, caught the eye of a klatchKeeper?

The peace between the oldeFolke—the witches converted from ancient races such as faeries and dwarves, and from creatures with no names understandable to human ears—and the rest of us was tenuous at best. This peace was a requirement of the Path, and not something born of the oldeFolke's free will.

It would serve him right to learn of the oldeFolke in some rude fashion. "Maybe I'll see you around," indeed.

"The pup cannot help his confusion," Rol muttered. "Why would you punish him for being himself, for trying to restore his life? After all, you wish him to restore ours."

"Silence," I snapped, careful to keep my hands on the table. Rol flinched nonetheless. Shame warmed my cheeks, adding fuel to my swelling anger.

Rol pushed his food around his plate, his fork clinking against the stoneware. In the kitchen, Acaw the elfling spoke with his crow-brother, so softly that not even my keen hearing could make out his words. From the stables came the piercing whinny of Rol's stallion, and in the distance, an eagle screamed in triumph as it captured its prey.

After several long minutes, I said, "I'm not punishing Bren for being confused or for making efforts to return to his life."

"For what, then?" Rol grimaced. "Wounding your pride? I would have preferred the first explanation. The second sounds too much like—"

"If you compare me to my father, I shall turn you into a snake and skin you," I warned. "Alive."

"*Hmph.*" Rol seized his tankard of ale. "I was going to say your mother."

A strange panic seized me, and I could no longer abide the training master's cool regard. Before he could speak again, I jumped to my feet and fled the dining room.

I'm not my mother. I'm not. I'm not! She was tense and unforgiving. So deliberately cold.

And I'm not my father, either. I have intelligence and foresight. I wasn't so innocent and blind, trusting fate or circumstance or all the wrong people. I wouldn't go blindly to my death and leave my family to fight my battles.

Even if Rol was the only "family" I had, and even if he thought I was awful.

My growing dread drove me harder than Rol's well-placed barbs. How could I have allowed Bren to leave? Alderon, yes—to be sure, it would have been a pleasure to watch him suffer—but Bren?

What was wrong with me?

Weakness . . . liberal amount of both to overcome . . .

Sweet fates, but I wished there was some spell to rip my mother's voice from my mind! Perhaps she was Nire. After all, Mother seemed intent on taking my sanity before she was captured.

If she had been captured. She could have been killed, her spirit thrown into the Shadows. I had no way to know for sure.

Shadowbridge seemed to resist my efforts to reach the door. Here a rug snagged my foot. There a chair sat just forward enough to trip me. Somehow I lurched to the entrance without falling and yanked on the metal ring handle.

The door swung open. A roar of anger reached my ears immediately—far away, from down the hill. By the Goddess! Bren had already arrived in the village. And he was already in trouble.

I could have cast a ceasing spell, halting everything within a few miles of me, but I had done that once already, only a short time ago. The oldeFolke would be so enraged, being spelled twice in one day—they would no doubt take some hideous revenge. Not an option. This problem I had to handle more directly.

"Wind!" I screamed, holding out my palms.

A crack announced my gift from the trees, torn loose and speeding on its way. The live oak branch landed in my hands with a rustle and thump. Its rough bark felt strong and sure, and its gnarled contours welcomed my legs as I straddled it.

One push of my feet sent me skyward, and I shot down Shadowbridge Hill toward Shallym.

It took only a moment for my sensitive vision to find the crowd—and Bren. He was a mile ahead, no more, sprawled across a merchant's cart on Main Square. Apples lay everywhere, and Bren had covered his head with his arms.

Wagons had stopped. Children covered their mouths with their hands. Even the horses were staring.

Wind rushed through my hair as I hurtled toward the village. At least twenty witches pelted Bren with fruit, curses, and stones. Some were regular witches, human by birth, as I was. But most were of the oldeFolke—creatures with magic so ancient and powerful it could scarcely be contained, even

by me. They looked none too pleased to find an unconverted human in a witch's refuge on the Path of Shadows.
Especially in Shallym, the oldest Sanctuary of all. I could tell
the oldeFolke were regretting their vow of peace, just by the
tension simmering brightly in the air.

" . . . you owe me!" the cartman was bellowing at Bren.
"My apples! My beautiful apples!"

"He isn't even a witch yet!" screamed the nearest hag to
her cronies. Her warty face twisted with rage, and her truly
dark hag-spirit hovered nearby, ready to strike like a snake
on her command.

Mother always said hags were descended from the union
of faeries with cobras and asps. Looking at the hideous
woman and her hateful familiar, I had no cause to doubt
that lineage.

Don't move, Bren, I pleaded in my mind as I flew toward
the marketplace. Not a twitch. Not a quiver.

Six hypnotically beautiful girls danced as one near Bren's
feet. Bren was still conscious and not trying to crawl toward
them, so I knew the girls must be a very young klatch-
Koven. Not yet at full strength or power. Manageable, at
least.

No Keeper in sight, thank the Goddess.

Otherwise, Bren might have been swearing his eternal
love for the klatchKoven—the result of faerie dalliances with
Greek Sirens—and I did not want to think of what surely
would happen next. Of all the oldeFolke, klatch witches dis-
liked humans the most, perhaps because human males
found them irresistible and refused to leave them alone. The

klatch certainly found means to avenge themselves for that particular human weakness, however.

Oh, dear. If that cartman finished his mutterings before my arrival, I might find myself searching for a mouse or lizard instead of a stubborn, insolent boy.

At the moment, though, Bren looked helpless, cowering in the muck.

I landed like a meteor, live oak branch flaming from the speed of the ride.

The crowd gasped as one and fell silent—and more importantly, they fell away, leaving Bren and me in the center of a large, quiet circle. Even the hag-spirits dared no movement. They hovered, scowling at me like the Shadowmaster's minions.

Perhaps they were, I reminded myself. Even with the vow, was evil not still evil? After all, it was Father who allowed hags to defect from their dark origins and enter the Path of Shadows, and Father's judgment was questionable, at best. More heart than mind, sometimes.

Like my own.

"Get up, Bren," I said.

Bren didn't move. He crouched on the ground near my legs, and I could feel anger rising from him like spell-driven steam. Mud obscured his hair and face, blending brown to brown, giving him the appearance of a puppy fresh from frolicking in a puddle.

Hags drooled and the klatchKoven clasped their hands. I knew they were waiting for me to spell the boy into oblivion. If I tried to use magic to set him on his feet and failed—

if Bren threw off my magic in front of them like he had when we first came to Shallym—no.

Too great a risk.

I gave him a gentle kick. "Get up, or die. I assure you that if I leave, the villagers will kill you."

Bren scrambled to his feet, all thumbs and stumbles, barely missing a hag as he staggered in the mud. "This is sooo not happening," he said to himself, but everyone heard. We were all witches, with hearing keener than owls.

The hag that Bren nearly bumped curled her fingers and hissed, but I raised my hands.

Everyone cowered.

"He offered you no insult." My voice echoed through the silent marketplace. "And he means you no harm. Any aggression toward him will be a breach of vow and cause for expulsion. You'll all do well to know that this boy is under my protection until his conversion, and even afterward."

Before the cartman could argue that his property damage was enough to warrant spellwork, I restored his wares with a wide sweep of my fingers. Down to the last shiny apple. He grunted and backed away, keeping a wary eye on my hands.

Hags—I counted seven in all—swore and threatened under their breaths, but their hag-spirits sulked close to their elbows as they raised cloaks and vanished. The klatchKoven shrank back, clawing the air like frightened cats. From a few streets over, I heard a reedy whistle.

A Keeper.

The klatch witches scattered, running for their mistress. I shivered, not desiring to encounter a klatchKeeper on this tiresome day. The remainder of the crowd seemed to agree. They stomped away, both merchant and customer, grumbling and shooting wicked glances in Bren's direction.

The Keeper sang out as her charges joined her, and for a moment, their eerie and beautiful chorus filled the air.

Bren glared at me with a mixture of hate and fear on his dirty face, and then his head turned. He began to drift toward the enticing music of the klatchKoven. In seconds, he almost tripped over the apple cart.

Too much to hope that he could resist a Keeper's song with no training. No, Bren was definitely not ready to meet a Keeper, and strangely, I wasn't ready to share Bren's attention with any woman who appeared to be that beautiful.

Not that he felt the same, I was certain.

"Quiet," I said, letting my hands make a circle above my head. The spell affected only the air around Bren and me, so the oldeFolke would not be offended.

Silence settled over the two of us like a pall, and Bren shook his muddy head. His normally bright eyes were still glazed from the Keeper's music. I took the spare moment to point at the dirt all over him, banishing it clump by smear back to the earth. By the time I finished, he sparkled. But he had sparkled before, even filthy.

"What did you do?" he asked, glancing around. His eyes lingered on the owner of the applecart, who glared back ferociously. "Why did everything get so quiet?"

"Come," I said, ignoring his question. "We're safest at Shadowbridge until you know enough not to be hexed into twenty pieces or entranced by the klatchKoven—and then, well, your fate wouldn't be pleasant."

"Go to h—" he began, but bit off his own sentence. Silver energy surged from his clenched fists, startling me.

What was that power?

I still hadn't figured out the source of his strength, but at least he couldn't see it yet. Soon, though, he would. Very soon. I didn't have much time left to understand this boy.

Raising my hand to dismiss the thought, I shouted, "Wind!"

The crack of wood startled Bren into raising his fists as though to strike what might come his way

"You don't have to wish me to hell," I told him in a voice that sounded all too much like my mother's. "I've already been, and yet remain. Trapped, just as yourself." One-handed, I caught the live oak branch as I added, "Now, come and ride with me. I won't save you from your own foolishness again."

chapter seven

"Save me from my foolishness?" I was so furious with Jazz that my arms shook. "You brought me to this creeped-out place. I am so sick of your high-and-mighty, better-than-everyone attitude! If you weren't a girl, I would— I would—" I clenched my fist and slammed it into the closest thing to me—which happened to be the apple cart. Wood splintered and crunched as my knuckles went straight through it. I yanked my hand back, expecting to feel pain, or at least numbness, but I felt . . . nothing. Nothing at all. The hole was at least a foot in diameter, the wooden planks an inch thick. Yet not a single scratch or cut was on me.

Apples tumbled through the hole, one after another. But the noise of apples hitting cobblestones faded. For a minute, I forgot about the village. Forgot about Jazz. I clenched and

BREN

51

unclenched my hand and stared at it. The really weird thing was that I thought I saw a glow on my arms. Like the glow I'd seen on Jazz, but silver instead of gold. And even more bizarre was this total power rush that went through me like an electrical charge.

My brother Todd would have freaked. He'd be so jealous he'd turn silver. Dad wouldn't believe it, of course. And Mom—who knows? She might have made an offering to the forces of the universe.

I lifted my head and looked from my hand to Jazz. Her dark lips were parted and her eyes wide. I felt a tickle in my chest, almost like fingers pushing into my skin. Was Jazz trying to read my mind again? Or something else—like touching my feelings? My essence.

My essence? Where did that come from?

A sick feeling settled in my gut. I shook my head, making sure to will Jazz—and anyone else for that matter—totally out of me.

Jazz blinked and stepped back, holding that tree branch she'd pulled out of the sky close to her body. She raised her chin and attempted to put on her better-than-anyone act, but I could see right through her. I had surprised her. Made her leave my brain.

How about that, Dad? Using my head enough for ya?

"You have some explaining to do," I said to Jazz, my voice low, but dead serious. "And you'd better start now."

"Yes. Well." She glanced around the street that was now almost empty. The only others around were the merchants and a couple of older-looking women who glared at me a lot.

She cocked her head as if she was listening for something. "It isn't safe for you here." Her eyes met mine. "Whether it pleases you or not, you have no choice but to trust me. We must go to Shadowbridge at once."

A snapping sound jerked her attention to the skies, and mine, too.

For a minute, I thought I saw a dark shadow pass above us. Not really in the sky, more like . . . behind it. I glanced at Jazz, and felt a new wave of cold wash down my back. She looked very, very scared.

"What's going on?" I muttered, keeping my eyes pinned to hers.

"We need to leave now, Bren," she said, and the concern in her voice shut down all my arguments.

I nodded. "Okay, but as soon as we get there, you're going to answer my questions."

Jazz waved her fingers, repairing the applecart again and sending every spilled apple back to the piles on its shelves. Then, she straddled the branch and motioned for me to get on. I hesitated a second, but I got on behind her. If I hadn't seen her fly in on her flaming broomstick, I would have thought she was totally nuts. But instead I just thought I had gone nuts.

"Hold on to me," she said.

I put my hands at Jazz's waist, barely touching her.

She glanced over her shoulder. "You'll need to hold tightly, or you'll fall. Perhaps to your death."

"You'd like that, wouldn't you?" I muttered as I wrapped my arms around her and squeezed so hard she gasped.

"Not quite so tightly," she wheezed.

Grinning in spite of myself, I eased up. She smelled good—that peaches and cinnamon scent. And she felt soft and warm in my arms, and it surprised me how much I liked holding her.

"Don't worry," Jazz said. "I'll fly a bit slower than usual." She waved one hand over her head and shouted, "Resume!" and the marketplace noise came back like it had never been muted.

Even though she'd pissed me off, I couldn't help but think how cool it was to know a really powerful girl, a girl who wasn't scared and didn't seem to be all wrapped up in herself. Jazz hesitated and stiffened in my arms as I had the sudden and strange desire to nuzzle her long black hair. But in the next moment, the only thing I thought about was holding on for my life.

We rose in the air, and at first it felt a lot like going up in the Ferris wheel at the state fair. I always hated that thing. My stomach dropped and my heart pounded as we went even higher. But then we sailed forward, and I felt a total rush, wind whipping through my hair and cooling off my sweaty skin.

I realized I was grinning like an idiot when something hit my teeth. Probably a bug. I spit over the left side of the broom and got a glimpse of the ocean. It looked cool, the oranges and pinks of the sunset reflecting on its waters. I glanced to the right to check out the sunset—

And realized the ocean was in the wrong direction. It shouldn't have been to the east.

But I shouldn't have been riding a broomstick with a witch, either.

"To answer your question, I wouldn't like it," Jazz said as she lowered us toward Shadowbridge's massive steps.

I drew my thoughts away from the sunset. "Wouldn't like what?"

"For you to fall." She glanced at me over her shoulder. "I wouldn't like to see you hurt—or worse."

Jazz turned her attention to setting us down. When we landed and stood on the manor's steps, I kept my hold on her as she flung the smoking branch onto a thick patch of grass. I could feel the tenseness in her body as she waved her fingers—and the branch stopped smoking. Like magic.

She tried to move away from me, but I wouldn't let go. There was something about her that made me want to hold on tight. My gut told me she was special—she wasn't some giggling, make-up-and-clothes-obsessed airhead. Yeah, she was beautiful, but she had brains and a kind of self-confidence that I'd never noticed in any other girl—or guy, for that matter.

"You may release me now." Her voice was low, and I felt her tremble.

I dropped my arms, and she spun around to stare up at me. God, she was beautiful. And as sudden as that, I knew I wasn't angry with her anymore. A stray lock of her hair was across her face, making her look young and vulnerable—and sweet. Without thinking, I pushed the strands of black hair behind her ear, brushing her cheek with my knuckles.

Jazz's gaze widened, and she caught her breath.

Those golden eyes—so deep and endless a guy could get lost in them. What made a girl like Jazz tick? How could she be so stiff one minute and so soft the next? But it wasn't her hard side that unnerved me, that made me feel like I was moving in slow motion, inside and out. No, it was moments like this, when she seemed kind of delicate, and like she needed someone's protection.

My protection.

"It is about time you returned with the pup." Rol's voice rumbled from the open door.

Jazz whirled to face Rol, and I stumbled back and almost fell off the step.

"We— we just arrived," Jazz said, sweeping past Rol with her chin in the air.

Rol raised his brows. "I see that."

As I walked by him, he winked at me and I grinned. Why couldn't my dad be more like that?

I followed Jazz, and Rol fell into step beside me. Torches were mounted in brackets along the walls, spitting and hissing like snakes as we passed by.

"In the drawing room, Your Majesty?" Rol asked.

Jazz gave a prim nod. "Yes."

Rol led us into a room that was cozy compared to the rest of the manor, lit with candles that gave off soft light. Jazz pointed to a wooden chair with red velvet cushions. "Sit, Bren."

I narrowed my gaze.

She lowered hers. "Please."

"Okay," I replied and sat down. "But if you don't start talking, I'm outta here, hexes or not."

With a sigh, she said, "I'll tell you at least as much as you can handle for tonight."

"Do you require anything more, my queen?" Rol asked before I could argue with Jazz.

"Nothing further." She waved him away. "Thank you, Rol."

Rol bowed himself out the door, and Jazz and I were alone.

Amazing. She still looked perfect—not a hair out of place, not a speck on her clothing. Me, I could feel my own hair standing on end after that wild ride, and I needed a bath, despite that little magic trick in the village where she got rid of all the dirt on me. How'd she do that?

"Tell me where I really am," I said a few seconds after Rol was gone. "I know I'm not in California any longer. Hell—um—heck, I don't even know if I'm on Earth anymore."

Jazz clasped her hands in front of her, her back straight and her shoulders squared as she sat at the edge of her seat. "You're correct that we're no longer in California; however, we are on Earth." She paused and stared at her black polished nails, and I imagined gold glowing around their edges. "We're in Massachusetts—only it's the year 12, almost two thousand years in your past."

My jaw about hit the floor. "12 AD, as in before King Arthur?"

"This village is called Shallym." Jazz looked everywhere but at me as she spoke. "A pre-medieval version of the

Salem you may have knowledge of from your history texts. Shallym existed before any other permanent villages on this continent. It has always been a haven for witches facing persecution in other civilizations, and one of the only places in time where there are no nonwitching humans."

I could barely focus on what Jazz was saying—my mind kept going back to the 12 AD thing. I forced myself to pay attention, even though I was thinking she was a little nuts.

For a moment she stared out the window, into the growing darkness. "In one form or another, in every time, there has been a Shallym. A Salem. A place of peace. That's what the name means, in fact. Peace. From the word *shalom*."

"A haven for witches," I repeated, not really believing a word. "A secret ancient town."

"Towns. Many of them." She turned her gaze back to me. "Shallym was the first safehaven. When my father created the Path of Shadows, a ribbon tying together all of our safehavens, he made Shallym the first Sanctuary connected to it." Her golden eyes looked a little sad when she mentioned her dad, but it was so brief I wasn't sure.

My knee bounced while I struggled to pay attention to what she was saying, and I started pulling at the lace of my tunic. "I don't get it. Your dad couldn't be that old, so he made this Path recently, right? Like within this century."

Jazz glanced at my bouncing knee as she nodded. "Only five years past."

"If we're really back in 12 AD, then how can Shall—uh, Shallwhatsit—be a part of this Path thing?" I gestured in the direction I thought the village was. "This place existed thousands of years ago, if what you said is true."

"Sh-aa-llim." Pursing her lips, she tilted her head and looked like she was trying to think of a way to respond. "My father's Path reaches through time, touching magical places where witches go to avoid torture and murder at the hands of those who don't understand us."

She stretched out her fingers and traced a line in the air— and the air between us started to glitter. The sparkles twisted and slid together, until it looked like some weird version of the yellow brick road. Floating in front of my nose.

"Think of the Path as a moving magnetic road," she said as her hand worked, "running from spot to spot, touching places where the magical energy is strong enough to attract it."

I blinked at it, trying not to let my mouth hang open. Jazz kept drawing in the air, and little silver bubbles drifted up and attached to the yellow ribbon.

Jazz pointed to the bubble on the end closest to me. "This is Shallym. At the beginning of witches' recorded time, where we are now."

All I could do was nod and stare at the floating colors.

"These are Sanctuaries in other times." She tapped a bubble closer to her. "Like Middle Salem in the 1600s."

"What's the one right next to you?" I nodded toward the last bubble, which was drifting beside Jazz's cheek.

She glanced at it, and for a second, she looked soft. Almost relaxed. "L.O.S.T. The Sanctuary I just made, where you entered the Path."

My frown was automatic. I was about to make some smart remark about being kidnapped, but Jazz waved her hand and the yellow ribbon and bubbles popped into nothing. I couldn't help staring at where they had been. Sort of neat, how she did that. I almost wanted her to put it back. "So, this Path is a place all witches can go?"

"With help entering the energy field, yes. It was." With a slight shake of her head, she continued, "At present, no witches may walk the Path unless I admit them. When I allow them on the Path, they must take the vow—a binding magical agreement to use magic against another witch only for self-protection. To save life or limb—their own or a family member's." Jazz looked at her black nails and back to me. "Now, with everything that has happened—with the evil we're fighting—once on the Path, it isn't possible for any witch but me to leave. Their magic simply isn't strong enough to survive more than one exposure to the moving road." She leaned forward, her face intent. "Thus, if a witch is expelled from the Path, they are simply banished into the Shadows, a sort of nonexistence. And they become vulnerable to corruption."

I rubbed my face with my hand, my head aching with all that had happened and all that she was telling me. "That's what you meant when you told those old crones that it would be a breach of their vow if they did anything to me. And what you're saying is that if they were expelled, it'd be almost like they didn't exist anymore."

Jazz's smile lit up her face. "Yes, you understand."

I frowned. "No, I don't. Not all the way."

Her smile vanished. "I see. Perhaps you require rest. I can explain more in the morning."

As stubborn as I felt, as much as I wanted to know what the hell was going on, she was right. I was beat. I couldn't absorb another word, even if I tried. And even if I could find my mom's truck tonight, I was too wiped out to drive without falling asleep at the wheel.

"Yeah," I said. "I could use some sleep."

Like a graceful cat, Jazz stood and led me from the drawing room, up a huge staircase, and into a dark room. She said "light," and in an instant, a fat candle burned on a bedside table.

Real magic? Or some kind of trick? Had all that I'd seen so far been a slick sleight of hand? I brushed the thoughts away, too tired to think about it right now.

"Rol's quarters are next door to yours." Jazz pointed to her left. "If you have need of anything, ask him. He sleeps lightly."

I yawned and stretched my arms. "Not me. I sleep like the dead." My vision blurred, and it was all I could do to keep my eyes open. "'Night, Jazz."

"Jasmina," she said softly, like a last-ditch effort to get me to stop calling her Jazz. But I had the feeling she didn't really mind anymore. "Good night, Bren."

When she left, I blew out the candle and collapsed face-first on the bed. The statue in my pocket dug into my thigh, and I groaned and turned onto my side.

Maybe the statue was bad luck or something. Look at the mess I was in.

But thoughts of it faded as I slid into a deep sleep.

Minutes later, I startled awake, heart pounding. I was awake, wasn't I? The air—it looked so strange. I was outside, not in a bed. More like a forest. No, wait. A village, close to the trees. I was standing outside an old village much smaller than Shallym.

A hollow *thock* made me jump.

It sounded like someone hammering once on wood, only louder. An image jumped into my mind of a huge, faceless monster pounding on a castle door—while the people inside the castle huddled and screamed.

Again I heard it. *Thock.*

Then *thock, thock, thock!*

And this time, people did scream. From inside the village. From inside little huts and buildings. The ground shook, and I fought not to fall down and start screaming, too. The wrongness of the night, the sounds, even the feeling of the air made me sick inside. Dizziness hit me harder than the knocking as the ground tremors came and went. A tearing sound above me made me grind my teeth.

What the hell was happening?

It sounded like the sky was ripping in half. Or maybe I was losing my mind.

Bizarre shadows flooded the night around me. My skin crawled as if spiders raced up my spine. I tried to yell, to run forward, but I couldn't move or breathe. The shadows bled through the air, appearing and vanishing, then appearing again.

Were they alive?

Wind came from nowhere, blowing and howling, drowning screams and awful, inhuman sounds from those shadow-things.

And then everything went quiet.

Soft laughter drew my attention, and I cut my gaze from the shadows. A dark form appeared against a moonlit backdrop of silver-shaded trees. Something about the silhouette was . . . familiar. Yet I couldn't see the being's face, couldn't tell who it was—or even what it was.

A witch, I thought. But no, something far more terrible. I felt that sharp pain in my gut, like a knife pressed under my ribs. My blood ran colder than cold. I watched the shadows flow through the night toward a village. Something told me it was a Sanctuary, like Jazz had talked about.

The next thing I knew, the wind sound came back, along with screaming, shouting, screeching. Shadows slipped through one dark building after another. The wicked being followed, a black form blending with darkness. As people—witches, I assumed—fled out into the night, purple sparks dripped from the being's fingertips. The . . . *thing* . . . threw purple ropes of power—I didn't know what else to call them—around the witches.

That was bad. I knew it. Very, very bad. The evil creature was planning to kill them all—for no reason I could see. I tried to do something to help, but I still couldn't move. Couldn't help anyone.

The being secured the witches tight with the magical ropes. Immediately, shadow-things attacked the bound victims.

Screams of the dying echoed through my head, and my own silent screams joined theirs.

When I woke again, this time for real, I bolted up in bed, shaking. Where was I? It wasn't my own room back in Yuma.

And then I realized I was in the bed in Shallym. I really was in another time, another place. My mouth hung open, and I kept coughing. My heart wouldn't slow down.

What had I heard?

I rubbed my sleep-coated eyes and tried to breathe normally.

What the hell had I seen?

chapter eight

I felt so tired.

I wished I could be in my bed back at Shadowbridge, tucked tightly beneath the covers and
dreaming just before the dawn—but such was not
the lot of the Queen of the Witches. A sense of distress and
disaster drove me from my sanctuary and into the air, moving from place to place and time to time until I located the
disturbance.

As I landed and threw away my burning branch, my
body ached, inside and out. Smoke stung my eyes, and
soot settled heavily on my cheeks. I couldn't see the sun in
this once beautiful, bright village outside of Trier. The two
witches kneeling before me looked as if they might never
see the sun again, so dark was the terror in their eyes.

"It happened so quickly, Your Majesty," said Grelda, a hag, in halting English. Her hag-spirit coiled tightly around her arm. I couldn't see its eyes, which unnerved me. Grelda had been from an older time in Germany. Two years ago, when she asked for asylum, I had brought her forward to the Trier area just before the year 1590, in hopes she would be happy in a somewhat familiar environment. I never imagined a horror like this.

"We heard sounds like knocking," said the second witch, a girl of only thirteen, who had been introduced to me as Helden. "An unearthly, evil sound. Another noise came, like wood splintering— and then— and then—"

She coughed and broke down, sobbing in Grelda's arms.

I bit my lip and forced myself to take stock of what was left of the village—a small churchlike structure and two hovels that looked to be storage bins, perhaps for corn or grain. Everything else had been burned. On a few fallen rafters, embers yet glowed, and an unnatural purple hue hung about the charred remnants of corpses and animals.

"How did Nire know of this place?" Grelda growled, casting a suspicious look upward. "Were we sacrificed? *Betrayed?*"

I knelt and placed a hand on her shoulder. With the other, I stroked Helden's arm. "Neither. I believe the Shadowmaster has been biding time, gaining power, and now is seeking Sanctuaries one at a time. It's happenstance, chance, but Nire is quickly growing more skilled at searching. Soon, nowhere will be safe."

Not here, not Shallym—and before long, not even L.O.S.T., my last hope.

"Nowhere will be safe as long as you are on the Path," the hag snarled. "It is *you* whom Nire seeks. Your power."

"Don't be a fool." Helden recovered herself and pushed away from the hag. "Without Jasmina's protection, the Shadowmaster would slaughter us all in days!"

"Protection." Grelda's sarcasm was unmistakable. "Some *protection* she has given us."

My stomach burned almost as hot as my cheeks. "You know the strength of Nire's magic when it's focused and at full strength. The Shadowmaster murdered your clan, and I saved you."

"For what?" The hag leapt to her feet. Her hag-spirit unfurled and took the form of a great, dark bird, wings spread, beak wide like a maw. "More massacres? More chaos? If you cannot contain Nire, perhaps we should dispose of you and find a proper leader from the oldeFolke!"

I couldn't double my fists, as Grelda might take it for the threat of a spell and act, harming all of us, or at the least, dooming herself to banishment.

"Consider your words," I urged through clenched teeth, forcing my hands to remain at my sides. "You are overwrought, and Helden may have need of you to make her choice."

At this, Helden expressed her confusion in a series of sobs, and by grabbing Grelda's clothing.

Grelda bared her teeth at me, but then took the young witch, of whom she was obviously fond, away from the devastation of the village to talk.

As soon as they were a distance away, I folded my arms, turned my back, and let a few of my own tears escape. How many had been killed this time? Two hundred, maybe more? Only two women left alive in an entire village—and to the world, it would probably seem that human witch hunters had exterminated a nest of devil-worshipping bitches.

The stench of burned flesh, of ruined wood and earth, hung thick in the air. Perhaps the hag was right. Who was I to take on a creature capable of this level of evil? I had power, true. And training and skill. But how could I defeat a being I couldn't even find, much less understand?

Grelda's voice rose, as did Helden's. I did my best to ignore the words, to leave them their privacy, but I knew what was happening. Grelda was explaining to the young witch that she should accompany me onto the Path, to a Sanctuary as yet inviolate, where she would have a better chance of survival. Now that Nire had broken through my protections and located Trier, no witch in this time period would be completely safe. The Shadows could return at any moment for another attack, or even the Shadowmaster. I wasn't strong enough to re-seal connections Nire had shattered and spelled.

My fists clenched, seemingly of their own accord, as Helden wailed. She had just lost everyone she knew and loved, and just learned that Grelda could not go with her. Because of Nire's dark magic, a second trip onto the Path would mean Grelda's death. No one but me, and perhaps the Shadowalker, could survive two exposures to Nire's evil spells without having our life forces drained.

"I will not leave you!" the girl cried, loud enough to hurt my sensitive ears.

And then once more, the two were whispering. Grelda's tone sounded commanding, definite, and harsh.

By the goddess. My heart ached. Sometimes I thought it would be better if I abdicated, or died in one of Nire's massacres. At least I would never have to know this bitterness again.

Some minutes later, Grelda presented Helden to me, and I took the girl's arm.

"Come," I said as gently as I could. "I'll take you to Shallym with me. It's an earlier time, and it will be strange to you, but—"

"She will go," said Grelda in a low, menacing whisper. "Take her now, before it is too late."

I took a slow breath to steady myself, then met the hag's eyes. Her hag-spirit, now a sinewy black cat, lay tense and watching in her arms. "What will you do, Grelda? Where in this time will you go?"

She shrugged and broke my gaze. "There are oldeFolke, and perhaps other villages who will have me. Somewhere far away from Trier."

Arguing would be pointless, as would asking her for definite plans so that I could check on her and offer what protection I could. Hags were proud, and could be deadly if that pride were trampled.

Instead, I gave her a formal half-bow of respect, and took charge of Helden.

Grelda returned the bow, but still would not look at me. Her judgment of my worth was clear, and I couldn't say I blamed her.

The girl and I turned away, toward the Path, and I carefully opened the bonds, steeling myself the assault of poisonous darkness. With Helden's arm in mine, lending what strength I could to her, I escorted her onto the ribbon of energy.

We hesitated only briefly as I raised one hand to close the Path.

At that second, Grelda flung herself inside, screaming along with her hag-spirit. I was too stunned to move—what was she thinking?

Tears streaming, Grelda reached for Helden. Helden reached for her with her free hand, but they never made contact.

Grelda howled and fell to her knees, already gasping and clutching at her chest. Screaming, Helden tried to kneel beside her, but I held the girl back even as I sealed the Path behind us. I had to get her to Shallym, get her off the Path as fast as possible. There was nothing I could do for Grelda, no matter what my heart urged.

As I dragged Helden with me, Grelda writhed. A pale white light rushed out of her skin, and her hag-spirit exploded with a miserable whimper. Seconds later, Grelda faded into a dark outline of herself, then melted into the shadowy cloud infesting the Path walls.

Helden sobbed without cease as I managed to haul her into Shallym and seal the Path behind us. The poor girl cried all the way to the village and outside a hut during the entire time I negotiated with the smallest hag clan to take her in as one of them. I spoke eloquently of Grelda's courage and her love for the fledgling witch. Helden could never be hag by birth, of course, but she could certainly become a hag in her heart, by Grelda's judgment.

This seemed to suffice for the clan leader, and she sent her sisters and their hag-spirits to collect the wailing girl outside.

As I left, Helden's eyes followed me, along with the rest of the hags.

Their gazes seemed to be accusing me of weakness I couldn't deny.

By the time I got back to Shadowbridge, I was heartsick and weary. The morning was yet fresh, but I didn't think I could enjoy it. I also didn't think I could abide breakfast or Bren's boundless energy. Nor could I tolerate the thought of coming upon him asleep, having to touch the muscled curve of his shoulder to wake him—no. No. Not this terrible hour of yet another failure, when it seemed night should still hold me captive in the darkness.

Were it anyone else I needed to wake, I would have nudged his thoughts—but Bren had resisted my mind-touch in the village yesterday. In fact, he shoved me out so hard I quite nearly fell on my backside. I felt certain he realized what he had done, accident or not. No doubt he would practice that skill and use it to shut me out evermore.

And so, Bren was Rol's problem. At least for the moment.

I ventured into Rol's room only long enough to give him news of the destruction of Trier and tell him to take charge of Bren for now. Then, I waited behind my door until I heard the training master greet Bren by dousing him with a pail of water.

The boy's shouts would have bothered a deaf slither.

Once I was certain Rol had Bren well in hand, I crept through Shadowbridge like a churchmouse and hid myself in the drawing room. The easternmost window offered a brilliant view of the new morning sun. As I leaned against the sill, the surge of clean light felt warm on my skin.

So little felt clean and fresh in my life anymore. So little felt hopeful. At least I had these quiet moments in my stronghold. Wherever I was along the Path, I could remember these quiet, sunlit hours when I had time to reflect. To remember what it was like to dream of the future, and not to worry.

Had I ever not worried?

I sighed and drew a yellow ribbon in the air. It coalesced and glittered, as if waiting for me to add colors or shapes. One at a time, I formed bubbles and added them. Sanctuaries. Havens. I had been drawing the Path for as long as it had been created.

Father taught me. Part fun, part lesson. When you were the only child of the King of Witches, there was little time to be carefree. That's why I had no grand history of romantic attachments or social events, as Bren no doubt could boast.

As soon as I could move my fingers, I had been in training to be the most powerful witch on the planet. From Father, I took my skill. But my strength—that came from Mother, along with an abiding knowledge of our history and my purpose. I was to be queen. I had to act the role at every moment. By the time I was eleven years of age, I could escort a new refugee to Father's Path of Shadows without a single breach of manners, whether they were human, olde, or anything in between.

The ribbon I had drawn twinkled in the air. The bubbles looked secure and inviting—golden, even. For that was a golden time. Father had been instrumental in making peace with the older creatures of Earth, the ones time and tradition had forgotten or all but destroyed. Hags, elves, klatch witches, and beings we couldn't name or understand—even nearly extinct creatures like slithers—had been brought back from the sharp edge of oblivion thanks to the Path. They could escape endless hunting by humans, and murder, and the simple exhaustion of always being prey.

Then, Father had prevailed upon human witches to stop being afraid of their more powerful olde ancestors, and he had convinced those ancestors not to use their powers for unfair advantage. It was a splendid achievement, even if Mother and many other cautious human-born witches believed he was making a mistake, trusting the oldeFolke.

Most of us thought he was a genius.

I traced the floating ribbon with one finger.

The oldeFolke were frightening, often odd—but they made such contributions. And then came Nire. The Shadowmaster. Unquestionably oldeFolke, unquestionably powerful. Horribly powerful. But we had learned from defecting hags like Grelda that Nire hated witches and oldeFolke alike. Nire hunted us all, even in our Sanctuaries.

Frowning, I drew a black X-mark on the Path. Dead center, blocking its golden flow.

We knew nothing tangible of Nire's true identity. The hags and klatch witches who fled—they had never seen the Shadowmaster—only sensed the presence and followed commands issued by minions. We had no idea where Nire came from or where the Shadowmaster's stronghold might be located. We didn't even know how such a creature broke into the Path.

As far as we knew, Father and I were the only witches capable of freely crossing on and off the Path. Other witches had to use Father's and my magic to push through the ribbon of energy and for release into the Sanctuaries. But Father and I had never escorted anything like Nire into our safehavens.

And that was before Nire fouled the Path's energy with dark magic, binding many entrances and exits. Sealing off the flow of energy and calling out the Shadows to pollute all they could touch.

Following the will of my mind, the X-mark on my drawn Path radiated darkness. A cloud filled the ribbon, and gray and black bands slowly extended around the Sanctuary bubbles, one at a time. Only a few remained untouched, like Shallym. The rest were invaded, broken, unsafe—destroyed like Trier. The violated, clouded Sanctuaries hovered there, taunting me, until I waved my hands and blew the picture away.

———————

Had Alderon succeeded in crossing the barrier and leaving the Path? No, that was ridiculous. No doubt Alderon became one of the Shadows like Grelda, just after he attempted to leave—as he well deserved.

Of course I knew I shouldn't wish ill on anyone. The Goddess taught that everything you wish upon another being will come back upon you threefold.

I sighed again.

The dawn was to be my respite, and I was spoiling it with worry, as usual. Why could I not think of my childhood or my old hobbies? Riding branches and horses, creating sculptures of air and leaves to amuse my father, showing off new spells to my mother—even changing Rol into various creatures. With his consent—most of the time.

Once I turned Rol into a toad and had to spend three days hunting him. "A lesson," he said, laughing as I changed him back. "A lesson in taking care what you wish for." I had missed him terribly. Mother and Father were so busy, and Rol—it was Rol who had the patience and time for me. Even the patience to be a frog to enhance my training.

All of that seemed so distant now. And foolish.

My eyes burned, and I rubbed them. Before I had left for Trier, I had barely slept, thinking of Bren's smile. Remembering his unkempt brown hair, his stubbled cheeks, and the look in his eyes when he touched my face. He had such power inside him, and his emotions ran so strong that I felt like I could grab them and hold them. Maybe even hold him.

No!

The image of smoldering, ruined Trier intruded on my irresponsible thoughts. I had no time to waste on banalities.

Why did I help Bren learn how to shut me out of his mind? What did that touch mean, the day before? What was he thinking?

By the Goddess. This childish obsession was enough to turn my stomach. Weakness. *Weakness!* Mother was right. I had so much to overcome.

And how could I even care about such trivia when Mother was still missing? My aunts, my cousins—every soul still living on the Path, plus all of Nire's hostages, were counting on me. Just because some ancient oldeFolke said the Shadowalker and I would join hearts. Honestly. I could die tomorrow, and some other witch might see Bren through this quest.

"If his soul is good,

If she trains him true,

If their hearts be joined . . ."

Bren's heart, bound to someone else. That thought sat queer in my belly. I frowned—and the drawing room door burst open.

I whirled around.

Bren stomped in, dressed in his unlaced tunic and brown leather breeches. He had a furious expression, a thick slice of toast in his fist, and wet hair still dripping from Rol's wake-up visit.

"What the—" he sputtered, then seemed to gather himself. "You told him to drown me, didn't you? And we had a date. You owe me some answers."

I couldn't help it. I smiled.

Rol chose that moment to stumble in. "My apologies, Your Highness. He said he had to relieve himself and stole away from the training yard—through the kitchen, I see."

Laughter rolled out before I could stop it. I covered my mouth but could not cease giggling.

Bren glared. Rol stared.

"Let him stay for now." I waved Rol away. "Go and ready the yard before you fetch him. Come back straightaway, though. I suspect he needs much swordwork."

Rol nodded, and his mouth puckered. I sensed the training master was more annoyed than confused. And perhaps a bit worried. Rol always became surly when he worried. Without another word, he bowed and left the drawing room.

Bren crammed the last bite of his apparently stolen toast into his mouth and sat on a small couch near the window. I took my favorite bench, still within arm's reach, and studied his rumpled hair and crumb-covered face. His strong jaw was clear of stubble but at least half a dozen nicks marred his now clean-shaven features. Obviously using Rol's shaving kit would take the boy some getting used to.

After a second, he stopped chewing. "Wha'?" he asked around the toast.

"Nothing," I said, feeling my cheeks heat. Drawing a deep breath, I struggled back to calmness before adding, "I hope your breakfast was pleasing."

Bren wiped his mouth on his hand and nodded. "Slept pretty good, too, except for the nightmares. Especially the one about my dad stringing me up by my toes."

His words had a caustic edge, but I could scarcely blame him. My gaze dropped to my nails, and I picked at the black paint before forcing myself to look up again. "Is your father the angry sort?"

"Yeah, I guess." Bren shrugged. "Mr. Perfection. All he sees are my mistakes, so this stolen-truck-disappearance routine's really going to rack up some points."

"I'm truly sorry." I leaned forward and placed my hand on his. Crumbs tickled my palms, and it was all I could do not to conjure a vat of water and plunge Bren's fingers in for a good cleaning. "My mother— she— well, I understand what you must go through with a parent like that. If there were any other way . . ."

I squeezed his fingers. "Bren, do you understand what your presence here means?"

He shook his head, staring at my hand.

Embarrassed, I pulled away and fought the almost killing urge to wipe my hand where the crumbs had touched me. "The Path of Shadows—without it, witches have no future. My father was a visionary, and wise enough to see this. To create the Path, he used his special royal strength, a strength born of centuries of breeding for the most powerful magic."

Grasping my seat cushion, I leaned forward as I spoke. "Father's creation worked. The Path was saving us, human witch and oldeFolke alike." I frowned and that familiar ache twisted in my belly. "Until Nire. The Shadowmaster invaded the energy and used dark spells to bind the Path. Since then, our Sanctuaries have become hunting grounds for evil."

Bren frowned as if thinking about some remembered dream. He seemed to consider saying something, then crammed his hand in his pocket, hesitated, and shrugged. "So? I mean, you're all witches, right? So you can't really get hurt or die, can you?"

"I assure you, we're as mortal and frail as the unconverted." I drew back and clenched my hands in my lap. "Even after witches are fully aware of their own powers, they live the lifespan of their species, and face the same diseases, the same risks. And the same vulnerability to murder and massacre."

A flash of rage singed my insides, and my back stiffened. Thoughts of the Shadowmaster, of the horrors perpetrated by Nire's minions, always stabbed at my soul.

Bren kept his eyes on my hands without comment, but started pulling at a loose thread on his tunic. I could tell he was listening. Perhaps not believing a word I spoke, but at least he saw fit to give me his attention.

"Nire raids the Sanctuaries at will," I said. "Stealing witches, killing them, holding them hostage. And the Shadows—lost souls who can't find a way to the afterlife—they were already difficult to manage along the Path, but now they're murderous."

Bren's expression didn't change, but his eyes moved from my hands and darted here and there, as if I were now boring him.

A spark of anger ignited in the pit of my chest. I curled my fingers into my palms to keep from using them to hex him. "Nire won't stop with us, with our world. Once witches have all perished, Nire will come for the nonwitching world, too. Humans and unconverted humans like you. Nire intends to take the planet for the Shadows."

"Is this Nire some kind of Hitler?" Bren settled back in his seat, finally bringing his gaze to mine. "The bastard goes around killing people and witches just because they're different from some ideal?"

I nodded. "Yes."

"Jeez." He scowled and rolled his eyes to the ceiling. "Even here there's intolerance. Can't people just get along?"

"Bren." I leaned forward again as his attention turned back to me. "Unless you help me defeat Nire, we will all die. Witches and humans alike."

An incredulous look passed across his features. "Yeah, right. You're trying to tell me that you think I can help you cream some Shadowmaster dictator who's been kidnapping and killing witches." He ran his hand through his thick hair and laughed, but it was hollow at best. "Jazz, you are out of your mind. I'm no hero."

It took all my years of training to keep my voice calm, to not let him see the fear his denial caused me. "I speak the truth. I need your assistance."

"Why me?" Bren's warm brown eyes focused on my face. "What's so special about me?"

"I— I don't know," I admitted, feeling that strange chill of fear again. I dismissed it. The twinge of concern made no sense, and it was beginning to make me angry. "But I went in search of the Shadowalker. The spell I cast—to bring me the soul who could stop Nire—delivered you to me. You, out of all the people in the nonwitching world."

Bren raised an eyebrow, and his mouth twitched. "Your magic made me feel like I had to pee?"

I smiled despite the heaviness in my soul. "Not . . . exactly. But the magic brought you, the true champion, to me."

"Can magic make a mistake?" Bren's face darkened. "I'm nobody's champion, except for maybe my baseball team— but even there, I make lots of errors. And my mom, she's the only other person who believes in me, always says how I'm destined for great things, but I think she's just being a mom." He flipped his hair out of his face with one hand. "This has all got to be a mistake."

"No." I shook my head. "Magic never makes a mistake. Only witches make mistakes."

"Sh- crap," he muttered. "I sure fit in with all the loonies here. I can't get anything right. My dad sure made that clear enough."

My heart ached at his words. It took everything in me not to grab his hand again, but I maintained control. "You don't believe in yourself. That's natural in the unconverted. Your talent is strong, though. I believe in you already. I know you can find the power to defeat Nire."

Bren began to bounce his knee in a nervous movement, as he had last night. "Assuming I agree to all this craziness, what makes you so sure I can do it?"

Because I feel it in my heart, I wanted to scream.

The thought shocked me near speechless. "I— I— er, well. Because I am sure. I . . . sense it."

Bren grinned at my discomfort.

I should have been angry, but seeing him happy for a moment thrilled me. My mind fished for something—

anything!—to relieve the strange tension now floating between us.

"You mentioned King Arthur," I said. "So, you must know Merlyn?"

"Yes." Bren pulled at the lacing on his tunic. "I know about him, I mean. Never met the guy."

"Merlyn is a shining example of what the Path accomplished before Nire's incursion." I got to my feet to walk off my own nervous energy. Which was in itself strange—I had never been nervous about anything before meeting Bren. "He's actually from your future, but his town turned on him. Tried to burn his home. Would have killed him in his sleep, but he walked the Path of Shadows back, back to a time when his knowledge and personality were of benefit to the world."

Bren looked amused and his eyes sparkled. "So, that's why the legend says Merlyn lived backward? Cool."

He stood and took a step toward me. Not to menace this time. No.

This time, I feared he meant to touch me.

"Witches of Merlyn's talents are very rare." I paused in midstep, struggling not to run out the door like a timid child. "Even Merlyn began as an unconverted. Raw talent, no belief, just like you. Human, I mean. Unlike the hags and klatchKoven witches you encountered in Shallym."

"Knew there was something weird about them." Bren smiled again, but his gaze deepened. He reached toward me, hand and heart, brushing against that part of myself I kept so carefully hidden.

A shiver coursed my spine as he touched my arm, letting his fingers slide down, across my wrist to my hand.

The warmth of his caress made me gasp, and I could not tear my eyes from his.

"So, what about you?" he murmured, his damp brown hair softening the rugged angles of his face. "Were you human before you became a witch . . . or were you something else?"

"Human," I whispered, trying not to tremble from his touch as he drew me closer to him. Once more I felt that indefinable power within him, and how his feelings surged free like the tides or the wind. What I wouldn't give to touch that freedom, or to grasp it for myself. "Most of us begin as humans, though my parents were witches, so I grew up knowing and believing in magic."

Bren's face was so close now, his palms burning the flesh of my arms.

I wanted him to fully show me that soft, vulnerable side that I had glimpsed occasionally since his arrival. I wanted him to kiss me, wanted it so much—but guilt welled like a spring, drowning my passion. My spells brought him here by force. My magic stole him from his family. For what?

To fight some hopeless war with me and end up a burned husk like those poor souls in Trier?

To keep me company so for once, I wouldn't be alone?

He leaned toward me, bringing his lips a hairsbreadth from mine, but I turned my head, gently pushing him away.

"No," I said, not daring to look into those now warm and inviting brown eyes. "I can't do this. Not . . . now."

chapter nine

So, Miss High-and-Mighty was giving me the brush-off. Thought she was too good for me.

I pulled back and folded my arms across my chest. "You can't *do* what?"

Jazz's cheeks went red, and she looked flustered. "Kiss you."

"Why would I want to kiss you?" I tried to look like it was the farthest thing from my mind. "You're the last person I'd want to kiss. Hell, I'd kiss Rol before you."

That did it.

Jazz looked like I had slapped her. I felt kind of bad, but not bad enough to apologize.

"At least we agree on something," she snapped, her chin in the air and her golden eyes flashing.

She was gorgeous. I really wanted to kiss her then. So hard and long it would make her head spin.

"Your Majesty," Rol said from the doorway.

Jazz and I whirled toward him at the same time.

"This imbecile is all yours, Rol." Jazz's eyes spit fire as she looked from him to me. "And Bren was just telling me how much he desires to kiss you."

With that, she stuck her chin even higher in the air and swept out past Rol.

He raised his eyebrows, and I held up my hands. "Uh, no. You're a nice guy and all, but I really don't want to kiss you."

Rol grunted. "I find that most reassuring."

Shaking my head, I grinned and said, "Jazz sure has some temper, doesn't she?"

"You have no idea how fearsome her temper can be." He gave a nod toward the hall. "Come now to the smithy. We have much to do today."

With a shrug, I headed toward the door. "Sure, why not. Maybe you can clue me in on what I have to do to get out of this place."

Rol kept silent, taking me down a long hall and into the kitchen, then out a back door and into the huge dirt yard. The sky was cloudy, and it was still cool enough to chill my wet head. The ocean smell was strong, even though we weren't right on the beach. My damp shirt clung to my chest and the leather pants felt strange, but comfortable. The boots, though, they would take some getting used to.

The nicks on my face from shaving stung as I followed Rol to a building that looked like a blacksmith's shop, which made sense since he said we were going to a "smithy." A big pit of fire blazed at the center and all kinds of tools and weapons lined the walls. It smelled of smoke and iron, not to mention a lot like the guys' locker room at my school.

Rol eyed me like he was sizing me up for something. "You are left-handed, are you not?"

The heat made me dizzy. I wiped sweat from my forehead with the back of my hand as I nodded.

He grabbed a leather belt with a long, wide thing on the side of it—a sheath for a sword, I guessed. Next thing I knew, he was strapping the belt around my waist. I felt like a gunslinger the way it settled on my hips.

"Stay here," Rol ordered before disappearing through a doorway.

While I waited for him, I wondered why I was going along with all of this. I didn't really believe that I was any kind of champion, but after what happened in the village yesterday, I had the feeling I might not be so lucky if I went there on my own again. Maybe Rol would help me get back to where I came from—if he dared to cross the royal pain in the ass.

With a sigh, I glanced at the manor, and for an instant, I thought I saw Jazz watching me from a window. But when I blinked, nothing was there. I had to grin, thinking about the look on Jazz's face when I told her I would rather kiss Rol than her.

Served the witch right.

My smile slowly changed to a frown.

Jazz really was a witch. And I really was in some premedieval fortress, above some pre-medieval town.

It was all too much to take in—witches, Shadowalkers, and some serious Nazi named Nire. The Shadowmaster.

Yeah, right.

I had to be losing my mind. Maybe Dad finally got to me, and I had some sort of psychotic breakdown on my way to the beach. That would be typical. Irresponsible Bren. Impulsive Bren. It would be just like me to go insane at an inconvenient time—and lose Mom's truck in the process.

Rol ducked back through the doorway, carrying a silver sword. The blade glittered in the dim light of the smithy. He handed it to me, handle first.

"No way." I stepped back. "I don't do knives and guns."

"Take it," Rol instructed. His voice sounded like gravel falling into a pit. "I believe it is yours."

"Uh-uh." I backed up another step. "It's a wonder I didn't slice my throat open with that shaving tool you made me use this morning. I'd cut my arm off with that thing for sure."

Rol closed the gap between us. "Take the sword." The giant's eyes glittered, and he seemed tense. Nervous. Like if I didn't take the sword, he'd get mad.

And he was my only friend here in freak-land. I definitely didn't want him pissed with me for real. Still, the thought of holding a sword made me nervous. The thought of holding anything sharp made me nervous. I had a bad habit of making disasters with dangerous objects. Like the time I was helping Dad prune Mom's rose bushes—and I almost chopped off one of his fingers with the shears because I wasn't paying attention to what I was doing. That episode ended with seventeen stitches in Dad's hand, my being grounded, and having to listen to a never-ending lecture.

"Irresponsible . . ." His voice was like a hammer in my mind. "Impulsive . . ."

Grinding my teeth, I reached forward and grabbed the handle of the sword. The moment I touched it, my hand tingled and a surge of energy flowed through my arm to every part of my body. I felt wired, like I'd had at least a dozen cups of coffee.

My skin glowed silver for the briefest of moments and then it was gone, and I was sure I must have imagined it. But the energy in my body stayed. I felt as enormous as Rol, and so alive. Like I'd just hit a grand slam to win the World Series.

How do you like that, Dad? Huh? Want to come cut me down now?

I moved away from Rol and swept the sword back and forth in the air. Strange designs flashed along the blade. I could tell the edge was sharper than sharp, and the weapon was heavy, but it felt comfortable, like my favorite baseball bat. It was about the same length, but wider. Like two bats put together.

When I looked from the sword to Rol, he was smiling as he said, "I wasn't certain before, but I had hoped."

"Hoped what?" The sword grabbed my attention again, and I made another smooth stroke through the air.

"That you would be the one to master this blade." Rol patted my shoulder. "You will do, boy. You will *do*. I should have known better than to doubt Jasmina. The queen is . . . tense, but quite accurate with her spellwork."

Excitement swelled through me, and as weird as it sounds, I couldn't wait for Rol to show me how to use that incredible sword.

And show me, he did.

He worked me all over that training yard, teaching me the proper way to hold the handle—which was really called a "hilt," Rol told me—swing the blade, block with it, and at least a dozen other things. Rol was a relentless coach, pushing me harder and harder—tougher than any baseball coach I'd ever had. But I didn't mind.

Training felt normal. Natural. I had trained off and on my whole life, every year since Mom started me in T-ball. Even then, I had wanted to be good at something. To have one thing in my life I didn't drop, break, lose, step on, or piss off. And I thought if I got really good at baseball, Dad could at least be proud of me for that.

Like that would ever happen.

I swung my blade so hard I almost spun around, but caught myself with my back foot.

A look of satisfaction covered Rol's dark face.

"Well met," he thundered, and I thought he might be about to give me a rest break since we had been at it for over an hour. Then he whacked my shoulder and said, "Again!"

After what seemed like endless drills on balance, positioning, and footwork, Rol said, "Enough play, boy." He raised his own sword. "Defend yourself."

He whirled and swung his blade at me, cutting a wide arc. I shifted my weight and blocked the blow, pivoting out of his path. He spun to attack me again, but my sword was already up and my stance set.

Rol charged once more. This time he angled suddenly to my right. Without thinking, I switched my sword to my right hand and slashed out at him. His momentum was so great he had to flip and roll forward to avoid my suddenly greater reach.

I spun on my heel and met him with my sword up as he scrambled to his feet. His eyes blazed and he raised his sword again, as if to attack.

Then a smile cracked his face, and he said, "Time for midday meal."

To my surprise, the cloud cover had burned away and the sun was already in the west. My stomach growled in agreement, and I laughed and sheathed the blade. Sweat soaked my hair and clothes, and my muscles felt that ache of a good workout. The sword slapped the side of my leg as I followed Rol across the training yard to the smithy.

"So tell me, Rol," I said as we poured cold water from a rain barrel over our heads. "How and when do I get back to where I came from?"

Rol wiped his hand over his wet face and looked puzzled. "Did the queen not explain to you about the Path of Shadows and the Shadowmaster?"

I pushed back my wet hair. "Yeah, she did."

He shrugged and poured another bucket of water over his head. "Then you know that anyone the queen takes onto the Path is trapped in his first Sanctuary until such time as the Shadowmaster kills him, or until the Shadowmaster is conquered."

Water dripped down my face as I processed what he said. He had said it all like it was matter-of-fact. No big deal.

"So," I replied very slowly, adding together all that Jazz had told me, "what you're saying is that Jazz purposely brought me here, knowing that I can't leave until the Shadowmaster is defeated, and that I might be killed."

Rol nodded. "Aye."

She had told me, in so many words. But, damn her. She knew I didn't fully understand that! Rage engulfed me like white-hot fire. My breathing got faster, and I ground my teeth so hard it made my head hurt.

When I got my hands around her neck . . .

Respond, don't react.

Take the sword up to that castle and make her send me home. She's got to know a way.

Respond, don't react.

Oh, shut the hell up.

Through gritted teeth, I growled, "I need to have a word with the queen."

Rol raised one eyebrow and shrugged again. "As you wish. But I will be watching to see that you do not harm her. Or try to leave for the village. We have already come too far to risk you being breakfast for a hag or sex slave to an enchantress."

I was so mad I barely registered the sex slave comment. In fact, I was so mad, I didn't care if ten beautiful women wanted me as a sex slave. All I could think of was Jazz, and how much I wanted to take my sword and hack up her entire mansion.

Rol stepped out of my way.

I clenched my fists and headed toward the manor.

chapter ten

JAZZ

He would rather kiss Rol, indeed! Well, I knew a few spells that could grant that tasty wish.

In my mind's eye, I saw Rol kissing a fire-lipped camel. This was but one of my moments of temper. I had been twelve, I think. And I'd conjured it just to make Rol kiss it because he had been teasing me. Rol was a master teaser.

Unlike Bren, who was nothing but a master falcon dropping.

I flicked my fingers and blasted a vase into sparkling dust. That vase had always bothered me—all the cracks and irregular patterns. It looked messy. Mother wouldn't have tolerated it.

Cleaning my stronghold helped me to spend my anger in productive ways. Defeat my inner weaknesses. After all, an ordered fortress was a successful fortress.

Between monitoring for the Shadowmaster and venting my frustrations by redecorating, my wrists had begun to ache before noon. A few of Shadowbridge's rooms wound up rather bare, but all were clean. Each time I removed a flaw or piece of dirt, the tight ball of panic in my belly eased. Until I saw the next out-of-place rug or dusty chair. Was my entire life contaminated with dirt? I glanced around, feeling tense pains in my chest.

No. No. Everything was clean. Clean and bright.

I felt thankful I had few servants to wonder over my actions or feel displaced by my efficiency. Only my training master directly attended me, as befitted a proper ruler of the witches. Rol had been with me and only me since birth, first as a protector, then a trainer, and now the one witch sworn to defend me to his death. If I died young, Rol would carry on with my battles and appoint my heir. If I had an heir, Rol would support the child until the child's second could be located. Perhaps Rol was slaying Bren at the smithy to preserve my honor. Or at least beating the brat-boy senseless.

What had I ever seen in Bren?

For the life of me, I didn't know. A goat had more charm, couth, and bearing. Bren was more like—like a donkey. A stubborn, smelly donkey.

Wonder how a donkey would fare against a slither?

Hmm. I would have to have Rol wake a slither for the training, first thing on the morning. No, no. Better yet, I would wake it myself and deliver it. With proper shielding, of course, since they were protected beasts.

Oh, why not now? My own little surprise, just for the initiate. He could not ask for a greater proving-challenge.

But it had been months since I transported an object as large as a slither. I knew I should practice at least once before I went to the smithy. The thought of making a fool of myself in front of Bren was profoundly unpleasant.

I strode into the kitchen, nearly startling my elfling cook beyond recovery. Acaw glared at me over a pot of stew large enough to roast three of his kind, and raised his thick eyebrows. In the window, his crow-brother ruffled his feathers and gave a sharp cry of rebuke, but Acaw said not a word.

Typical.

Even the masters of the wood dared not speak against the Queen of the Witches. I barely heard three words out of Acaw on a favorable day; therefore, I didn't bother with conversation. He grunted as I headed for the back door, already concentrating, already working the transport spell.

The back bailey stretched before me, quiet and deserted. Overhead, the sun was midsky and waning. My hands whirled before me, over and over, building speed. Building power. I picked a spot close on the path in front of me, around a blind curve from the smithy so Bren and Rol couldn't observe my trial transport.

Drawing a breath, I reached out with my hearing, deep into the nearby woods. Small heartbeats. Large. Larger still. Ah! Huge and doubled! A slither!

My fingers curled to a fist, and my muscles shook with the effort of concentration. A bang—well, in truth, a small explosion—announced the success of my spell.

When I opened my eyes, I was but five lengths away from one of the largest slithers I had ever seen. Barely wakened from its day sleep, it was too sluggish to react in good time.

Luminous green scales shifted along its enormous neck as it turned its stupid eyes in my direction. Ground trembled beneath the lash of its ridged tail. Claws as large as my leg dug into the earth, and the beast opened its cavernous, toothy mouth. The stench of charred, rotten flesh filled the air as it spread wings almost the length of the bailey.

I threw up my hand just in time to shield myself from a massive blast of fire.

Yes, I thought as the flames broiled around my protective veil. This beast would do quite nicely. Perhaps Bren would wish to kiss it, too.

The slither stopped its attack. Scales crinkled as it turned its neck once more, tracking something behind it—and my heart ceased beating.

By the Goddess! Bren. Here, now!

The boy had come to a halt near the slither, obviously stunned into inactivity. His eyes were wide and his arms hung straight by his side.

Smoke poured from the slither's nostrils and it roared.

My skin crawled. I nearly gagged from the beast's odor. I scarce had a chance to throw a shield around Bren before the beast breathed a wall of fire right on his head.

Of all the ridiculous luck!

As the fire dispersed, Bren staggered and grabbed for his sword. He yanked at it, but thank the fates, the sheath held the blade well. He wasn't yet accustomed to the weapon.

The slither swung its head back and forth and flicked its wings as I worked feverishly on my transport spell. My mouth had gone dry, and my head pounded. This was not the satisfying scene of vengeance I had planned. I couldn't allow the beast to hurt Bren. Moreover, I could not risk Bren hurting the slither. Part of Father's peace accord with the oldeFolke had involved protecting endangered species needed for their spellwork.

Weakness. Mind and blood. Mother was right.

The hags would mutiny. Never mind the klatchKovens and all other witches. The oldeFolke would come unhinged if Bren damaged one scale on the slither's ugly head.

Leave it to me to cause the Shadowalker to violate the protection of sacred beasts. I could just hear my mother. If I had to banish Bren to the shadows and consign all witches to their doom over something I did . . .

My fingers ached from spellmoving. Another few seconds yet. Just a few.

Bren was yelling so loudly his voice drowned the hammer of the slither's dual heart. Clearly in shock, he yanked again on his sword hilt, stumbled, and fell on his backside.

The slither charged just as I curled my fingers to a fist.

The afternoon exploded with the force of my spell. Grass and leaves, even stones, swirled, sucked into the vortex. Bren began to slide forward. A huge crash echoed through the bailey, and the beast disappeared.

With every ounce of energy I possessed, I held the spell, and held and held until I was sure the slither had been returned to its day lair. Then, exhausted, I dropped to my knees, rocks biting into my flesh as I hit the ground.

I could barely breathe.

Bren was up now, having recovered his senses. He strode back and forth across the bailey, raking one hand through his hair, and still shouting. "What was that thing? A dragon? Why was it here? What did you do with it?"

Rol's angry voice cut through the chaos. "It was a slither, boy." The training master treated me to a foul-humored glare as he came to a stop at Bren's side. "A dragon, yes. And a beast with no earthly business out from its lair in daylight."

Rol's judging tone lodged beneath my skin. I forced myself to my feet, returning his wicked stare. In a few seconds, Rol looked away.

Not a victory, no. My training master was choosing not to fight with me. Somehow, that hurt worse than a tongue-lashing.

He clapped his hand against Bren's back. "Never fear. You will have opportunity to face beasts much worse than slithers in a fair fight one day."

Bren grinned at Rol like an old friend before smirking at me.

Fire ignited in my belly, hotter than any slither might offer. Had Bren won my training master away from me so easily? Rol was loyal to me. Only me! If I lost him, I would have— I would have no one.

No one and nothing.

Nothing at all.

Bren sauntered toward me across the grass, swaying as arrogant boys tend to do. In the background, Rol stood with arms folded, refusing my attempts to meet his eyes.

"You and I, we gotta talk," Bren said.

"No," I snapped. "*We* do not. Go inside. Or go and kiss Rol, as you so fondly desire. The two of you seem quite close now."

Bren frowned, coming to a halt mere inches from me. "Rol told me what you did. About the Path and how you decided to trap me. Was there some reason you left that tidbit out of our little heart-to-heart this morning?"

My fingers bent of their own accord, and Rol moved quickly out of my line of sight. "I didn't leave it out. You simply failed to understand. We were both distracted this morning. Speak whatever lies you will, but you're as transparent to me as flat sandglass."

"Am I?" Bren grinned, and I wanted to sear him a new mouth. "Read my thoughts. Go ahead. And while you're at it, maybe you want to be more careful about conjuring up dragons in the yard. They don't seem too friendly."

"Leave me be," I warned. "I have better things to do than spar with the likes of you."

Bren snorted. "The likes of me? You're the one who's a liar! And you cheat, and you— you steal people off a public highway by making them have to take a piss. How could you do something like that to anyone? How could you do that to me?"

"Bren," Rol said. He sounded worried.

"I did nothing to you on purpose!" I shouted. "Do you think I'd deliberately seek the one boy on Earth who would drive me to the brink of madness? I can't believe I have to turn the fate of my mother—my entire kingdom—over to you!"

In one surprisingly fluid motion, Bren ripped his sword from his scabbard and threw it at my feet. "I didn't ask for this, remember? Don't witches have good memories?"

"Bren," Rol said again, but I scarcely heard him over the rush of blood in my ears.

"By the Goddess, but I wish I could forget," I growled. "Forget my father and hundreds more, murdered in ways you cannot imagine. Forget my people, hunted and terrified. Forget my mother, missing and in the grip of the worst evil that ever existed." I lifted my chin and glared at him. "You're the most callous cretin I've ever known!"

"You're the cretin!" Bren yelled.

Rage poured energy through my every fiber. My hand moved before the next words even left his mouth. A flick of the wrist, and Bren flared like a falling star.

In seconds, he took on an appearance more befitting his personality. The huge ears were particularly to my liking, and the black hooves, too.

So there. You haven't learned to resist my magic completely. How does it feel to be your true self?

Bren flicked his tail and blinked at me, and I smiled.

He made a much better donkey than a person, after all.

Laughing harder than I had laughed in months, I turned on my heel and fairly skipped through the kitchen door.

chapter eleven

BREN

I felt weird. Beyond weird. And I had the sudden desire to bray.

Jazz had done something to me, but I wasn't exactly sure what it was. For a moment, I was too stunned to move. My limbs tingled and I felt a little dizzy, and I had a hard time focusing. It was all I could do to watch her go back into the manor, cackling her stupid head off.

And it was like I was standing on my hands and feet, but taller. My ear twitched and rotated toward the sound of her laughter, and my tail swished.

My tail?

I tried to look at Rol, but I couldn't see him by looking straight at him—as if my eyes were on either side of my head. I had to look out of one eye.

He was crouched down and staring at the ground, his arms resting on his thighs and his hands clasped.

"What happened?" My mouth felt huge and strange as I spoke. At least the witch hadn't made me mute.

Rol shook his head and looked at me. "It is most unwise to upset the queen."

"Whatever." My hip started to itch and my skin shivered. "What did she do to me?"

"You are an ass," he said.

"Well, thanks a lot." I stomped a back hoof. "You're no prince yourself."

His lips twitched. "I mean to say that Her Majesty turned you into a jackass. A donkey."

"A donkey?" My tail swished again and I shook my head. Hair flopped across my neck.

Rol sighed. "Aye."

"What a total witch."

"That she is."

I bared my teeth and felt my lips curling. "Oh, I don't just mean a witch, I mean a b— never mind." My coat itched some more, like flies were crawling over my hide, and my skin shivered. "You're a witch, too, right? So can you change me back?"

Rol sighed again and shook his head. "I am a witch. But I cannot alter the spell of the Queen of Witches."

My stomach rumbled. I had a sudden craving for sweet oats and hay. A horsey smell met my nose, and I glanced around to see what it was.

Oh wait. That must be me.

I shook my head and stomped a hoof. "I guess I'll just have to hunt her down and make her change me back."

Rol's gaze cut to me and his face twisted into a horrified expression that was almost comical. I would have laughed if I wasn't so ticked at Jazz.

"Nay," he said. "Dare not cross Her Majesty again. You had best remain here until she comes to her senses."

"Bull." I backed up, stumbled, and nearly fell over. When I tried to turn, I ended up going in circles a few times, making myself dizzier than I was before. I kicked out my hind legs, got my bearings, and headed toward the manor.

I pictured myself kicking my hind legs again, but this time right at Jazz, and knocking her to the moon. Or better yet, my donkey teeth biting her right on the ass. But, no. Even if she was a witch, she was still a girl—a female. I was stronger than her, at least physically, and I wouldn't hurt her like that. No. I'd think up a better way to get even, no matter how long it took.

Behind me, Rol said, "It is most unwise . . ."

With my strange vision, my perception was off and I scraped my shoulder against the doorframe as I walked into the manor. I was so mad I barely felt a thing. My hooves clattered across the stone floor as I trotted through the kitchen.

"Where's Jazz?" I asked a short man whom I suspected might be an elf.

The elf-dude dropped the bag of flour he was holding, and a cloud of white powder coated him, causing him to look like a small, white statue. His mouth and eyes were wide, like he couldn't believe what I was asking. Though maybe he just hadn't had a donkey talk to him before.

"Well?" I asked.

"Drawing room," he squeaked. Behind him, in one of the wide kitchen windows, a crow fluttered and squawked.

"Thanks," I muttered.

I never remembered being so mad in my life. My head was on fire, and I wanted to smash my fist—well, hoof—into a wall. But the walls were stone, and I would probably just have broken some bones.

One thing about having four legs was that I could run pretty fast. But when I rounded a corner, I skidded on the stone floor and my hooves almost went out from under me. I regained my balance, barreled into the drawing room, and stopped just short of running over Jazz. Right then I would have liked nothing better than to trample her under my hooves for humiliating me, but I managed to control myself.

Jazz stumbled back, then straightened and gave me that snotty look of hers. "Leave before I turn you into a worm and grind you beneath my heel."

It really ticked me off that I couldn't look straight at her, that I had to stare out of one eye.

"You can't stand it if someone talks back to you or has a difference of opinion."

She narrowed her gaze. "That's not true."

"Yeah, it is." I took a couple of steps toward her so that my donkey nose was practically in her face. "And it was wrong to use your magic on me like this. You're no better than bullies who beat up a kid who isn't as strong as them. I didn't have a chance to fight back."

Jazz clenched her fists, her cheeks turning bright red. "I'm warning you. Leave, or—"

"Or what?" I stamped a hoof and swished my tail. "You're going to kill me maybe? Oh, wait, I know. Turn me into a monkey to humiliate me some more. If this were a fair fight, I could take you down."

She raised her hand. "Bren—"

"What's with you?" I cut her off and blew air out my nostrils. "You take me away from my life, my family, my world, and shove me into this— this— *hell hole,* where there's no way for me to get back unless I do what you need me to. And to top it all, you get off on turning me into a donkey."

I tossed my head and stamped another hoof, hoping I was getting dirt all over her stupid floor. "Yeah, I have no choice, just like you said. You have chosen me. But I don't give a sh- crap about you or your family or any other witch. I'll go fight your stupid Shadowmaster and then get the hell out of here, because I'd like nothing better than to never see your face ever again."

Jazz had turned so white that her eyes looked as bright as gold coins. I almost thought she looked ready to cry, but I didn't feel a bit sorry for her. She clenched and unclenched her fists, and her lips moved, but nothing came out.

My idiotic tail swished as I glared at her out of one eye. At least I hoped it looked like I was glaring, if that was something donkeys could do. My heart pounded and my hide bristled. What if she did turn me into a worm and stomp on me?

She backed away, and then her hands moved so fast I could hardly see them. A flash of light blinded me and my body tingled, like ants crawling over my skin. When I could see again, I staggered and fell to one knee.

Knee. Leather pants. Hands! I was me again.

My legs were shaky as I stumbled to my feet and faced her. Still she said nothing, her chin raised and a defiant glint in her eyes.

"While I'm being honest," I said, standing so close I could have wrung her neck. "I really did want to kiss you this morning, and I know you wanted to kiss me, too. But after this little stunt, I can see what kind of person or witch you really are." I folded my arms across my chest. "As far as I'm concerned, I want as little to do with you as possible. So let's just get this training crap out of the way and get this whole mess over with so I can go home."

Jazz went even paler and kept her mouth shut tight. Her fingers twitched as she raised her hand to her throat, and it was all I could do not to flinch.

Before she could say or do another thing, I spun away from her and stomped out the door of the drawing room. My skin crawled, as if her eyes were burning holes through my back. Ignoring her, I stormed through the strangely empty and spotless mansion.

I didn't stop walking until I reached the yard, where I picked up my sword. When I didn't see Rol, I sheathed the weapon and headed across the training yard toward the smithy. I found him there, sharpening his own blade.

He raised his eyebrows and stopped in mid-swipe. "The queen returned you to your normal form."

"Yeah." I rotated my shoulders, trying to work the knots out of my muscles. "We had another little heart-to-heart."

With a nod, Rol stood and sheathed his sword. "You begged Her Majesty's forgiveness."

I snorted. "Like hell. I told her exactly what I thought about her. She's nothing but a control freak, and when we get rid of Nire, I don't ever want to see her again."

"And she let you . . . live?" Rol looked so shocked that I was afraid he was going to pass out on me.

"Yeah." I shrugged.

He kept shaking his head, and he had this stupid smile. The kind a dad gets—a good dad—when his kid does something special. "By the Goddess. Never would I have dreamed to see the day."

"Whatever." A sense of unease nagged at me as I kicked at the dark soil with my boot. "Rol, has Jazz actually killed? People, I mean."

Rol wrinkled his forehead and looked thoughtful. "Jasmina is so very powerful. Centuries of breeding stand behind the queen. The strongest magical blood runs through her veins. Her threats have been sufficient enough so far, but I have never doubted she would kill, if need be—or if she were angered to such a point."

Relief poured through me. At least she wasn't a murderer—yet, anyway. I had a strong feeling she'd been way tempted with me.

My stomach growled. "Hey, I'm hungry, but I don't want to eat around Jazz. Can we just grab something from the kitchen and eat out here?"

"Aye." Rol grinned and clapped me on my back with his huge palm, nearly pitching me head first into the rain barrel. "It is most unbelievable to think the queen has met her match."

chapter twelve

There was nothing left in the drawing room but
the bench beneath my favorite window. Even the
cushions on it were gone.

My fingers ached from the work. My wrists felt
like I had plunged them into dull fire and knives. And my
head—that same pounding behind my eyes. As if something
wished to crawl out of my skull.

Turning Bren into a donkey had been wrong. Cowardly,
even, but I would be damned to the Shadows before I told
him that. Still, I couldn't allow such lapses in judgment in
the future. No more using magic against the Shadowalker.
Period. I was making that vow to myself, for his sake, and for
my own.

And because I was not a bully.

What was wrong with me? Was I losing my sanity?

Mother always said if I didn't keep to the highest training standard, my "weak blood," the blood she was so sure came from my ever-careless father, would win. I would disappoint her and let the kingdom down like he did, when he admitted the oldeFolke to the path. And when he tried to reason with the insane people in Middle Salem.

Pictures flashed through my mind as I sat on the floor and hugged my knees.

I could still see Father, with his affable grin and loose white shirt, meeting with the witches of Middle Salem, the Salem of 1692. Laying the plans for our escape. And that awful night, September 19, 1692, when he gave his life for us. Father died due to human folly and fear, a "full death," unlike those killed too young by accident or evil purpose. His soul would have moved into Summerland, beyond Talamadden, death's haven—and maybe even beyond our understanding, to become one with the universe. He made the sacrifice willingly, believing his death would allow the rest of us to escape the persecutions to come.

Instead, we walked into the Shadowmaster's trap.

That was four years past, in absolute moments—but it was over three hundred years ago in Bren's nonwitching world and in L.O.S.T. And yet in Shallym, it was over a thousand years in the future.

Such a reality would certainly boggle an untrained human mind.

"The land is the key," Father had told the witches in the Middle Salem meeting. "The city officials are only accusing you of witchcraft so they might take possession of your lands, as the law allows. Stand your ground! If we expose the true motives of these accusers, how can this madness continue?"

Mother had been sitting next to me in that meeting. Her stern face was inches from mine when she leaned to whisper, "Your father is a fool, Jasmina. He trusts too much in the good nature of others. These unconverted will turn on him like mad dogs. Mind what you see and mark my words. Soon, ruling the witches will be your task, for he will no doubt get himself killed in this pursuit."

I sighed and rubbed my temples. At the time, I thought it was more of her vicious criticism.

But she had been right, my mother.

In days, my father had been murdered by the humans and the unconverted, pressed to death in Middle Salem. On purpose. By "pious" men who believed they were ridding the village of witches.

As his only direct descendant, I became Queen of the Witches. Guardian of the precious Path. The Path Father created with his brilliant mind, despite what Mother thought of his skill and intellect. For he had been truly brilliant.

I could almost see Father sitting beside me now, laughing at the bare drawing room, pointing his graceful fingers at empty spaces and restoring what I had destroyed.

"Quite the temper, my love," he would no doubt say, as he had so many times. "Are you angry with your mother again? Well, she certainly is a complex being—but do not think to judge her until you know her true heart as I do. Come, come, sweet Jasmina. Next, you'll be accusing her of being Nire. Give me my hug and go and find us some fresh mushrooms for a rabbit stew."

A tear slid to my cheek and I slapped it away.

So many times I had brought him mushrooms. Stew after stew. Eating with him was like a warm hug, filling me with joy and love.

Gone forever now.

I scrubbed another tear from my cheek.

Sentiment was useless. Sobbing was for the ailing and the weak. Not for a queen who must see to her people. Besides, it was well past time for monitoring, and the very air about Shallym had been thick with trouble since Bren's appearance in the market.

As though the Shadowmaster had found my Sanctuary. As though Nire knew the Shadowalker was here.

But that was impossible. If Nire had found Shallym, we would be as dead as the witches in Trier.

Still, something bothered me.

I thought of Bren, and the room around me blurred. I smelled flowers and cinnamon spice and knew I was about to have a vision. I'd had them since childhood, though less and less frequently of late. Drawing on years of training, I cleared my mind and kept my eyes unfocused.

The image that formed was all too familiar.

My teeth slammed together, and I felt the day's fatigue like a harsh yoke on my neck and chest. Still, I didn't reject this gift from the Goddess, this rare prescience that might give me needed information.

Blinking, but keeping my gaze adjusted to nothing, I knew it was Bren standing before me, laughing. His eyes were no longer the warm brown I had come to like—but the awful, bright bruise-blue I had known and hated. *Alderon.* Bren had Alderon's eyes!

And then his features twisted horribly, shrinking, forming into something small and squat, more hideous doll than human being.

I'm coming for you, the Bren-thing rasped in a high, skin-grating voice I had never before heard. *Alderon wasn't strong enough to light the way, but I am. You can't hide forever, Jasmina Corey.*

The Bren-creature sneered.

Queen of Nothing. Nothing at all.

With that, the vision vanished.

I was left gasping and horrified, and wondering what on earth to make of that.

As usual in my life, the answers weren't immediately forthcoming, and I had no minutes to waste seeking them.

I'm coming for you, Jasmina Corey, Queen of Nothing.

At least that part was bitterly clear. I chewed my lip, trying not to faint from the vision's draining, evil sensation. We needed to double our efforts with Bren's training. Time was definitely running out.

On the dawn of the third day after I turned Bren into an ass, he had made more progress in weapons training than I might have imagined.

I wasn't altogether certain that was a good thing for me, however. Likely most of his elegant sword strokes were made with images of my head ready for the chopping. And yet, he was such a gentleman with Rol, so relaxed and easy and . . . so himself. Hiding, watching, I saw flashes of brilliance in his movements, and I heard the range of his humor and knowledge. Quite impressive, really. With Rol,

Bren became the boy I sensed behind that raging wall of emotions I seemed barred from moving through.

As if I want to move through? Goddess, spare me.

Remnants of my vision clung to my consciousness, troubling me whenever Bren laughed and, for some reason, whenever he placed his hand in his pocket and shrugged. I kept having an urge to rip off his pockets so he couldn't do that again—but I feared my meaning would be less than clear if I did.

Instead, I had repaired to the study again to give myself some peace, but no queen has peace for long. With a sigh, I made myself stand and prepare for the task of checking my kingdom, monitoring each Sanctuary whether intact or violated. I had to do what I could to protect the witches forced to stay behind—and to track and estimate Nire's movements.

Clearing my thoughts was no easy endeavor, but I focused on a simple mantra given to me by my mother.

"Soar, the spirit.

Soar, the spirit."

Slowly, the clutter between my ears swept itself left and right, forging a clear path to my center, to my ability to focus, and to the endless bounty of the earth and the Goddess.

"Soar, the spirit.

Soar, the spirit."

My mind stretched toward the ceiling. It was a trick of concentration, separating consciousness from the physical body—much like shifting the eyes to see something close, and then far away. Since the age of four, I had been a master of such feats. Better, even, than Father. And Mother, though she would perish before admitting it.

A rush of air and the lurch of my belly told me that I had broken free. I had become part of the air and wind, free of the earth, and yet more connected than ever.

My body, my shell, yet stood beneath me, eyes closed, muscles as rigid as any armor. I did not fear for my body's safety, for Shadowbridge's protections were my own—and thus the strongest magic along the Path.

My arms, now the wings of a falcon, stretched to lift me higher and higher—through the ceiling and out of Shadowbridge. The afternoon sky was a splendid, brilliant blue, banishing thoughts of my parents and Bren, clearing my senses for a proper search.

With studied precision, I covered diagonals over Shallym. Back and forth. Up and down. Listening. Watching.

Wind whipped against me, forcing me high before allowing me to drop low. I tested the air with my feathers and instincts.

Only the oldeFolke noticed me in my falcon form as I passed through the market. A hag leading a young girl—Helden—pointed. The hag's hag-spirit, this one a scraggy black cat, hissed and swiped a paw at me. Helden looked as if she'd like to do the same. An elfling shoe merchant bowed to me on my next pass, causing his green cap to fall into a puddle. I dove and retrieved it, tossing it to his eagle-brother when I came through again.

All seemed peaceful. All seemed in order.

One by one, I opened the Path's eleven doors, through the eleven different points in time, and flew patrol over each Sanctuary. As I entered each door and slipped into each Sanctuary, I took care to re-seal the Path behind me.

Even Middle Salem received a fair share of my attention, though I hated every moment of being there. As was typical when it was daylight in Shallym, it was night in Middle Salem. It was as if the two Sanctuaries moved on an opposite clock.

As I passed over Ipswich Road, I glanced left and right. Salem Village, the farming section, was quiet and dark. Salem Town, on the port and alive with British trade, seemed brighter and more inviting. If only the witches had stayed on the port side of that invisible boundary—but as the humans moved in from Europe, the witches moved west.

And the humans came west with us, until they overtook us and kept going—miles out of the township proper, to the rocky farmland where we had made our homes. We tried to exist in peace with them, set up businesses and offered goods to both the villagers and the townspeople, but by the Goddess, Puritans saw the devil behind every tree—behind every lost crop and fever blister. Especially the poorer villagers—they were the most superstitious lot of all.

Wind whipped my face, and I turned my feathers to avoid the worst of the chill. As if the worst of anything could be avoided in Middle Salem.

The villagers were terrified enough before Nire interfered, twisting the mind of Samuel Parris, the spiritual leader of Salem Village. This much we learned from the hags who defected to our side. The Shadowmaster had whispered powerful poison, turning an otherwise good man into a murderous zealot. It was Nire who made Parris obsessed with and terrified of witches, using visions of witches ruling the world and slaughtering Christians by the score. It was Nire's influence that heated the minister's tongue until the good reverend's sermons fanned jealousy and mistrust into raging, hateful fires.

The people of Salem Village turned on the people of Salem Town. All along the imaginary line between village and town, the same line I now flew above, anyone with any land or prosperity was accused of witchcraft. Under British law, the penalty for witchcraft was death by hanging, and of course, the town officials could seize the "criminal's" land.

Land and money. Typical human pursuits. My wings ached from the tension filling my falcon-body.

As usual, human pursuits left real witches caught in the middle, though none of us were actually accused of consorting with the devil. Not until Father volunteered himself, "accusing" my mother, his own wife.

Salem Village was stunned and entranced.

That was Father's plan, to draw attention to himself, in hopes the fools would do what they had done so many times before: accuse the accuser. Father thought that if the villagers spent their time and attention on him, it would spare more innocents from accusation—and deflect attention from the true witches, who were preparing to flee onto the Path. Father refused trial, and refused comment, drawing the ire of the judges and ministers, keeping everyone's focus on him just as he planned, and giving us precious time to disappear.

The memories overran me, and I slowed—almost too much. The breeze eased, letting me drift toward the ground.

We had to flee Middle Salem that day. We had no choice. In that, Mother had been right.

But Father feared that if we left without stopping the insanity, innocent humans would be executed in our stead.

And he was right. So terribly and brutally right.

The very hour we tried to leave, Father was supposed to pretend to endure his "execution" by pressing. The magistrates hoped this form of torture would make him "confess" his sins. The entire village turned out to watch, and while their attention was elsewhere, I opened and closed the Path as fast as I could. One at a time, I escorted witches to the barrier and across, instructed them to wait, and went back for the next.

Nire wasn't yet strong enough to walk the Path freely and without limits, but definitely strong enough to interfere. We just didn't know—I just didn't know—how powerful the Shadowmaster had become.

The Path itself seemed to fight me, and it became harder and harder to get people safely through the energy bands supporting the road through time. My limbs grew heavy, and my mind began to drown in nothing at all. The moon caught my attention. The wind. The stars. I forgot opening and closing spells. I didn't think to concentrate. It no longer seemed important to hurry, and I felt compelled to have long conversations with many witches each time I opened the barrier. Outside the Path, waiting witches dozed or moved off, plucking blades of grass.

But the clock kept ticking outside of the dark spell holding us ignorant, and the weights on Father's chest grew heavier. But he dared not speak out or use magic to stop his torture until I gave him the signal that all witches were safely on the Path . . .

Ah, what a horrid mess.

I nearly stopped flying at the memories, pulling out of my steep dive at the last second.

What had happened next to my father—I didn't want to remember, but I couldn't shut it from my mind.

Even now, I could see myself as I at last realized Nire's evil enchantment. Consciousness waking with screams of alarm, I battled the magic and broke it. So much time had passed. Not an hour—but a day! Almost two. Immediately, I sensed Father dying. His life ebbed and his spirit moving to the next plane before I could complete my task.

And even now, four years later, I could still feel the loss of my father ripping through my soul as I at last hurried back to the Path to get my mother and the others. Forcing myself to leave Father's empty shell behind as I took the last witch through the barrier with me, to join those who were waiting.

The last witch was Rol, of course. He had stayed to help me. Only, once we arrived back on the Path, it was empty. The fifty-odd witches I had escorted to the Path's safety were missing, including my mother.

Nire had them. The nearby Shadows made that only too clear, and the hag defectors confirmed it over time. Nire had my family and our friends, and the Shadowmaster would kill them if I did not leave Middle Salem immediately. I didn't understand why, past the fact that Nire couldn't yet challenge me directly, but wanted me off balance and far from everything I found comfortable and familiar. I didn't know where the Shadowmaster's Sanctuary was, or even where to begin the search—though I remained alert for clues everywhere I went.

My father was dead, and my mother was missing, and virtually everyone I had ever known was gone. Hostage to the Shadowmaster.

And back in Middle Salem, humans went on killing each other for imaginary witchcraft, in order to gain land, money, and power. No doubt Nire thought it amusing. The Shadowmaster would have been delighted if the humans had murdered each other down to the last soul.

How did any creature learn to hate so deeply?

I pumped my wings and rose higher over the cursed ground.

As always, Middle Salem began to weigh too heavily on my heart. Even four years later, I could still sense the spot where Father died.

If only the Path of Shadows could take us back in time to a moment of our choosing—but time is not so kind. It rushes ahead, relentless. Once a moment is lived, it cannot be revisited, for time has moved on. The Path actually allowed me to move across time, but not through it. I could not go back and save my father, or prevent my mother and the rest of the witches from rushing into Nire's dark arms.

And so I flew above the cemetery, past crumbled angels, stark crosses, and shadowy crypts, to the spot where my father's bones lay in unhallowed ground. Nothing marked his final resting place save a clump of bushes. Witches didn't get headstones in Old Salem. Thanks to Nire, Father died for nothing and went on to this ignoble burial. I couldn't save the others, and neither could he. In fact, other than Rol, the only witch we saved from Middle Salem was me.

What good was I, after all?

It had been four years, and Nire was nothing but stronger, as the recent, more direct and complete destruction of Trier had shown me—not to mention the queer vision of Bren, giving me what could only be the Shadowmaster's message.

I'm coming for you, Jasmina Corey, Queen of Nothing. Nothing at all.

Weakness. Mind and blood . . .

I would never defeat the Shadowmaster.

Yet, I had to. Somehow, I had to.

So great was my level of distraction that I almost failed to notice the chill ripple of the air. The dank smell choking away the clean breeze.

And then I heard the unearthly screams.

Shadows! My heart squeezed in my chest. Nire's minions were afoot in Salem.

Wheeling to meet the oncoming threat, I saw them. Twenty, maybe more. Dark blots against the moon's pale light. They flew hard for me, even as I steadied my flight and readied a spell of light.

Cold air punched me like closed fists. The stench of rot and death clogged my senses.

"Stop!" I screeched, but the foul creatures resisted me.

Damnation!

I tried again to cast a ceasing spell, but I couldn't complete it. My sense of dread doubled. What arrogance had led me to believe I could perform a proper ceasing spell outside my body? Or were these beasts simply too strong for me?

Weakness, Jasmina. *Weakness!*

The lead Shadow snarled and wailed, bearing down on my position. My feathers and wings flexed, and bolts of light spread outward like a fan. The flare made my own eyes ache.

With a shriek, the first line of minion-attackers fell away, only to circle and join the onrushing Shadows from behind.

Once more, the wind bit my face, my wings. My feathers turned so cold I could barely flex them.

By the Goddess. The beasts are stronger than they should be!

They had never battled me head-to-head like this. I couldn't let them wound me, or everything would fall to ruin.

With all of my strength, I flew hard for Shallym, streaking across Sanctuary after Sanctuary, slicing openings and attempting to seal them behind me.

The Shadows followed!

How was that possible? They couldn't be strong enough to enter and exit the path on their own—could they? But that meant Nire's strength and understanding of the Path had grown beyond imagination. And I was leading the Shadowmaster's minions straight to L.O.S.T.

Holding my breath against fear and the hideous odor of the Shadows, I stopped in one of the oldest Sanctuaries, turned in midair, and fired again.

Light blazed over the dark junglelike growth below. Shadows screamed and scattered. One veered crazily and struck my tailfeathers.

I spiraled down, trying to flap, but failing. I picked up speed as I plummeted. The cold numbed me beyond measure. Behind me came Nire's horrible rushing servants. And for all I knew, Nire as well.

Bren! Help me. The ground loomed as I fell. *Help me!*

chapter thirteen

My stomach lurched as I swung my sword. Rol laughed when I missed my target—his head. Frowning, I belched, then missed again.

BREN →

Bren...

Jazz's mental whisper poked at my brain like a migraine. I shoved it out and fought Rol twice as hard. A small tornado of dust swirled around us.

"Concentrate," Rol barked.

Damn Jazz. Turning me into a donkey, ignoring me for the past few days, and now trying to make nice by whispering in my head. An ass, I reminded myself. Here, in witchworld, I wasn't just a donkey. They called me an ass.

"I'm not an ass," I muttered as I fended off a rush from Rol. He didn't seem to hear me talking to myself. Thank the universe for small favors.

The training yard felt hot. Too hot. And I kept seeing spots out of the corner of my eye. Dark, floaty ones. Part of me wanted to ask Rol what they were, and another part of me knew hallucinations were bad news in any culture. So I kept fighting, even though I wanted to puke.

Bren . . .

Jazz again. This time, more urgent. I felt my face blaze red. God, but she was pissing me off. *You had your fun,* I shot back. *Now you can wait for me to have mine.*

With a feint to the right, Rol disarmed me. My sword clattered as it hit the dirt. The blade gleamed in the afternoon sunlight, and I flinched as silver flares pierced my eyes like darts.

"Your mind is elsewhere," Rol grumbled. "Thinking of the queen, perhaps?"

"In her dreams." I rubbed my head and wished it would quit throbbing. "Must have been that . . . uh, whatever it was on that sandwich you made me for lunch."

Rol frowned. "Squid. Baked, not broiled. My favorite."

"Whatever. It didn't agree with me." I belched again, loud enough to puncture an eardrum.

"Mmm." Rol's oh-sure expression said it all. He didn't think I was sick. He thought I was mooning over Jazz.

Half-lunging, half-falling, I managed to grab my sword and wheel on him.

Mooning. Over that witch. No way!

Our swords crossed with a clang. Sunlight from both blades seared my eyes, and that was it. I couldn't take it. I don't know if I threw up before I fell or after, but the result was the same.

Me, lying in the dirt, sword in one hand and recycled squid in the other.

Rol started laughing, but then his voice faded into the distance. I was so dizzy I couldn't tell up from down.

Bren! For the sake of the Goddess, hear me!

Jazz's voice broke through my defenses like bats swirling out of a cave. In seconds, my brain felt battered. Seized. She was everywhere inside my mind, all at once—and she was scared. In pain.

Under attack.

"Damn!" I scraped squid vomit off my palm and fought to stand. From somewhere, big hands helped me, then held me steady as I turned left, then right, squinting.

No Jazz.

But I felt her somewhere above me. In the sky.

And those things I had seen out of the corner of my eye . . . were they chasing her?

"Bren! Come awake! Bren!" Rol shouts came from miles away, or so it seemed. He shook me. I felt like a rickety puppet in his massive mitts.

For a second, I was above him, looking down. Out of my body.

Oh, shit. Am I dying? What's with this crazy stuff?

With a jerk, I fell back into myself. For two seconds, the world straightened back out. Rol's fingers crushed my biceps, but otherwise, I was okay. Not dead. And then it started back.

"Jazz." I squirmed in Rol's grip. "Damn. Not again!" Rol let me go and I stumbled back, keeping my sword up, all the while trying to block Jazz's intrusion.

Rol didn't try to attack while I was battling Jazz. In fact, he dropped his sword and put his hands on the sides of his head. Like he was a radio trying to broadcast.

"She's screwing with you, too, right?" I shook my head, then wished I hadn't. A new wave of dizziness made me half-green. "What's her problem?"

No answer.

"Where is she? Is something really wrong?" I lowered my blade.

Rol continued his impersonation of a satellite dish.

The hairs on my neck prickled. "What is it?"

Light rose from the top of Rol's head and divided into long lines. Arrows. With a roar, he fired them into the sky.

"What are you doing?" I ran to him as a new bunch of arrows formed.

Rol kept his eyes closed and his hands attached to the sides of his head. "I am helping the queen." His voice was tense. Serious. "She is under attack."

Those shadow-things. Chasing her. Fear for Jazz shot through me, and I squeezed the hilt of my sword. "Let's go."

"Cannot cross onto the Path without her," Rol murmured. "Cannot reach the other Sanctuaries."

"Well, we have to try, don't we?" I punched him in his shoulder and winced when my fingers hurt.

"Concentrate," he told me. "Give her your energy. Not too much, not enough to harm you." More light arrows fired from his head.

"You're nuts, man. I don't know how to do that." I whirled around, opening my mind to Jazz. Wishing I hadn't closed her out.

Where are you? I'll come if you tell me.

Help me! Jazz's plea was immediate and so strong it almost drove me to my knees. The planet spun funny, her emotions were so strong. Like a tide, nearly separating my thoughts from my body again. For the briefest moment, I realized I could do it. I could leave my body, if I wanted to. If I tried.

Magic.

No!

I rammed my sword into its sheath and took off across the training yard. One way or another, I would find Jazz. Something was after her. Whatever it was, it would be sorry because I was going to kick its ass.

Bren!

Jazz's voice drew me like a magnet. I stumbled and nearly fell—and then a powerful arm wrapped around my waist and snatched me right off my feet. I didn't yell or fight as I dangled, because I recognized the grip.

It was Rol. On a broom-branch.

As we flew higher off the ground, he held me tight in one arm, like I was a toddler or a sack of dog food. After one glance down, my head spun and I refused to look back at the earth racing beneath my dangling feet.

Instinctively, I tried to grab at my sword, but Rol's voice rose over the rushing wind as we flew. "Your blade will do us no good, boy. Jasmina is not in Shallym. I'm taking us to the barrier, next to the Path. From there, we will share our energy."

"I don't know how!" Frustration held me tighter than Rol. I wanted to punch him, just to have something to punch.

All I could think about was getting to Jazz before . . .

Before what? Before it was too late? Before something hurt her?

Why should I care? But damn it, I did. More than I wanted to. The thought made my gut ache.

In seconds, we reached a shimmer in the air, and Rol took us down, down, to a patch of grass in a thicket of trees. The branch he had ridden was flaming like mad. He doused the fire with a flick of his wrist and chucked the broom out of sight.

I started to run toward the shimmer—I knew Jazz had to be on the other side—but Rol snagged my arm and held me back. "You cannot pass through the barrier—the Path—without the queen."

"Then how can we help her?" I shouted, flinging off his grasp.

"Concentrate." He grabbed the sides of his head again. "Imagine your power, your strength, flowing out of you like a river. Imagine it rushing toward Jasmina."

The urge to hit him nearly overtook me this time. There was no way I could do that. And no way it would work. I had a sword. The hell with this advanced magic bullshit I'd never understand. Why couldn't I get to Jazz and use the blade?

Biting back a howl of complete rage, I put my hands to the side of my head.

River. River. Make my strength a river.

Nothing happened.

Rol was firing arrows off his head like some sort of weird human bow, and I couldn't do a thing.

Doubling my effort, I really tried hard to imagine the river thing. I did. And it wasn't working.

By the Goddess!

Jazz's mental shout ripped into my soul. I had never felt so helpless. So useless. When the dizziness hit me, I welcomed it and wished it would knock me out so I didn't have to feel what a huge failure I was.

"God dammit!" I staggered and drew my sword for no good reason. Everything was spinning and spinning.

Roaring like some nut, I bashed into the barrier and felt it give. I fell forward, into what felt like humming pudding, through screaming shadows and sickly deathlike smells— and then out, into moonlit darkness.

I stumbled to my hands and knees, and lived only because I was bending over. A huge bird swept over me, giving a screech like a dinosaur from a bad science-fiction movie.

Because it *was* a dinosaur. A pterodactyl, to be exact. The second I looked up, I recognized the prehistoric bird's outline against the huge moon and unbelievably bright stars. It flapped a few times and disappeared from view.

Before I could react, I heard more wings, different wings, and screaming. A girl. Jazz! She was close. Her essence hovered like light perfume on the breeze—and then something else screamed.

Something inhuman and evil. Whatever it was smelled like a sewer with an attitude problem.

Still fighting major dizziness, I lurched toward the nerve-grating sounds and smells. On instinct, I raised my sword and my skin glowed with a faint silver sheen.

Silvery light arched into the darkness.

The inhuman things screamed again, and they sounded—and smelled—closer. I coughed. Fear poked through my chest, cold and harsh, but I ignored it.

Something flapped past me so hard it spun me around.

I swung my blade in its wake. Light blazed, showing me a bat-thing, only bigger and uglier. This was no prehistoric creature, unless the history books missed a breed. This was a monster. Something unnatural.

Golden arrows suddenly rained down from the sky, directly at the monster.

"Rol!" I yelled, realizing what was happening. The big guy was still sending light beams out of his head, trying to help.

More wings flapped. I lashed out with the sword, connecting with something soft, yet powerful. A shriek filled the night.

Then more flapping, and more golden arrows hit their mark. A flock of smelly, cold things pushed past me as they fled like big bat-chickens. I felt like I was in a hurricane without rain. And then I fell.

"Jazz! Where are you?" I kicked against the ground, trying to orient myself. "Where the hell are you?"

Nasty dirt filled my mouth, and I hacked it out. Using every bit of strength I could muster, I stood up again.

My sword quit glowing, and night closed around me. Even the moon was blocked by clouds.

I'm down. Jazz spoke in my mind even as I saw a ghostly image of her run—no, drift—out of the nearby skyscraper trees. *On the ground, in spirit-form. Do not touch me. You aren't strong enough to survive it.*

"What do I do?" I stupidly swung the sword and wished I had something to fight. At least I was good at that. "I came to save you!"

And, as usual, I will have to save you instead. Go back to Shadowbridge. It was foolish of you to come here. Her voice in my head sounded snotty as usual. *And you have risked Shallym by leaving the Path open. Hurry through so that I might seal it before Shadows find the breach and discover our last free Sanctuary.*

"Hello?" I shook my blade at her. "'Thank you, Bren'? 'I'm so glad you showed up and saved my ass, Bren'?"

I thought you and Rol would send me energy. Jazz's you're-such-a-screw-up tone turned up to full blast. She reminded me of my dad. *Please, stop jabbering and get out of here! The risk is too great. Go back through the barrier.*

My teeth ground together. "I don't know how to get back. I don't even know how I got here."

I felt Jazz sigh, and she seemed stronger. As she approached, her fresh, clean scent cleared the air, and the darkness seemed . . . brighter.

Relief competed with an urge to slice her ghost body in two.

She raised her hand, still ten feet or more from me, and I felt a little push. *Move. Straight back.*

I started to say something sarcastic, but apparently, I didn't move fast enough for her. She muttered something about wind and power, and the air suddenly howled around me.

No use fighting. It was stronger than ten bouncers with bad B.O.

"Thanks! Thanks a lot!" Spinning and pinwheeling, I tumbled through a gash in the barrier. Shadows screamed around me and the sick odor filled my nose and mouth, and then I stumbled out the other side.

Behind me I heard Jazz mumble, "I'll see you at Shadowbridge." Then the stink vanished, along with the strange shrieks from the bizarre darkness.

I hit the ground, face down, right on top of Rol's smelly feet.

Perfect. Just perfect.

chapter fourteen

As I flew in my falcon form, back from the darkness of the ancient Sanctuary where I had been
struck down and into the daylight of Shallym, my
heart thumped with the knowledge that Bren had
managed to breach the Path. No one save my father, myself,
and Nire had ever been able to accomplish that. Moreover,
he'd survived two more doses of the Shadowmaster's evil
magic. He didn't even seem fazed!

That Bren had done these things by accident filled me
with a mixture of hope—and fear.

What did it mean? How could he have accomplished so
much with so little training?

The prophecy. Bren was the Shadowalker.

In short order, my ears picked up the sound of splashes
from the rain barrel by the smithy and Bren grumbling

something to Rol about washing off vomit and dinosaur shit.

Rol's voice rumbled in the training yard, and then Bren shouted, "What the hell was that about? No! Let go of me. I'm going to the house to have a word with that bitch. Again!"

"Hold, Bren." Rol's footsteps echoed as he ran, no doubt not keeping up.

Circling over Shadowbridge, I tried to catch a full breath. The shock of the attack, my near defeat—and Bren's sudden, reckless, and surprising appearance—it was all too much.

And now another tantrum.

I would have preferred the Shadows to facing Bren in a temper, especially since he would be full of arrogance from what he thought was his "victory." I could not believe he had taken such a chance, risked everything—risked himself—for me. Should I berate him or hug him for hours?

His bravery coated me like some protective force. It maddened me. He maddened me. I wasn't sure I didn't like it, though.

Stop this! I must remind him who is queen. He needs to remember who has the power here. Otherwise, he'll be an insufferable ass.

And somewhere deeper in my mind, a more deliberate part of me added, and he'll most assuredly fail his destiny.

"Where did all the furniture go? And what's wrong with her?" donkey-boy was saying. "Why isn't she back in her body yet?"

"Careful," Rol replied. "If you touch the queen's body while she is traveling, you will die instantly—Bren!"

A smack—and then, "Ow, Rol! What did you do that for?"

"If you had so much as brushed her flesh, you would be naught but ashes now." Rol's voice was harsh. "This is no teasing matter, boy. Shadowbridge is protected in many ways, and protections make no distinction between the foul and the fair. Do you understand?"

"I get it," Bren said. "More of the Queen of the Nutcases and her black-magic circus."

With one furious flap, I shot back to myself faster than an arrow fired from a bow. Through the roof, into the drawing room, and straight into my body with a jerk and a gasp. My flesh felt heavy and clumsy, but I forced open my eyes and glared at Bren. "Queen of the what, donkey fodder?"

Bren stood at arm's length, gazing at me with a mixture of loathing and rage. Water dripped down his face and arms onto the drawing room floor and his brown eyes glinted harshly. He smelled of sweat and rainwater, and his hair was wild. He had a huge bruise from sparring, peeking from beneath his tunic. Its angry green hue pleased me to my core.

Or perhaps he had earned it while battling Shadows—a thought that unsettled me, although I didn't understand why.

Rol stepped away from Bren and spoke in a rush, as if to distract me. "Your Majesty. I was quite concerned."

"No need." I tried to sound nonchalant, which made Bren turn near purple. "A close call, but I'm fine. Your pupil, however, risked his life and future, rushing headlong into peril. I hope you'll address judgment in his future sessions."

"You—" Bren started, but Rol cut him off with a sharp gesture.

"Bren has completed only his conditioning sessions," Rol explained. "He will learn battle strategy by Summer Solstice, I have no doubt. His magic, however—you said to bring him to you at three o'clock. It is three."

"What?" Bren wheeled on the training master, hands fisted. "No way. I am not staying here with— with that!"

"Are you fearful?" I asked. "Because if you are—"

"You shut up," Bren snapped. "I'm talking to Rol."

I sucked in my breath and clenched my hands, barely gaining control in time.

Rol gave me an annoyed glance and backed from the room, holding his hands in front of him to block any charge Bren might consider. Bren tried to follow, but Rol slammed the door. A sharp thunk told me the training master had barred the exit behind him.

Bren threw himself against the wood shoulder first, trying to knock the door open. Of course, it didn't move. He tried again, and once more before turning back and pointing his finger at me. "Let me out. I've had enough today, and I'm not speaking to you. I saved your ass back there in Jurassic Park Land. And you know it."

I thought about teaching Bren's finger some manners, thought about how funny it would look if I caused flowers or feathers to grow from its tip. But I did nothing. The sting of his words burned deep within, and I feared becoming angry beyond control . . . or repair.

"Open the door yourself," I murmured, battling a wave of fatigue. "If you do, you may leave. Better still, no one can lock you behind a physical door again."

Bren started to say something, then broke off. He glanced from me to the door, and back to me again. "Do you mean I'm supposed to open the door by magic?"

He sounded more fearful than sarcastic, which I didn't expect—or know how to address. So, he believed now, in his own magical potential. Even though it scared him to death.

"Yes." I sat on the bare floor and flinched at a speck of dirt that had fallen from Bren's shoe. "Most magic is quite natural. From the supply of energy within your own body. Moving or transforming objects is simply a matter of concentration, just like leaving your physical body—or breaking onto the Path."

The boy eyed me as if I might be mad, but he kept looking from me to the door. From the door to me. "Okay," he said finally. "But like I said before, I'll do your stupid training and kill your stupid Shadowmaster, except from now on, nothing is free. We'll start with straight answers, like what the hell happened out there. Got that? But for starters, before I try to open this door, I want to know what happened to the furniture."

The empty room seemed to press in on me, and that speck of dirt ate away at my sense of well-being. My belly tensed, and my breathing grew more rapid. "I blew it all to dust. With my fingers. Like this." I zapped the damnable dirt to oblivion. "Because I was angry with you. Does that give you pleasure?"

Bren grinned, treating me to a full view of his handsome face. "Well, what do you know. A straight answer."

His eyes gleamed, and my heart sank. The sarcasm—I didn't think I could bear it. Especially not for hours, alone with Bren in this room, trying to teach him to tap into his own skill. After he indeed saved my life.

"All right, all right." Bren smiled again as he scrubbed his palm over his wet face. "Tell me how, and I'll do it."

I opened my mouth to tell him, but out came a long and rattling sigh.

Bren raised his eyebrows.

He looked curious, and—for the moment—like a real and free champion, making his real and free choice to battle by my side.

The mere thought of Bren actually electing to help me was too much, and I started to cry. The first tears loosed the rest, and to my great humiliation, I sobbed so hard I leaned forward on the floor.

"Aw, man," Bren said. "Rol? Hey, Rol! Get back here!"

I turned my back to Bren and put my face in my hands. To keep my own promise to myself, I couldn't even make him disappear.

chapter fifteen

Jazz was crying. The Queen of the Witches was sobbing so hard her shoulders were shaking. And Rol
wasn't coming back.

I looked from Jazz to the door and then back to
her. I felt helpless—and guilty. A heavy sensation filled my
stomach, like I'd swallowed a dozen baseballs. I had been
pretty mean to her the past couple of days, except for the
saving-her-life part.

My mother's voice popped into my head, telling me to
choose my words with care—that words had tremendous
power.

I rubbed at the aching bruise on my chest as I realized I
had used my words to hurt Jazz. What was I supposed to do
now?

I walked over to Jazz and knelt beside her. "Are you, uh, okay?"

"Leave me," she whispered.

"The door's still locked." I raked my fingers through my hair. "I don't understand how to use magic to unlock it."

She raised her hand, as if waving me away, and the bar scraped against the door.

Freedom.

I could just walk away and let her cry her heart out. It was what she deserved, wasn't it? After all, look at what she had done to me. Kidnapped me, brought me to this oddball place knowing that I couldn't leave and that I might die. And she had turned me into a donkey, then pretended I didn't risk my neck to pull her ass out of a jam.

"Go," Jazz said, her voice hoarse, and she still refused to look at me. "I've humiliated myself enough." She wrapped her arms around her knees, her face buried against her thighs. Her black hair fell forward, completely covering her features and her arms.

Shit.

What was I supposed to do? Pat her on the back and say everything will be okay? I sat down next to her and started to touch her, then pulled away. For a moment I just stared at Jazz's trembling shoulders, feeling an overwhelming urge to comfort her.

Before I could think better of it, I wrapped my arms around her and brought her head against my chest. Jazz stiffened, but I only tightened my hold. After a couple of seconds, she shuddered and then relaxed, as if she had melted against me. Like the weight of the world was pressing her down.

The weight of the world.

That was it. She was only sixteen, yet she was responsible for hundreds, maybe thousands of people. And she was doing what she had to in order to save them. One of those "for the greater good" type of things my mom was always harping on.

I really did feel like an ass.

Irresponsible . . .

Impulsive . . .

Lower than the worm she had threatened to turn me into and grind under her heel. All I had been concerned about was myself, and she was thinking about countless lives.

"I'm sorry, Jazz," I whispered, and kissed the top of her head. She smelled so good and felt so soft and warm in my arms. "I wasn't trying to hurt your feelings. I was just mad, and I— I really didn't mean all the things I said after you turned me into a donkey. I just, well . . . I don't think you should have used your magic against me, and I think you should be more grateful I helped you out. But otherwise, I was a real ass. Okay?"

Jazz froze. After a moment she sniffed, her words muffled against my chest. "It was wrong of me to turn you into a donkey. And to deny how you helped me in the ancient Sanctuary. You have my apologies."

"Let's start over." Her hair was soft and silky, and I found myself stroking it as I talked. "We can be friends. But we need to be upfront about everything."

"Friends?" She sounded surprised as she lifted her head and looked at me. For the first time she didn't look absolutely perfect. Her dark makeup was splotchy, and her eyes were red and swollen. Yet she still managed to look beautiful. Golden light crept around the black smears on her face, as if her natural glow was trying to break free and shine.

I wiped a smudge from her cheek, freeing another speck of light. "Sure. Why not?"

Jazz glanced away, her expression distant and sad. "I've never had a friend, save Rol. And well, as much as I love him, it's not the same."

"You've never had a friend?" I stopped stroking her hair. On impulse, I took her chin in my hand, and made her look at me. "Not even one?"

"No." She closed her golden eyes, and it was like the light in the room had dimmed. "From the moment I was born, I've trained to be queen. My mother believed that having friends would make me vulnerable. Weak."

No friends, ever. And I thought having ADHD was a pain in the ass.

"You have me for a friend now." I pulled her back against my chest and hugged her. Holding her seemed so right. "I'll help you find Nire."

She sighed and relaxed against me. "Thank you, Bren."

I rested my chin on top of her head, breathing in her cinnamon-and-peaches scent. The figurine, now in the pocket of my pants, popped into my thoughts. It burned against my thigh, and as I held Jazz, my own words haunted me.

We need to be upfront about everything.

What was the big deal about a dumb little statue? Why would I need to tell her about it?

Why didn't I want to?

Later. I'd tell her later.

"Did you say your dad was killed by that Shadowmaster?" I asked against her hair.

"In a manner of speaking." Jazz nodded, her head bumping my nose. "Father gave his life to help the witches escape Middle Salem, to make sure they were safe from a disaster Nire created." She sighed again. "But Father was killed by humans in a frenzy of fear—a natural death in the order of the universe. Such a death barred him from Talamadden, the special haven within Summerland, and a possible second chance."

I frowned in concentration, trying to keep focused on what she was saying, trying to make sense of it. "If he'd had an unnatural death, directly from spells or something, he would've had a second chance?"

"Yes." Another sniffle. "But Father's soul is gone forever . . . and the worst thing is that he died for nothing."

Absently I rested my hand on hers and slowly stroked the soft skin on the back of her fingers. My face and arms were almost dry—although after sitting so close to me, Jazz was probably a bit on the damp side now. "What do you mean, that he died for nothing?" I asked.

"I got caught in one of Nire's enchantments, and I couldn't get everyone onto the Path fast enough." Jazz said it quietly and so matter-of-fact. "Nire captured my mother and the rest of Middle Salem's witches, save for me and Rol. That was four years ago, when I became queen."

Twelve. She had been queen since she was twelve years old. And she blamed herself for her father's death. When I was twelve, all I thought about was goofing around with my friends, listening to my favorite CDs, playing video games, and baseball. And the only headache in my life was my dad on my case all the time.

When I looked at her again, I felt like I was seeing her differently. All her pointy edges seemed understandable, and somehow softer. Completely cool by me.

"I'm sorry about your parents, Jazz." I rubbed my thumb in circles on the back of her hand. "My dad is rough to live with, but I'd hate it if anything happened to him. Or my mom and brother. I'd do anything for them."

"Then you understand." Her voice was so soft I could barely hear her.

"Yeah, now I do." I lifted my head and stroked her hair behind her ear. "I'm sorry I've given you such a hard time. I'll work harder at learning this magic business, all right?"

She sighed and leaned against my chest. "The progress you have made in a few days time is quite remarkable. You should be well and truly pleased with yourself."

"I don't know about that." I shrugged. "My dad would just point out all of my screw-ups."

"Your skill with the sword," she went on, her voice low and serious, "I have never witnessed such rapid development in abilities. Have you always excelled in athletic pursuits?"

"Uh, yeah. Thanks," I said. Jazz's praise felt good, but it kind of embarrassed me, too. "Mom got me started in baseball when I was really little. She always goes on about how I'm destined for greatness, and about how discipline and practice would bring me closer to that destiny." I shook my head and laughed. "I never cared about that crap. I just love to play baseball."

"Your mother is a wise woman," Jazz said.

"Whatever." I shrugged again and then hurried to change the subject. Talking about myself always made me feel uncomfortable. Besides, I wanted to know more about her. "So, what kind of fun does a kid have when she's growing up as the future Queen of Witches?"

Jazz shifted in my arms and seemed to relax as she started telling me about her childhood, about her family, and her life before Nire had taken everything away from her. But she didn't talk about what she'd lost, just the happy times, the way things used to be.

In turn, I told her about some of the fun stuff I did as a kid: playing baseball and football with the guys, swimming at the Y, racing bikes down our neighborhood street, and toilet-papering the old hag's house around the corner. Fun stuff.

We talked for hours, just sitting there on the floor of the drawing room until my ass was numb. It was really cool, and everything would have been perfect if I didn't feel so damn guilty for not telling her about that statue in my pocket.

The following afternoon, after I finished training with Rol, I went to the drawing room to try and learn magic from Jazz. I found her sitting on that lone bench by the window. I guess she didn't hear me come in because she was staring out the crystal-clear pane with a soft, wistful expression on her face.

What was she thinking about? Was she thinking about me, maybe even us?

Get your head out of your ass, Bren. It's just like you to be selfish and think it's all about you. More than likely she was trying to figure out how to beat Nire and get her family and friends back.

No teenage girl or guy I'd ever known had Jazz's depth. She could be serious and scary as hell, but she could also be caring and sweet, and even funny.

Last night had been amazing. We'd talked for hours and didn't argue once. I'd loved hearing about the things she'd done when she was a little girl. Like the time when she was five and she'd turned Acaw into a rainbow-colored parrot just because he wouldn't talk to her. He'd just sat where she'd zapped him and called out, "A-caw, A-caw, A-caw." Having had one too many run-ins with the uptight elf, this image really made me laugh.

Yeah, it had been pretty cool really talking with Jazz.

She turned her gaze from the window and smiled when she saw me. "Are you ready for your lesson?"

"Sure." I returned her smile as I stepped into the drawing room, over to where she was sitting. "I was wondering something though . . . could you explain some more about this Path and the Shadowmaster?"

Jazz went sort of still, like it surprised her that I wanted to know more. "All right." She nodded and gestured to the bench beside her. "It's a long story."

I slid onto the bench and had the sudden urge to touch her again. Like I needed her to ground me. I took her hand in mine and I looked into her eyes. "Okay, tell me about Nire. I need to know everything."

Jazz's cheeks went red as she glanced at our hands and back to me. I squeezed them tighter, telling her I wasn't going to leave her.

"It would be best if I show you." She pulled her hands away from mine and gracefully moved from the bench to sit crosslegged on the floor. "Come." She gestured for me to sit in front of her.

I didn't know what she had in mind, but I figured it was probably the only way I'd get some answers. I followed her lead and sat crosslegged, but without the grace she had. My scabbard banged on the floor, and I had to adjust it so that my sword hilt wasn't in my way. When I finally got settled, our knees were touching, and this time she took my hands and held them tight.

"Sharing a vision is difficult and takes much of my magical strength," she said. "It will leave us vulnerable to attack by Nire or Shadows, so we can't stay in the vision long."

The idea of being open to attack didn't sound so good to me, but I figured she wouldn't take the chance if she thought there was any real danger to us or to Shallym.

She leaned forward and I did too, until my head was against hers. Her skin felt cool next to mine. "Clear your mind and concentrate on the energy around us," she said and closed her eyes.

I closed mine and immediately found myself going through all the weird stuff that had been happening to me. To think I'd been playing baseball just weeks ago, knocking the ball around with my brother Todd—

"Concentrate," she said, this time louder.

Oh yeah. Concentrate. Damn ADHD anyway. It was such a pain in the ass to forget where I was at the moment and have my mind on other things than what I should be thinking about. Like that time—

"Bren . . ." This time Jazz's voice held a note of warning, and I dragged my thoughts back to the moment. "Clear your mind and concentrate on the energy around us. Now."

Shit. There I went again.

This time I forced myself to focus on nothing but where we were at and the moment. The more I got into it, the more I felt what she meant about the energy in the room. It was a kind of electrical charge that seemed to get more and more intense.

A burst of light flashed through my head, and then I felt like I was being jerked out of my skin.

In the next moment I found myself standing in the middle of a dark village. A shiver skittered down my spine. Evil surrounding the place was tangible, as if I could reach out and grab it—or kill it with my sword.

Jazz stood beside me. "You will now see what Nire does to our people."

I glanced down at Jazz, but her form was shadowy. "I'm ready."

"The Shadowmaster is of the oldeFolke." Her voice was quiet, but steady. "OldeFolke are witches who were never human to begin with. Most are faerie halflings, crossed with animals or other magical creatures. They live longer, with stronger magic—many are older than anyone knows."

I looked up ahead, squinting as if I'd see the Shadow-master somewhere in that dark place. "So, Nire could be hundreds of years old?"

"Far older." Jazz raised her chin and searched the skies. "Some suspect the Shadowmaster has existed since the dawn of time. No one knows what Nire looks like or who is loyal to the forces of darkness." Her ghostly hand tugged at my arm, and we moved forward through the village.

Shadows clung to buildings around us and my skin crawled. The Shadows started to move. They crept down the walls and vanished through the wood.

Screams came from inside the buildings. In moments, witches and other beings fled out into the street, running through doors, jumping from windows, flying away on branches.

I tried to draw my sword, but Jazz's tense fingers gripped my arm. "There is nothing we can do. This is a vision of the past, the second sanctuary Nire invaded."

It was like the dream I'd had, only this time there were more Shadows, more witches being herded into the center of the village. My heart pounded and my gut twisted at the sight of all those people screaming and trying to escape. I wanted to do something, anything, but all I could do was stand there and watch.

One Shadow swooped down and raked vicious nails across a witch's cheek, and she screamed. Immediately the wound squirmed with what looked like mini-shadows, and black blood flowed down her face. She dropped to the ground and writhed in obvious agony, the sound of her cries making my blood run cold.

The nightmare vision continued, and I clenched my vision-fists. Shadows attacked and rounded up witches until the ones who weren't already dead or turned to Shadows themselves were cowering in the street.

Jazz's fingers dug into my arm so hard it felt real. "Nire," she whispered, fury in her voice.

A purple glow blazed. The form from my nightmare appeared, as ghostly as we were and hard to make out.

The Shadowmaster. I had dreamed about Nire. And now, here the monster was—only not here, at the same time. Somehow, I had the sense that Nire could only appear in spirit-form, that the Shadowmaster hadn't grown strong enough to show up in person.

When that happened—well, I wouldn't want to be anywhere around.

Even as Nire approached the witches, something struck me as incredibly familiar about the Shadowmaster. It didn't make sense at all, the way I felt.

I ground my teeth, waiting for Shadows to attack the witches. But this time the Shadowmaster spoke in a voice that was unworldly, neither here nor there. The language Nire used I shouldn't have understood, but somehow I did.

"Amongst you are many of my kindred, the oldeFolke," the Shadowmaster said. "Those of you who choose to serve me will be allowed to live and prosper. Any of you who choose otherwise will be sent to the Shadows, along with all witches of weak powers and weak blood. I will cleanse the earth of all that is vile and impure, and right what is wrong with our world."

Whimpers and cries rang out. Fury tore at my gut as I saw what the Shadowmaster was doing. My heart wrenched for those who would likely not survive.

"I will join ye." A hag moved from the center of the crowd and knelt before the Shadowmaster. "I never held well with that Jasmina Corey. Queen of Witches, indeed."

My jaws ached, I ground my teeth so hard.

"I will serve you as well." A male witch stepped forward and dropped to one knee. "It will be my honor, Shadowmaster."

Several more of the oldeFolke chose to join Nire. But most of the witches remained where they stood. Frightened witches whimpered and huddled with those who whispered gentle words of support. "Talamadden," I heard them say. "There is always Talamadden."

Wise oldeFolke merely eyed the Shadowmaster with a kind of calm that must have come from centuries of wisdom.

Nire's gaze raked over the oldeFolke and fury was evident in the Shadowmaster's trembling hands. "Join with me," the being shouted, "or you shall perish, now!"

No one else moved.

My gut twisted, and I wanted to shield my eyes from what I knew would happen next. I didn't want to see Nire throwing those blazing purple ropes around the witches. Didn't want to see the Shadows devour them. Didn't want to hear the screams of the dying. Didn't want to see them turned into Shadows.

Thock.

That hollow knocking sound from my dream!

Thock. Thock. Thock.

An incredible force slammed into me.

Jazz and I both flew back, and I landed on my ass. The second I cut my gaze to Jazz's, I knew that wasn't supposed to happen.

We both scrambled to our vision-feet.

At the same time I heard a bizarre giggle, and I felt the wriggling sensation in my pocket.

"We've got to get back!" Jazz shouted. "I think Shadow-bridge is under attack. Focus as hard as you can on returning to your body."

She didn't have to tell me twice. This time I had no problem concentrating.

I jumped back into my body with enough force to tear my real hands from Jazz's. We scrambled to our feet. I ripped my sword from its sheath, and Jazz held up her hands, gold sparks glittering at the end of her fingers.

I held my breath as my gaze darted around the room. Sunlight poured in through the window. Complete silence filled the room, except for the sound of our breathing.

Slowly, Jazz let her hands drop to her sides, and the gold sparks twinkled out. I lowered my sword. Our gazes locked.

Jazz's chest rose as she took a deep breath. "I believe Nire is closer to finding Shallym than I had thought."

Not good. Not good at all. Because I had the same gut feeling, even though I couldn't say why.

I raked my hand through my hair. It was all too much. But I had to know more. After my heart started beating normally again and color returned to Jazz's face, I asked, "Why don't you go after Nire before the bastard finds this Sanctuary?"

"We don't know where to find the door to Nire's stronghold." Jazz gave a shaky sigh and moved to the bench by the window. "The place where the fiend enters our Path. For all we know, Nire could be among us at any time."

I sheathed my sword and eased onto the bench, but I felt completely on edge, like I should be attacking something rather than talking about it. "The Shadowmaster could be anyone around us?"

"Yes." With a nod, Jazz added, "And as I explained before, Nire desires to kill or enslave all witches and humans, too. We've learned this from hags and other oldeFolke who defected from Nire's service, or escaped from areas the Shadowmaster controls, or those who survived the attacks. And through my visions."

Everything she said, and everything that had just happened, was so unreal, like that Japanese animé my brother used to watch every afternoon when he got home from school. It was hard to absorb it all. A witch-strongman going around and wiping out witches and humans. How could anyone be that sick?

"Shadows are Nire's minions," Jazz continued, still looking frazzled and out of breath. "Souls of dark witches gone before, and souls of those lost on their way to the afterlife. Even without their bodies, these Shadows are capable of physical, magical, or mental assault against anyone on the Path of Shadows."

She laced her fingers together in her lap as she talked. "Little by little, Nire is conquering the Sanctuaries along the Path, killing witches or trapping them in the timeline so they'll be killed in the inevitable persecution to come."

"Hold it. Hold it." My head started to hurt more than it already was. "Trapped in the timeline? What do you mean?"

"It's confusing, I know." Jazz looked at the ceiling as if searching for Shadows there. "Father designed the Path so that witches could enter a Sanctuary in a time of peace and acceptance. If the witch was young, or had a long lifespan, then as time moved forward in that Sanctuary, peace and acceptance might end. Then, the witch could flee back to the Path, to a new Sanctuary."

"Okay, so, once somebody enters a Sanctuary, time keeps moving, and things might get bad for witches again." I rubbed my temples. It was all so confusing, yet in a way it made sense.

Jazz nodded, her black hair gleaming in the afternoon sunlight pouring in through the window. "And now, Nire has put spells on the Path. Barriers of dark magic. Obstacles of Shadows. Witches with lesser strength than mine are forced to stay in the first Sanctuary they visit." She crossed her legs at her knees and leaned back in the seat. "When time moves on and problems begin, I can't save them a second time. I can't take them to a new Sanctuary because a second exposure to Nire's poisonous magic would kill them."

A deep cold rippled along my skin as what she said sank in. "Then how did I get into that prehistoric Sanctuary and back to this one? Wasn't I exposed to Nire's black magic twice, too?"

For a moment Jazz looked almost afraid to answer. Finally she said, "Three times. On the way to Shallym, and then twice more when you entered the ancient Sanctuary to save me and came back. You have great strength, both physical and spiritual. It means your mother was right, that you're destined for great things."

I wasn't ready to deal with that yet. My brain was really starting to throb, and I had to struggle to keep my focus. "So, what you're saying is that normally witches can only go into one Sanctuary, and that's it. Which means they're trapped in the timeline."

"Yes. Until they die of natural causes or fall victim to violence." Jazz's gaze locked with mine. "Because it always comes, Bren. Violence and persecution for witches. No matter what time or place."

I leaned forward and took one of her clenched hands and held it within mine again. "And your family? You faced this persecution, too?"

"We lived in Middle Salem, at first in peace, and then the Salem witch trials started. We had to flee." She raised her chin and her eyes glittered. "That's when I lost Mother, all of my family, and all of the oldeFolke living with us. When we tried to flee to Shallym on the Path."

She swallowed and her voice faltered. "Nire took them hostage to make certain my father died. And to torture me, hoping one day I will suffer too much and turn to evil, or accept it, in order to have relief."

"What?" I practically shouted and almost jumped to my feet. "Wait a second. How could that bastard expect you to become evil?"

Jazz shrugged, but the tension in her body told me how much it bothered her. "It has been known to happen. Witches and oldeFolke lured to Nire's side to try to save a loved one— or for greed and power."

She made a face, and for a minute, I wondered who she was thinking about. Did Jazz know someone who had gone bad? I didn't know whether to ask or leave it alone. Finally, because she seemed so stressed out, I went for leaving it alone.

Everything was so overwhelming that my thoughts threatened to scatter, but I fought to maintain my concentration. "Why does the Shadowmaster want to torture you? I'm glad he hasn't killed the rest of your family, but what's the point?"

She looked embarrassed, and lowered her eyes. "I'm a pure descendant of Shallym's original witches. I have power that no other witch queen or king has ever had, save for my father." She paused for a moment. "The Shadowmaster wants to steal my energy and magic—join with it and take it over. If Nire accomplishes this—well, Nire would be invincible if my power were added to the Shadows."

Whoa. No way was I going to let Nire get hold of Jazz.

"An ancient prophecy foretold all of this," she said. "And it predicted one who could defeat the Shadowmaster. The Shadowalker. Only he can wield the sword forged by the oldeFolke, the sword designed to break Nire's spells. Only the Shadowalker will have the strength to journey with me into Nire's stronghold, sever the Shadowmaster's dark energy at its very source, and free the Path."

I swallowed hard. "And that Shadowalker—"

She interrupted me, her words coming in a rush. "I moved through door after door in witch time and witch place. We call it 'walking the Shadows,' because those connections are where the Shadows lurk. Going through those doors can accidentally release Shadows into the time and place the witch goes, so there's always danger. That's why I was so upset that you had breached the Path and hadn't sealed it behind you."

Her eyes looked tortured, almost frantic as she continued, "I walked the Shadows in search of the true champion—the Shadowalker, a powerful witch in his own right with a special energy that can drive the Shadows back and ultimately destroy Nire in his own lair. In every time and place, I set up spells, but no champion came."

Jazz squeezed my hand so tight her nails dug into my flesh, yet I barely felt the pain. Her golden eyes stared into mine, pleading. Begging me to understand.

"Finally," she said, "I set up spells in your time, in the non-witching world. I called out for the champion, and you came, Bren. And yesterday—when you saved me—you entered the Path without my help. It's certain, after that. You are the Shadowalker."

My gut twisted up in a funny way. I shook my head. "No way. You've got to be wrong."

She raised her chin in that arrogant way that made me want to choke her—or kiss her. "It is the truth."

"I'm not a champion." I pulled my hand out of her grasp and straightened. "Not for you. Not for anybody."

chapter sixteen

JAZZ The vision had been terrible, as soul-wrenching as I imagined it might be—but even after that experience, Bren didn't believe me, about the level of his powers or his role. Even before he had told me as much, I had seen it in his eyes, along with something else. A flicker of darkness I couldn't read.

That flicker troubled me, like his ability to resist some of my magic. And yet, he had just asked that we be totally honest with each other. He had touched me so sweetly and vowed friendship last night. And then today . . . he had smiled like he'd been genuinely glad to see me, and took my hand. My cheeks flushed at his nearness, and his kindness warmed my heart. I didn't want to offend him with suspicion. Bren seemed open, and I was beginning to believe I could trust him. As much as Rol.

Maybe more than Rol.

The thought made my belly tighten. All of a sudden, the filth on Bren's shoes drove me near to distraction. I had to close my eyes to keep from zapping his boots and risking a few of his toes in the process.

With a flick of my wrist, I closed the drawing room door and lowered its outer bar into place. "Enough of my useless weeping. You must learn basic spellwork, or Nire will destroy you instantly."

When I glanced at Bren, he was frowning. "Thanks. That's reassuring."

"You wished us to be truthful with each other." I stood, dusting off my hands—and once more, that flicker of darkness marred Bren's handsome face. "That— that's what you wanted? Honesty?"

Bren nodded, but he didn't speak. Instead, he got to his feet and studied the door, as if glaring at the wood would make it move. I had a sudden image of him running through it. Breaking down the wood as he fled out of Shadowbridge, out of Shallym, and straight into the ocean to meet his doom.

"You have to see it in your thoughts." I moved to stand beside him, as much to steady him as feel his nearness. "Close your eyes, but keep the image of the door and the outer bar. Make it bright, and colorful, and real."

Bren closed his eyes. And opened them. He fidgeted and tried again. Once more, his eyes popped open.

He clenched his fists. "'See it in your thoughts'," he muttered. "You sound like one of those television psychics.

Call Miss Jazz. She'll read your future, right here in the Tarot cards."

"Please take this seriously." My weariness returned at the speed of light. "All you have to do is put your mind to it."

"'All you have to do is put your mind to it'," Bren mimicked in a voice much higher and more annoying than I thought mine had been.

What was making him so angry? Before I could ask, he squeezed his eyes shut. Immediately, his foot started to tap. In a few seconds, his entire leg was jiggling.

I touched his elbow, and he jerked away.

"Damn—darn—oh, screw it!" He turned his back to me. "I can't do this."

"Center yourself." Even at arm's length from him, I could feel his unfocused energy, leaping like toads from his mind. "Draw your thoughts together, and—"

"I can't, okay?" Bren's voice was hard, and his gaze was suddenly furious. "I have—problems with focusing. It's called ADHD. At home, I've got medicine. But here, it's just going to be a problem."

"But if you try—"

"It's not about trying!" Bren whirled and grabbed my arms, startling me so badly that I almost hexed him into a snail. "God damn it, if all I had to do was try to pay attention and concentrate, don't you think I'd do it? You think I like making rotten grades, pissing my dad off constantly, losing everything I own—having to work four times as hard as other kids to learn anything? Would that be fun to you, Jazz? Something you'd do on purpose?"

I stood still as a piece of rock in Bren's grasp. His eyes were wide and shining with pain. He seemed to want me to speak, but words failed me.

As my nervousness increased, the dirt on his shoes seemed to grow larger and more threatening. I started to shake, worrying that if it touched me, that if flakes of the filth actually made contact with my skin, something awful would happen. I didn't know what, but something awful. My eyes kept darting to the dirt, no matter how hard I tried to keep them on Bren's face.

His mouth twitched.

I jumped and zapped his boots.

Just a little. Just enough to rid them of the dangerous dirt.

Instantly, the knot in my stomach turned loose, and that feeling of impending doom receded.

Bren glanced at his clean boots, then stared into my face. I felt my cheeks heating up beneath his scrutiny.

"The dirt." He shook his head. "I was trying to talk to you, and you— the dirt. Everything has to be perfect, doesn't it? In order, no flaws, just right, or it freaks you out. You can't stand anything that doesn't meet your little mark in the sky." With a snort of disgust, he let me go and strode toward the window. "You're just like my father."

I stared at Bren's stiff back, and I wanted to go to him. My feet tried to move, but shame held me back like hot iron hands. My skin was on fire, and all I could do was quietly use my magic to remove the bar from the door, hang my head, and slip out of the drawing room.

———

For a few days, Bren and I spoke without really speaking—about the weather and training sessions and whether all hags were ugly. Sometimes, when he looked at me, I sensed even more intense emotions roiling out of him. Was it confusion, perhaps? Anger more likely, perhaps even hatred.

I could scarcely blame him. After all, I had wrecked his life, and now he knew about me—my weaknesses, and my failures, and my . . . problem with dirt.

By now, he had sensed the real truth, that I was not a fit partner in the battle with Nire, and that we were certain to fail in our quest.

Because of me.

With Rol's help, I tried to teach Bren simple spellwork, but as he had warned, he had terrible difficulty keeping his mind on the task. Even after several days we were still where we began—lifting the wooden bar. A toddler's game.

I didn't wish to widen the chasm between Bren and me. And so at dinner, when he asked me to clarify how time passes in the Sanctuaries, I nearly choked on a mushroom in my soup.

Rol looked uncomfortable as well, but the training master kept his large hands on his leg of mutton and his eyes on his plate.

"Well?" Bren's gaze was suddenly intense. "If we defeat this Nire bastard, can you drop me back in the parking lot—with Mom's truck—the same day you took me? You know, go out of the Sanctuary and back in at the beginning?"

My food stuck in my throat as I swallowed. I took a slow drink of ale and tried not to notice the crumbs all over the dining table. Dozens of answers and apologies rushed through my thoughts, but all I could manage was, "No."

Rol coughed. I glared at him, and he returned his attention to the mutton.

Bren put his silverware down. He looked angry again. "Why not?"

My stomach started to hurt. How could I explain everything to him and make him understand this time? "Because . . . it doesn't work that way. I can't go back in time."

Bren smiled as if he thought I was kidding, then slowly frowned. "You trot back and forth between times every day. And how else did we end up here, two thousand years away from where we started?"

"It's true that I can move across time on the Path, from location to location." The ache in my stomach turned into knifelike pains, spreading to my chest. I closed my eyes. The crumbs were overwhelming me. I opened my eyes again and forced myself to meet his gaze. "But, time is always passing. Yesterday is yesterday, in your time, or this time—or any other."

"I don't get it." Bren's deepening frown clearly communicated his belief that I was holding back the truth.

"You have my apologies." I tried to sound sure of myself, but my voice was hushed. Ashamed. No wonder he didn't believe me. "When you return home, it will be on whatever day we complete our task. A month, two months—the time will have passed, here in Shallym, and in L.O.S.T., too."

"Great. That's just great." Bren shoved his plate away.

I flinched.

Rol turned his eyes to me, waiting for me to react.

By the Goddess. One minute Rol adores me, the next he waits for me to blunder! It's maddening. Well, if he's so certain I'll show my ire, why disappoint him?

I stood. With a flourish of my aching fingers, I blasted the crumbs from the table.

Bren sat like a post, his frown glued to his face. I thought about blasting it from his lips, but I didn't want to hurt him. Besides, I had vowed that I wouldn't cause harm to the Shadowalker.

Not that he would give me the same consideration.

I turned and fled toward the drawing room. My footsteps echoed as I ran, but I didn't care. I had no place at that table, with those people. I had no place left anywhere, in any world, and the only one I could blame for that was myself.

It was early that same afternoon, and the sunlight held a particularly gray cast as Bren failed once more. How could he have breached the Path so easily, yet fail at every minor enchantment?

"Try the bar movement again." I gestured to the closed door, wishing Rol would hurry back from the smithy. "Put the force of your thought behind it this time. Moving natural objects is basic—our simplest option."

Bren glared at me before turning his angry eyes toward the door. He put his hands on his temples, pressing as he closed his eyes. Even with such an effort toward focus, his feet moved against the leather of his boots.

Seconds passed.

Bren's skin took on a silvery sheen, and my hopes rose. Whatever his power, perhaps he could use it productively.

More seconds passed.

My hopes fluttered back to resting position and became still, like the bar on the other side of the drawing room door.

"Damn." Bren's eyes flew open. "I'll just fight with my sword. I'm better at that kind of stuff. This is stupid."

I sighed. "No doubt because this kind of stuff is what I want you to do."

"Do you still think I'm screwing this up on purpose?" Bren wheeled around and lunged toward me, stopping only a few feet away. "Failure's always deliberate, right? No mistakes allowed. No flaws, no imperfections."

Images of Mother berating Father for every mistake he made flashed through my mind. More images followed, of myself blaming Father for dying and speaking angrily to his memory.

No!

Heat rose to my cheeks. "I never should have told you about my problem. Why not shout it from the rooftops to be certain I'm properly humiliated by my shortcomings?"

Bren hesitated, then smirked. "Now that's a thought. You're working hard to make sure I'm humiliated by mine."

"I am not." I straightened myself, outraged. "I merely want you to give the task proper effort."

His smirk faltered a bit. "You don't listen to me. You don't even listen to yourself, I swear. I've tried to explain about my attention problems, but you just won't hear me. I guess selective hearing goes along with your dirt thing."

Once more, my face filled with fire. "If I must be reminded of that fault every five minutes, what does it matter if I push you to do better with your spells training?"

"Fu- shi- *crap!*" Bren clenched his hands and bounced up and down as though he wished to hit me. A full sheen of silver covered him. "Don't you get it? I *can't.* If I could just point at that damn bar and zap it, I would!" He jabbed a finger toward the door—and I heard the bar rattle. Something shattered, there was a loud thump, and someone swore.

Rol.

Bren blinked as the training master pushed the door open, holding the wooden bar in his large hands.

"Very good," Rol murmured. "Though I fear one of the royal urns has been eliminated."

"I didn't do that." Bren shook his head, his hair flopping into his eyes.

"Yes, you did." My cheeks were slowly returning to normal temperature. The bare drawing room seemed brighter, and I realized my heart was beating rapidly. "Perhaps overdid it a bit, but you did it nonetheless. Excellent!"

"'Excellent'," Bren mimicked. He snatched the wooden bar from Rol's grasp, and for a moment, I feared he would launch it in my direction. "You're just trying to make me feel better. Admit it. You moved the damn thing."

My hands lifted on instinct, and my fingers flexed. "I did no such thing."

Bren didn't believe me. I could tell from his furious stare, and it was all I could do to hold back a hex. He was distracted, and thus probably couldn't concentrate enough to resist my spell—as when I turned him to a donkey. At the moment, I wanted to turn him into a snake so badly I could feel it in my toes. The energy of the earth cried out for me to act, but I held myself in check. Barely.

"You moved the bar, boy." Rol's voice was gruff but proud.

"How do you know?" Bren's gaze flicked from the bar in his hands to the training master and back to me.

Rol shrugged. "Her Majesty would never break a vase during a simple spell—or make the wood behave like a sword."

"Of course not." Anger left Bren's expression, but his infuriating smirk returned. "That would be dangerous. And very messy."

"*Ooob!*" I fired a blasting spell over Bren's head, blowing a round hole in the wall behind him.

Rol's gasp was audible, and for a moment, Bren looked almost frightened. I felt a charge of satisfaction before being overcome with horror at my loss of control.

There were too many people in the drawing room. I tried to breathe, but the air felt stale. I needed to take a walk. Monitor. Fly to the village. Anything but stand in that room for another instant.

"Are you—" Rol began, but I didn't wait for him to finish. In seconds, I was running down the hall, down the front steps, and out—out toward Shallym.

What was wrong with me? I had never been one to flee—but if I didn't get away from Rol and Bren, I might do something I would forever regret.

It took me no time to call a proper live oak branch, and with a push of my feet, I sped down Shadowbridge Hill.

It was afternoon by the time I finished routine monitoring and landed in Shallym. The town was fairly busy with trade and conversation, though my arrival at the market was greeted with nervous stares and sideways glances. Hags scattered like fat ants as I landed just before the branch caught fire. The wood smoldered as I discarded it, lacing the rich smells of fruit, meat, and spices with an edge of acrid smoke.

A few witches were brave enough to nod at me.

I nodded back, wishing I could find it within myself to speak to them. They would probably scream.

Was I so formidable? I folded my arms and shook my head. When I sighed, a nearby elfling dodged beneath a cart bearing pears and peaches. The cartman shivered, but kept a false smile pasted on his heavy-jowled face.

Why were these people so infernally concerned with my slightest mood? I had never harmed a single one of them. Ever. A few moments of temper, here and there, but I only ever blasted stones and old sticks. What had I done to earn such tremendous fear?

A mother tugged the hand of a child who strayed too close to me. The child, so much smaller, fairly lifted off the ground, but not before I saw the look of frightened respect flicker across her face. Not respect for me, but respect for her mother. The way I respected my mother— and feared her.

Of course . . .

That was it.

My arms relaxed as the realization trickled through me. The villagers didn't fear me because I had hurt them. They feared me because I *could* hurt them. Because of my greater power and my control over the Path.

Those who didn't show outright fear gave me glances of grudging respect or anger, like Bren.

Did Bren stay angry with me because he feared I would hurt him with my power? Or—no. Perhaps he stayed angry because I could hurt him with my tongue. Because I was hurting him with my disapproval.

Dear Goddess. Did my opinions cause him pain?

The bustle of the marketplace swelled around me as my mouth fell open.

Bren's opinions of me certainly caused me pain. Why had I not realized that he might care what I think of him?

I was selfish. I was completely selfish.

My stomach knotted, and I found it difficult to breathe. That instant—seeing myself through Bren's eyes—stabbed me deeply. My breath came short.

"No. Stop being ridiculous. He doesn't care about me." My voice sounded low and hollow to my own ears. "I ruined his life. I'm impossible, obsessed with cleanliness. He's said so a hundred times, at least."

Tears made the village blur and distort.

I *was* being ridiculous. If I allowed myself to think Bren cared about me as deeply as I was beginning to care about him, I'd be in for nothing but pain.

My duty came before such trivialities, anyway. It was time for me to get my focus back. And to do that, I had to rid myself of the fantasy that Bren ever would come to feel anything but contempt for me.

My cheeks burned.

It would be unpleasant proving the truth to myself, but I could see no other way.

The market was emptying quickly, and from nearby came the reedy keening of a klatchKoven Keeper, singing to her beautiful brood.

Most of the villagers hurried away as it became clear that the Keeper intended to enter the market with her charges. Even I shivered, though I had learned as a child how to contend with klatch hypnosis. A few cartmen put cotton or wax in their ears and held their ground. Brave fools. But they had learned some measure of resistance, living here so long.

The song grew louder, and the young witches spilled into the square, dancing. The six were slight and beautiful, fair of hair and eye and demonstrating impeccable grace. Behind them, the Keeper walked with assurance. She was even more striking than usual, with glittering golden tresses and flawless lines beneath her billowing white robes. Her eyes met mine, and I nodded—and then I felt a jolt of awareness.

Yes. They would meet my needs quite nicely.

"Keeper," I said in my most respectful tone. "I would ask a favor of you and yours."

chapter seventeen

Jazz's chin had been high in the air as she practically ran from the drawing room and disappeared out the door. A chunk of rock fell from the hole she had blasted into the wall, and it landed on the floor with a loud thunk.

The smoky-sulfurish smell drifting across the room reminded me of Todd's plastic cap gun from when he was a little kid. When my brother was six, he used to sneak up and scare the crap out of me with it. I wondered how the twit was doing. I had a hard time keeping track of the days, but I figured it had been at least a week or more since I had seen him, and I had to admit I missed him.

Rol shook his bald head and sighed. "Apparently your training is in my hands for this afternoon."

I clenched the wooden bar and gave a quick nod. Good. Anything was better than being cooped up inside with Jazz. Tension that had knotted my shoulders began to ease. Shards of the shattered vase crunched under our boots as I followed Rol out of the drawing room. Purple and green ceramic littered the floor, from what used to be a pretty cool urn.

Did I really do that?

Just as I was about to ask Rol if we should clean up the broken pieces, Acaw and his crow-brother appeared out of nowhere. Rol nodded to the elf, who zapped the mess and disappeared into the drawing room, probably to take care of the hole in the wall. How did the little guy know what had happened?

Did Jazz tell him somehow? Or Rol? Maybe the crow-brother knew. Jazz had said the bird was some sort of "familiar"—a magical partner who helped Acaw survive and kept him company.

After I slid the bar back into the door, I followed Rol through the manor, and I thought about what happened with the vase. Did I really do magic? Did I make that bar fly off and smack into the vase and Rol?

We stepped into the courtyard, and I shook my head. No.

Yet I had felt a surge of something when I pointed my finger at the door. Like lava bubbling inside me and heat shooting through my arm. My skin had shimmered silver as the feeling of power flooded me, and then the shimmer and the power vanished as quickly as they had come.

Our boots kicked up dust as we strode toward the smithy, and I drew my sword from its sheath. The blade glittered in the afternoon light as I thrust my sword into the air, jabbing at an imaginary opponent.

I couldn't wait to work out my frustrations and could almost feel the satisfaction of my muscles aching from physical combat. "Are we going to spar some more?"

"Nay." Rol barked the response, and for a second I wondered if he was ticked at me. But when we reached the smithy, he turned and the corner of his mouth quirked. "It is about time you discovered your magic."

I shook my head. "I still don't believe I moved that bar." Well, maybe I sort of believed it. But I wasn't convinced. Yet.

"Certainly, you did." He held out his hand. "Your weapon."

With reluctance, I gave him my sword and he laid it on a workbench, then set his own beside it. The smithy smelled of wood smoke and iron. Heat from the forge warmed my face and sweat broke out across my forehead.

"Come, pup." Rol led me back out into the courtyard, and a breeze cooled my skin.

I scowled. "Could you knock it off with the 'pup' crap already?"

"Silence." Rol stopped in the center of the training yard and raised his face to the sky.

Rol closed his eyes, his dark shoulders and arms glistening in the sunlight like some oil-coated pro bodybuilder. He took a deep breath and raised his powerful arms, his muscles cording. A vein popped out on his thick neck.

While Rol was doing his impersonation of a statue, my gaze wandered to the courtyard.

And I saw a giant dragon thing appear out of nowhere. Only ten feet in front of us.

"Rol!" I shouted as I whirled toward the smithy to grab my sword.

"Stay." Rol opened his eyes and snatched my arm in his vice grip before I got past him. He jerked me around to face the beast.

The dragon blinked at me as I struggled to free myself from Rol's grasp. The creature was so massive it blotted out the sun, casting an enormous shadow over us. Wind whooshed by my ears as the dragon stretched its wings from one end of the training yard to the other. The ground rumbled and the creature's scales glowed an iridescent green as it moved toward Rol and me.

"What's the matter with you?" My heart pounded and blood rushed in my ears. "It's coming after us!"

Even as the dragon reared back its head, I knew we were toast. It roared and let loose a blast of fire from its cavelike mouth. I closed my eyes and flung up my free arm as if that could shield me.

And felt nothing.

Slowly lowering my arm, I peeked through one eye and saw the dragon was gone. Vanished.

My other eye popped open.

Chuckling, Rol released his hold.

Whipping around, I glared at him, wanting to slug the big jerk. "That was an illusion, wasn't it?"

Rol grinned. "Aye. And an excellent one."

I clenched my fists. Okay, so Rol was bigger than me. A lot bigger. No matter. I still wanted to take him on. "Why the hell didn't you warn me?"

"A lesson, my boy." Rol's white teeth flashed against his dark skin. "So that you might see what a powerful tool the art of illusion can be."

The damn "tool" still had my heart pounding so fast that I thought it would never slow down. "Great. Next time think you could give me some clue?"

He clapped me on the back. "Now it is your turn to conjure a slither illusion."

I stumbled forward and rubbed my shoulder as I glared at him. "Oh, sure. One dragon coming right up."

Rol arched his eyebrow.

"All right, all right." I folded my arms across my chest. "Tell me how I'm supposed to make a stupid dragon out of thin air."

"It requires concentration and focus."

I rolled my eyes. "Just terrific. What I'm worst at: concentrating and focusing."

Rol frowned. "You are able to do both well with sword fighting. It is much the same with magic."

He had me there. When it came to physical stuff, like baseball and swordplay, I had no problem concentrating. Maybe magic was the same way? That is, if I really could *do* magic.

I dragged my hand through my hair and sighed. "So, how do I whip up a dragon?"

"A slither." Rol straightened his shoulders. "You must visualize the beast in your mind as alive and real. It shall appear as you have imagined it to be."

"Okay. Right. Picture a dragon—I mean slither." I shook out my hands and bounced on the balls of my feet, like I was getting ready to step into the batter's box. After taking a deep breath and exhaling, I closed my eyes and tried to visualize that up-close-and-personal view I had just gotten of Rol's imaginary slither.

Nothing happened. I couldn't even focus on its image. My knee started to bounce and that jittery feeling spread over me. Like I'd had a mega-jolt of caffeine. That same feeling always took hold of me when I tried to concentrate on schoolwork, or when I tried to practice magic with Jazz. Stupid ADHD made my life miserable.

Concentrate. I furrowed my brows and tried to force my brain to cooperate. My knee bounced harder, and I wanted to squirm out of my skin.

My eyes flew open, and I got a good look at Rol's disapproving frown.

"I can't do this." My gut flamed and failure burned like acid in my throat. Before Rol could respond, I turned on my heel and marched away across the training yard.

I half expected him to yell or come after me, but all I heard was his deep sigh.

So I was a disappointment to Rol. And to Jazz. Like that was some big surprise. After all, I had been nothing but a disappointment to my dad since the day I was born.

At first I didn't know where I was headed, I just knew I had to get away from Rol. From everyone and everything. Moving felt good and cleared my head, but my failures continued to gnaw at my insides. Why couldn't I be normal like everyone else, and be able to concentrate when it was important?

Not that magic was something normal people could do.

Not that magic was something I could do.

It wasn't long before I started walking toward my place. I had discovered it the day after Jazz had zapped the dirt off my boots. Rol had let me wander off, after we'd spent the afternoon sparring. Of course, he made sure that I knew Shadowbridge's grounds were protected by some kind of spellwork, so I could only go so far.

Not one to ignore a challenge, I had walked across the courtyard and through a grove of trees until I smacked into an invisible wall. I bounced off of it, like it was made of rubber, and landed on my ass. The barrier had glittered gold, reminding me of the way the sky had looked when Jazz trapped me in this timeline.

For almost the whole time I had been a prisoner, whenever I had free time, I tried to find a way around it, but no dice. So, like a trained dog behind an electric fence, I stopped trying to get past the invisible wall and found a place to kick back and be alone. At least I hoped I was alone, with no one spying on me in a crystal ball or something. I wouldn't have put it past Jazz.

Humiliation at disappointing Rol settled inside me as I reached my hideout. It was beside a stream, in the middle of a bunch of pine trees. My hearing seemed sharper, and in the distance I could hear ocean waves crashing against the shore. I smelled salt and brine mixed with the pine of the forest.

Sometimes, it was like I could sense the witches around me, too. From Jazz and Rol to the freaks down in Shallym. Like we were all connected.

That was friggin' weird.

I scooped up a stone and skipped it across the stream—it was so narrow that the stone only bounced twice on the water's surface before landing on the other bank. I pitched the next rock into the air, but like I expected, it struck the invisible wall and dropped to the ground. The only other sign of the barrier was that golden glitter that rippled across its surface.

With a sigh, I crouched beside the stream and started flinging rocks into it. I wondered what my parents were doing, and if Brandon's folks had called them when I never showed up in San Diego. More than likely, Mom was totally freaked out, and I bet Dad was telling her how they never should have let me go off on my own.

Todd was probably asking if he could have my room.

Shifting to sit on the bank, I propped my elbows on my knees and smiled at the thought of my brother. His pet menagerie would fit better in my room than his own, that was for sure. My parents had converted the back porch into a pretty cool bedroom for me, extending from one end of the house to the other. Yeah, I could picture Todd's boa constrictor and his glass tank of lizards all set up in one corner. I bet he would really go nuts over seeing a slither.

Mom had taken over my old room and used it for all her bizarre stuff—we started calling it the "backroom," even though technically, mine was at the back of the house. The backroom was where she took all her strange horticulture friends when they came over to visit, and where she kept her mushroom collection (she called it a "blind") and a bunch of other plants that only grew under black lights. I never understood what was so exciting about fungi. But most parents were terminally weird. At least Mom didn't collect old Barbie stuff or something really lame.

Sounds of wind through the pine trees and the stream gurgling over rocks had the effect of relaxing me every time I came to my hideout. I even felt like I could concentrate on anything I needed to.

Maybe that's it. Maybe I just need to practice alone, without an audience. Yeah. Alone, like I was most of the time, before I came here.

Excitement stirred inside as I remembered all the hours I had practiced hitting. When I was in Little League, Mom would drop me off at the city park's batting cage with a pocketful of quarters, and I would hit one ball after another until my muscles ached. No audience. No pressure. Eventually I had gotten so good that it didn't matter if anyone was watching me.

The same for throwing. I used to throw a baseball across our backyard at various targets, over and over and over, until I could just about hit any spot I wanted with my eyes closed.

With renewed determination, I stood and searched the area for something to lift with magic, like I had supposedly lifted the bar earlier. My gaze rested on a good-sized rock a few feet away, one that was as big as a basketball.

I shook out my hands and jogged in place, trying to limber up. After a few deep breaths, I concentrated on moving the rock with magic.

It didn't budge.

Again and again I tried to move the rock, but nothing happened. I must have spent a good half hour trying to move the rock, frustration building with each attempt.

Okay. I could do it—sure I could. I was alone, no distractions, nobody watching me.

I forced myself to calm down. To concentrate. To focus.
I can do this.

This time I closed my eyes, and remembered how Jazz told me to visualize what I wanted to move, to make it seem real in my mind. Warmth stirred in my gut along with a tickle of that power I'd felt earlier, when I had moved the bar.

Yes. I did move the bar.

The warm sensation grew as I pictured the rock. I opened my eyes, but the rock hadn't budged. I frowned, then realized my skin was glowing like it had that time I hit the applecart in the marketplace. A glow like Jazz's, only mine was silver. That had to mean something, right?

Again, I closed my eyes, and I heard Jazz's voice echoing in my head, "Put the force of your thought behind it."

Force of thought. Force of thought.

Fire curled inside, flames licking up into my chest and along my arms. Heat built and expanded, like lava flowing from a volcano. I raised my hand as I visualized the rock, imagining it as light as a basketball twirling on my fingertip.

I felt the power growing, so much I thought I would explode. I opened my eyes . . .

And saw the rock spinning in the air, a good four feet off the ground.

"Woohoo!" I shouted and pumped my fist. A flock of birds scattered from the trees, and I stumbled back. The rock dropped to the ground and rolled toward me, almost landing on my foot.

I couldn't stop grinning. I did it!

If I hadn't been afraid of feeling like an idiot, I probably would have danced around like a football player after scoring the winning touchdown in the Super Bowl. Energized by success, I started practicing on anything I could find. A piece of driftwood, a log, and then several baseball-sized rocks—all at once. The more I practiced, the easier it got. If nothing else, I'd be a hit at kids' birthday parties, dressed up like Bozo and juggling a dozen rocks at once.

Of course, I found I had to be careful, too. One time, I grabbed onto a dead branch with my magic, and yanked it toward me so hard that it shot through the air and almost took off my own head.

When I ran out of things to manipulate with magic, I decided to try an illusion. My victory at learning one kind of magic made me feel like I could do anything—at least when I was alone.

I closed my eyes and tried to remember what Rol had taught me about illusions. The now-familiar warmth sizzled inside my chest.

Picture a slither. Picture a slither.

Only I couldn't quite visualize the beast Rol had conjured up.

This time, when I opened my eyes, I felt disappointment. There was no imaginary dragon lumbering my way.

But then something closer to the ground caught my eye.

I narrowed my gaze at the thing inching toward me. It was about the size of a cat, but it had wings sprouting from its back and flames curling out of its mouth. The tiny creature roared, only it sounded more like a cartoon duck's quack.

Well, I had managed to create an illusion that might frighten a mouse.

Shaking my head, I laughed, and the mini-slither vanished. I couldn't stop laughing. I laughed so hard my stomach hurt and my eyes watered. I wiped the moisture from my eyes with the back of my hand and started to head back toward the manor.

Wait till I showed Jazz and Rol what I could do.

No.

While I walked, I slid my hand into my pocket and smoothed my fingers over the statue. For a second, I thought it wriggled in my hand, but I knew that was impossible. A lead fist settled in my gut. I frowned. Why didn't I want to tell Rol and Jazz about my success? I would wait until I was really good. Yeah, that was it. I would probably just make a fool of myself, anyway. They would think I made up the whole thing.

While I strode toward the manor, my thoughts once again turned back to the day that Jazz and I had talked the whole afternoon and half the night, too. Why couldn't we get along like that all the time? Why did we always end up fighting? I really liked her, despite everything. Or maybe it was because of everything. Whatever it was, I wished I could figure her out.

My stomach was rumbling by the time I reached the back door to the manor. But then I heard a sound. Women singing. The most beautiful song—familiar, yet I couldn't quite place it.

The singing drew me closer. I had to get to them. My heart rate picked up as I hurried through the manor and practically ran to the front door. I flung it open—and saw the most gorgeous beings I had ever seen.

Their glittery blonde hair floated around their faces, and I knew I was in love. I had to be with them. I had to get to them. Now.

chapter eighteen

Bren seemed to float down the front steps of Shadowbridge, entranced by the Keeper's insidious
music. Sunlight made his scruffy hint of beard seem
rugged and handsome, and I clenched my fists.
Already, the klatchKoven had begun to dance, waving graceful hands at the glittering sky.

JAZZ

I needed to see this. I needed to watch Bren under the
spell of other witches, even faithless flesh-eaters such as
these, to remind myself that my first duty was training him,
and that if he didn't take this seriously, he'd die. And
maybe I needed some distance, too. Seeing other witches
touch him might be just what I needed to snap me out of
lovesick self-pity. I really was getting tired of myself.

Rol stood in the doorway. His hands covered his ears. He
was shaking and sweating—and glaring at me in between

181

nervous glances at the Keeper, who stood to my right. Her expression was . . . smug. And hungry.

As for Bren, oblivion described him in full. For one who claimed difficulty with concentration, he was certainly well focused on the six pairs of swaying hips before him.

Bren reached the ground and stood atop Shadowbridge Hill, and the klatch surrounded him like golden panthers pacing around their prey.

The air smelled faintly of mulberry and hazelnut. Exotic and intoxicating. Rol was near collapse as Bren allowed himself to be drawn into the dancing circle. I could tell the training master would have risked his sanity to interfere, but my cold stare warned him away. Rol stumbled backward, and the heavy oak door of Shadowbridge Manor closed with a resounding thump.

The klatchKoven circled Bren, running long, pale fingers over his skin. Bren was breathing hard, making little effort to resist their charms.

I drew a centering breath and spoke through the beautiful singing. "Lovely, aren't they?"

Bren managed a nod as hands caressed his chest.

"You feel you should trust them." I sighed. "That they have eyes only for you."

Again, Bren nodded.

My frown must have been intense, because the Keeper beside me shuddered. Still, she didn't step away. KlatchKoven Keepers gave ground for no one, even the Queen of the Witches. Her formidable teeth gnashed once, but of course, Bren was far too occupied with physical sensation to notice.

The sight of other witches touching him, and of him enjoying it, made my stomach roil.

The klatch ceased singing and began to whisper, urging Bren to relax, to believe their message of love. And he wanted to. I could tell.

"Most beings are not to be trusted." My fists pressed into my legs, and my chest ached. "Mark me, Bren. Until you know every aspect of a being, especially if they're of the oldeFolke, don't drop your guard. Not until you've heard the oath sworn by their hearts, even as other words spill from their lips."

"Nice lips," he muttered to the nearest klatch witch.

"Try to regain your balance." My voice sounded like a goose's honk against the silken tones of the klatch. "Nire could have a dozen klatchKovens waiting to tempt you when we go to battle."

Bren didn't seem interested in balance or in tapping into his unusual ability to shrug off enchantments, spells, and magical commands. The sun kissed his hair with soft streaks, and he smiled with an expression close to rapture at the nearest witch. Below us, at the foot of the hill, I imagined all of Shallym, paused and watching.

Shadowbridge was silent and still, but I had no doubt that Rol was inside, bound in ropes of his own spells to keep himself safe, praying to the universe on Bren's behalf. Acaw might have been watching as well. Elves were immune to klatchKoven charms, as were many of the oldeFolke, but Acaw appreciated beautiful women no less than the next man.

Beside me, the Keeper began to sway.

"Don't forget my instructions," I said to her through clenched teeth.

Her response was a guttural purr.

"Resist, damn you!" I snapped my fingers at Bren, and the noise echoed like cannonfire.

He startled, and for a moment, his eyes met mine.

"Resist," I said again. "Focus on something else. Reclaim your thoughts, and realize the danger all around you."

"What danger?" Bren sounded drugged and harsh. "You're such a— a tightass, Jazz. Chill out."

My fingers flexed. "Tightass." That could be arranged.

The Keeper gnashed her teeth and whistled to the klatch, and they doubled their efforts to persuade Bren to drop to his knees.

With a final cutting glance at me, Bren sank to the ground. He closed his eyes as the beautiful witches stroked his shoulders, loosening him up, lulling him into a dreadful stupor.

I almost yelled that he was not trying, but remembered how angry such comments made him. Pressuring Bren would not help. I tugged at my hair. What would make a difference?

Anything?

He was completely vulnerable now, arms to his side, head back, lost in the klatch caresses.

A rustle of fabric told me the Keeper had moved before I saw her streak toward Bren's exposed flesh.

"Cease!" I commanded, spreading my hands wide.

Just as the day when I first brought Bren to Shallym, everything froze. Not even the air moved. The villagers, the ocean—everything was still, except Bren. He was swaying back and forth, even as the Keeper stood immobile before him, arms spread wide.

I eased between the Keeper and Bren. "Open your eyes."

Bren kept swaying.

The urge to slap him was powerful, but I contained myself. "Open your eyes, Bren, and gaze at your fate."

With a grunt, Bren did as I asked—and yelled. He fell backward, away from the statuesque klatch witches, pointing at the robed Keeper—at her true face, now revealed for him in the moment just before she would have eaten him whole.

All of her false beauty had been erased. Her purplish skin was warty and pocked, and her hideous head had grown three sizes to accommodate her sharp-toothed maw.

"What is it?" Bren yelled, scooting farther out of the klatchKoven circle. "Looks like a monster eggplant or something."

He got to his feet as I shook my head. "She would have been your doom had I allowed it. And she might be again." I pointed to the Keeper's rows of fangs. "Nire could have her under his sway, or a hundred like her."

"No way." Bren dusted off his clothes. "Anyway, I was just playing. I wasn't really going to let her near me."

My cheeks instantly burned. "Lying is an unbecoming trait, even to soothe your dignity."

"Well, what did you expect?" Rather than stand in front of the Keeper, Bren headed toward me—though he made a wide arc around the klatch—and stopped near my shoulder. "You didn't give me a clue about them, or how I was supposed to handle this. That wasn't fair."

"Do you think Nire will be fair?" My tone was cool, even to me. "Do you think Nire will hand you battle plans and encourage you to focus? I offered assistance. You didn't even try, Bren."

"Damn you." He kicked dirt all over my shoes, and I stiffened. The urge to clean it off was so strong it nearly overwhelmed me. "I've told you all I'm telling you—I try. I just can't."

"Owl dung." I turned to face him, and we were almost nose to nose. "I've seen you make effort and fail, and I've seen you fail to bother. This was the latter."

Bren's hair flopped into his eyes even as he tried to brush it to the side. "You don't know that."

I placed my hand against his chest and pushed him back a step. "This time, you failed to try. I'm not stupid, Bren. There's a difference between inability and inactivity."

"Whatever." His face was turning red. "You sprung this on me."

"Nire will spring things on you, too." I nodded toward the Keeper. "This, and worse. Will you simply not bother if the Shadowmaster acts unfairly?"

Bren's eyes narrowed. "Shut up."

"I won't."

"God, I swear!" He kicked dirt again, this time missing me. "You get more like my father every day."

"Insulting me is a convenient way to make me angry, so that I'll cease telling you the truth." I glared at Bren. My heart was racing. "It won't work. Did you ever stop to think your father had reasons to be angry with you?"

"*Aww, man!*" Bren let his head roll backward. "Did you ever stop to think that I failed him so many times I stopped trying?"

The bare honesty of Bren's angry confession stunned me. For one long, horrible moment, I felt like I was talking to a mirror, a twin, some dark aspect of myself that I refused to allow to the surface.

How many times had I wanted to give up trying to please my mother? And even now, how many times a day did the same thought cross my mind?

Even as I stared into the full might and bluster of Bren's arrogance, I stopped seeing it, as if some clever witch had cast a spell banishing my blindness to Bren's true heart. He seemed whole to me all of a sudden, and older, and more burdened. My anger yet boiled, but it took on a desperate, frightened feeling, as if I were suddenly fighting only for Bren's life and survival.

My hand flew to my throat, and I tried to measure my next words carefully. "I understand and accept that you have problems with learning and attention. But you need to understand that those problems don't give you license to offer half-efforts and lies. You're— you're much better than that."

At this, Bren's face became the color of a rising sun. "What do you know about it, Jazz? You've been so busy doing everything Mommy told you to do, you turned into a total pain in the ass. Nobody likes you. Not me and not them." He gestured to the klatch and the village. "And why should they? All of us—we're nothing but pieces on your little chessboard."

His words sliced me like a sword, and my head spun with the effort of holding back my tears and my spells. "Mind your tongue."

"Fine!" Bren snatched a handful of dirt and flung it in my direction. The filth struck me full in the face and scattered down my clothing. My breath caught in my throat, only to explode in a scream of rage.

In a single blast of my fingers, I removed the dirt and knocked Bren to his backside. The dirt that had been on me pelted him like brown rain.

"And when you're mad," he said, standing, letting the dirt fall to the ground, "anything goes. Isn't that right?"

My teeth were clenched so tightly I could scarcely speak. "You provoked me."

"So?" Bren's tone was mocking. "You think Nire won't provoke you?"

I whirled away from him and spelled the klatchKoven and Keeper back to Shallym. To appease the Keeper, I transferred a small squirrel with them, so she would not go completely hungry. Without looking at Bren, I shouted, "Resume!"

The keening scream of the Keeper snaked up Shadow-bridge Hill. She was no doubt enraged.

"Go inside," I told Bren as I summoned a branch. "She might return. Rol will help you."

Bren snorted. "Let her come back. I don't care."

Tears flowing, I mounted the live oak's gift, hiding my face from Bren. "As you wish. You'll make a fine dinner."

As I rose from the ground, I heard his bellow of rage. And then, "*Wait,* would you? I didn't— I'm— oh hell." Then, more distant, "Dammit, Jazz. I'm not the only one with problems around here! And you can't keep running away every time I don't do what you want."

His voice faded as I flew away, winnowed to almost nothing, and still his next words seemed as loud as thunder in my heart. "Sooner or later, we have to be our own sanctuary. You and me. Safe together—or we'll never beat Nire."

High above him, I hesitated, feeling the air press against my aching jaws. The urge to turn back swelled, but equally strong was the urge to fly until I didn't feel nervous and hurt and frustrated any longer. If he had made some effort—any effort—to focus on something besides the klatch, he might have triumphed. Such strong magic!

But he failed.

I failed.

When I glanced down. Bren was staring at the ground. For a moment, I hoped he might say something to suggest he understood what happened, or why I did what I did. Instead, as I drifted toward the Path's barrier, I heard an emphatic "whatever."

chapter nineteen

BREN

Pressing my nose against the cool glass, I stared out my bedroom window. The early morning sky was the same odd color of blue as my mom's eyes. Homesickness settled inside, like someone had put a sandbag on my chest. I missed Mom and Todd, and I had to admit, I missed Dad, too.

Yet, even as I thought about my family, I wondered at how Shadowbridge Manor had begun to feel like home in just the two weeks or so that I had been here. It was like I belonged in Jazz's world. Kind of like I had come home. When all this was over with, and we had defeated Nire, it was going to be tough to leave.

If we did beat Nire.

It had been about a week since the klatch witches had almost had me for an afternoon snack, and I still had a hollow feeling in my gut over the whole mess. I felt pretty crappy about the way I had treated Jazz, throwing dirt on her like a five-year-old. But she had made me so angry. Just like my dad, she knew all the right buttons to push.

Pulling at the lacing of my tunic, I sighed as Jazz walked down the manor's steps and to the end of the dirt path. I wondered if she knew that I watched her every morning before I headed downstairs to breakfast.

She opened her message box, took out the notes, and tilted her head, listening to her Shadowhispers. Since our conversations always seemed to go nowhere, I probably should have started leaving her notes in the stupid box. Maybe then she would have listened to me.

Jazz nodded at the box as she tucked a strand of her black hair behind her ear. Something inside me twisted, an ache I couldn't name. Well, maybe I could. Despite her tricking me into being there in the first place, our arguing, her being on my case like my dad, and everything having to be perfect—I cared about her, and I cared what she thought about me.

Why?

And if it mattered that much, why couldn't I tell her that I was learning magic and getting better at it every day? She and Rol still thought I was a failure at everything but swordplay. Rol had all but given up, focusing on drilling me over and over at driving my blade into the earth.

"In Nire's Sanctuary," he kept saying. "The earth will be different. Not earth—just space under spell. Everything Nire does and has is false, boy. False and unnatural. Remember that."

And then he would frown and look like he ate something bad. "Nire does not have even a natural Sanctuary, or we would have discovered it by now. No. Nire lives in some foul lair, stitched to the Path by filthy magic. You will have to use all of your strength, all of your cunning and belief in yourself—and in right and in magic—to destroy it. Drive hard. Drive to split that putrid spell-ground."

I had been practicing that. Driving my sword into the earth over and over. Once or twice, I'd even made a small earthquake in the training yard. It was pretty cool, though I couldn't really control it.

But at my hideaway, I was getting good at controlling objects, illusions, and even levitating my own body. My hearing was getting sharper, and if I'd wanted to be nosy, I could listen in on those Shadowhispers.

Down below the mansion, Jazz stilled as if she had heard my thoughts, but I knew she couldn't. I had become an expert at blocking her out. In fact, I was pretty sure if she tried to turn me into an octopus or feed me to a bunch of carnivorous witches, I'd be able to block the spells and hypnosis, or whatever.

As I imagined myself levitating a klatchKoven, Jazz lifted her head and looked straight up at my window, and her golden gaze met mine. I couldn't tear my eyes from hers. I wanted to be close to her, hold her, get in that zone again where we could talk for hours. But how?

Dammit!

Clenching my jaw, I forced myself away from the window. I grabbed my sword belt off the chest at the foot of my bed and strapped it on. The weapon felt good against my thigh as I strode out of the room and jogged downstairs. Warm smells of fresh baked biscuits and sausage made my stomach grumble.

Rol was eating breakfast when I reached the dining room. "Fair morning," he grunted.

"Backatcha." I plopped into my chair, shoveled piles of scrambled eggs and sausages onto my plate, and slathered butter and honey on a couple of biscuits. Acaw was an awesome cook, and there was always more than enough food.

Jazz came in a couple minutes later. She and I did a good job of ignoring each other while we ate, yet I'd catch her studying me from under her lashes every now and then. And she noticed me glancing at her, too.

When Rol finished, he nodded to Jazz and got up to leave. In a hurry to keep up with him, I gulped some milk, pushed my chair back, and grabbed what was left of my biscuit.

Just as I crammed the hunk into my mouth, Jazz said, "You won't be training with Rol this morning. You'll spend the day with me."

I choked on the biscuit, and Rol paused behind me to slap my back, damn near pitching my face into my plate.

Before I had totally recovered, Rol bowed himself out the door and said, "I shall be in the smithy if you have need of me." I wasn't sure if he was talking to me or Jazz, but I had half a mind to follow him.

As I swallowed another drink of milk to chase down the biscuit still stuck in my throat, I noticed Jazz staring at my shirt. I set the glass down and saw crumbs all over me, then I met her gaze. She blushed when she realized I had caught her, and I smirked.

Jazz's cheeks turned redder yet and she sprang from her chair, looking everywhere but at me and my dirty shirt. "Come," she ordered and swept out of the room, her chin in the air.

With a grin, I tossed my napkin onto my plate and followed her out the door.

We landed beside the ocean, and I jumped off the broomstick and onto the beach, my sword bouncing against my thigh. Angry black cliffs surrounded the small stretch of pebbles and shale. Wind carried smells of fish and brine and the screeches of seagulls circling overhead. Shells of all sizes and shapes were scattered within the kelp along the waterline.

I picked up a football-sized conch. "Are you going to teach me to fly a broom?"

She sighed and tossed the smoking live oak branch onto the shale. "When you master moving objects and levitating, you'll be able to fly as well. It'll be instinct, a part of you, like walking."

"Really?" I ran my thumb along the shiny inside of the conch. Cool. I would practice that the next time I was at my hideout. I was getting bored with what I had been working on.

Nodding, she folded her arms across her chest and stared at the Atlantic Ocean. By her frown, I had the feeling she was starting to lose hope that I would ever succeed at magic.

Waves pounded the shore, and the ocean's roar stirred something inside me. Kind of crazy, I know, but it was like my soul and my magic were in tune with the ocean. With all of nature.

"Uh, Jazz . . ." I started to tell her about my practicing, but it was like a force clamped my jaws together. I swore I felt the statue in my pocket wiggle.

"Yes?" She looked wary and tense, her spine stiff and her shoulders back.

"Well, I— uh." I bit the inside of my cheek and waved at the ocean. "So, what are we doing here?"

Her frown deepened, and I wondered if she suspected I was hiding something from her. Guilt twisted inside like a hot iron from Rol's forge. I had promised to be upfront, but I still hadn't told her about the statue, or my magic. Sometimes it even felt like the statue egged me on when Jazz and I argued. But that was ridiculous.

The damp breeze blew a strand of hair across Jazz's face, and she pushed the hair behind her ear. "Do you remember what I told you about the Path?"

"Yeah." I shrugged and tossed the conch onto the beach. "It's like a ribbon through time. And Sanctuaries—they're like bubbles attached to the ribbon."

She gestured to the ocean. "Do you see the Path? Part of the ribbon runs before us."

My gaze followed hers, and I squinted, trying to see what she was talking about. "All I see is a whole lot of water."

"Look carefully." Jazz spoke softly as she moved within inches of me, and I wanted to ease my arm around her shoulders—to draw her close and feel her softness against me. "Do you see the golden sheen," she was saying, "right here at the water's edge?"

I started to shake my head, but a shimmer caught my attention—it was like the barrier I had crashed through that day I'd helped Jazz fight off those shadow creatures. The glitter ran along a short section of the beach and into the ocean and beyond, like a tube snaking into the distance. I walked away from her, to where the water lapped the shore and where the shimmer was the closest. I reached out my hand to touch it and felt its smooth surface beneath the pads of my fingers.

Yes—that same rubbery texture—like the wall at my hideout. It wasn't an invisible wall that bordered my hideout. It was the Path. I opened my mouth to say something about it to Jazz, then snapped my mouth shut. The statue wiggled in my pocket. Nope. The hideout was my secret.

Jazz moved beside me, and her cinnamon-and-peaches scent mixed with the salty breeze. "Excellent." Her voice was soft and approving. "After my father died, I've been the only one able to open the Path and travel from one Sanctuary to another. Until you sliced through it that day you—ah—*aided* me."

"That was an accident." Her nearness was now distracting me, and I backed away. "What makes you think I could do it again?"

Hurt flickered across her face, and I knew she thought I didn't want to be near her. Before I could say anything, her queen-of-ice mask slipped into place and her tone hardened. "What makes you think you can't open the Path? Your fear of failure?"

I ground my teeth. "I'm not afraid to fail."

Jazz's golden eyes flashed. "You're also afraid to try."

I clenched my fists.

Mom's voice echoed in my head, "Respond, don't react."

I folded my arms across my chest, trying not to react. "Get off my case already and show me what I'm supposed to try to do. And be careful you don't open the damn thing right on top of Nire or something."

"Nire's entrance is hidden from us." Raising her chin, Jazz moved closer to the Path and slid her finger in a vertical line—like she had that time she'd trapped me and I chased her through that weird store.

Air crackled and sparkled gold, then a black slit appeared, like she had sliced open a piece of the sky. Cold air blasted out. It smelled of mold and dirt, just like the dark place Jazz had dragged me through when she had trapped me and the place where I had slashed through the shimmering wall.

She ran her hand back up the opening, and it vanished. "As quickly as possible, the Path must be resealed, or the consequences could be disastrous." She turned her glare back to me. "Opening and closing the Path requires the same concentration, focus, and strength of will as performing other spellwork."

"Great," I muttered. "So show me again."

She chose another place a few feet down the Path and opened it the same way. Only this time, she stepped through the slit. Just as I was about to follow her, the entrance closed. My face bounced against the Path, and I stumbled back.

"Witch," I muttered, waiting for her to return.

When she didn't come back, I shook my head and figured she had gone off in a snit to some Sanctuary. That or she was waiting for me to open the Path and follow her.

"Fine. Whatever." I imitated the movements she had made when she opened the Path, but it just felt like I was running my finger down the side of a balloon.

Surf pounded the shore as I tried again and again to open the Path. My frustration grew more intense with every attempt. I would have slammed my fist into the barrier if I hadn't already known I would just bounce off and land on my ass. If only I could hack at it with my sword.

My sword. Yeah, that was it! That was how I got through it the last time. And if I was really the Shadowalker, I was supposed to use my sword to slice through the Path. At least according to that prophecy Jazz had talked about.

Grinning, I drew my weapon. Now, swordwork was something I was good at. The hilt felt good in my hands as I limbered up. When I felt loose, I moved a little way down the Path, just in case Jazz was on the other side waiting for me.

I gripped my weapon with both hands, raised it over my head. With all my might, I swung my sword down.

My blade connected with the Path—and bounced off.

The force of the rebound yanked my weapon out of my hands and threw me backward, onto my ass. The blade flashed in the sunlight as it flipped through the air, end over end, landing point down in the shale a few feet away from me.

What the hell?

My breath came in ragged gasps as I stared at the sword, still quivering where it had struck. "Shit," I muttered. The realization that I could have taken off my own head was sobering. Maybe I needed to be a little more careful when trying something new. But how was I able to do it the last time, when I had blindly charged at the wall?

I scrambled to my feet and retrieved my weapon, swiping the blade across my leather breeches. The next time I tried to open the Path, I carefully slid the point down the barrier.

Nothing. Not even a little hole. What was the matter? I was alone. No audience. Maybe it was the thought of Jazz being on the other side that kept me from doing it.

Disgust twisted in my gut, and I gave up.

I rammed my sword into its sheath and stared at the ocean. Sunlight sparkled on the water, and I noticed something floating a few feet from shore. What was it?

Water sloshed inside my boots as I waded into the surf to get a closer look.

The thing bobbed up and down with the waves. It was colorful, like a big bowl of orange, red, and purple flowers. I was in up to my knees, and the undercurrent sucked at my legs.

Just a little closer. What was it? When I was inches away, I reached for one of the red petals—

And it blinked.

My heart pounded, and I started to back away. Water boiled around me.

From under the flowers an enormous head reared out of the water. It was a monster—a giant water serpent! Sunlight glinted on its fangs, and its eyes glowed a wicked red.

I yanked out my sword as I stumbled closer to the shore, and squared off with the beast. The serpent lunged. Using both hands, I swung my weapon. The blade connected with a fang and deflected the serpent's attack.

I backed up, reaching the beach as the beast hissed and dove toward me again. Blood thundered in my ears, but my movements were automatic from countless hours of training with Rol. I dropped to one knee on the shore, dodging the fangs, and aiming my blade toward the beast's neck.

Just as my sword slid into the serpent's flesh, I heard Jazz scream, "Cease!"

Even as everything around me froze, the force of my momentum continued. My blade sliced all the way through the neck—and I fell onto my ass, again. Drops of blood from the creature hung in the air; the serpent's head tilted at an odd angle.

The flowerlike thing had been on top of its head. It had been waiting for unsuspecting prey, and I had been stupid enough to fall for it. Again. Fury built up in me as I turned and saw Jazz standing a few feet away. Her face was white and her hand fluttered to her throat. I clenched my sword hilt and strode toward her.

She stood her ground and raised her head.

My body shook with adrenaline and anger. "Another one of your tests?"

"Another example of your foolishness?" Her glare matched mine. "Haven't I warned you that most beings are not to be trusted? Didn't I tell you never to drop your guard until you know every aspect of a being?"

"I thought it was a bunch of flowers!" I pointed my sword at the frozen serpent. "How the hell was I supposed to know it was a monster snake?"

"You killed it! It didn't have to be robbed of its life. It just needed to be left alone!" Jazz jabbed her finger at my chest. "If I had planned this, I couldn't have come up with a better opportunity to show your unbelievable arrogance."

I jammed my sword into its sheath. "And that's your job, isn't it? To make me into a total fool?"

She whirled on her heel and marched away from me. "May the Goddess forgive me for my folly."

While sitting alongside the stream at my hideaway, I cleaned salt water and serpent's blood from my sword's blade with a piece of soft leather. When I finished, I got to my feet, sheathed my weapon and crammed the leather into my pocket.

I started kicking rock after rock into the stream while glaring at the Path. It glittered on the opposite bank, taunting me.

As soon as Jazz and I had arrived at the manor, she had sailed into her drawing room and slammed the door with a flick of her fingers. Without stopping to say hello to Rol, I had stomped off to be alone.

To think about my foolishness. My failures.

I scooped up a rock, clenching it so hard that its jagged edges bit into my palm.

What did Jazz mean when she said I was afraid to try? I tried all the time.

Well, mostly when I was alone. When it came to something I wasn't good at, I didn't want to blow it in front of an audience. Too many times when I was growing up, I was told what a failure I was—not only by my dad but by teachers and other people, too. How I didn't pay attention. How I fidgeted and disrupted the class. How my handwriting sucked. How messy and disorganized I was. How I didn't even try.

Screw 'em. Screw 'em all.

I flung the rock into the stream and water splashed onto my boots. If I could open the damn Path intentionally, I would just disappear and find my way back to the place I came in—

Hey, wait a minute.

If I opened the Path, I could leave. I could take off and let Jazz find another stupid Shadowalker to grind under her perfect heel.

But didn't she say that I couldn't leave the Path until Nire was defeated? Or was it only witches who didn't have the power to open the Path who couldn't leave? If I did have the power to open it, maybe I could move along the Path like Jazz did. That would show her.

Determined to succeed this time, I hopped the stream, stones crunching under my boots as I landed. When I reached the barrier, I withdrew my sword and took a deep breath. I searched for that same focus, that same concentration and power that was starting to become second nature, like my swordplay. At least when I was alone.

When warmth and power filled me and my skin shimmered silver, I raised my sword and eased the point down the side of the barrier. This time I felt a connection with the Path. The same connection I had felt with the ocean and had been feeling with the forest. With every living thing.

I was born to do this. I knew it in my gut.

I'm a witch.

All the training over the past couple of weeks, all the practicing, had led me to that exact moment.

Cold air eased through the six-inch slit I made in the Path, chased by the smell of dirt and mold. I started to make the opening longer, large enough for me to pass through, but I paused. Maybe I should make sure I could close it first. I might have been pissed at Jazz, but I didn't want to leave her with an even bigger mess than she already had.

With the same focus I had used when I stared from the batter's box at the best strikeout pitcher in the league, I slid my sword point along the opening and sealed the Path.

Home run.

Satisfaction swept over me like cheering fans at a championship game.

I raised my sword and sliced an opening large enough to walk through. The Path was cold and dark as I sealed it behind me, but I could see, unlike the first time I had been on the Path with Jazz.

And I didn't like what I saw.

Shadows screeched and hissed from the walls and clawed at me—kind of like the ones I had battled when I'd helped Jazz. I raised my sword and my skin flashed brilliant silver. The Shadows cringed away from my light.

Interesting.

Why hadn't the same thing happened when I struck at them in that prehistoric freak-land I landed in when I fell through the Path trying to get to Jazz? My skin had a much brighter silver sheen this time. Maybe it was because my magic was getting stronger. Maybe these Shadows weren't as powerful. Or maybe it was both.

For the first time, I didn't feel nauseous and my head wasn't spinning. Without any more hesitation, I strode along the Path. Toward freedom. Away from Jazz.

It still felt like I was walking backward along an escalator, but I was steady on my feet. For a while I saw nothing but hissing Shadows. But then a darker patch appeared in the wall. Could it be a doorway, an entrance to a Sanctuary? Maybe it was L.O.S.T., the place I had come in with Jazz. Concentrating and focusing my magic, I slit a tiny opening with my sword point and peeked through.

A procession of armored knights on horseback trotted past, hooves splashing through mud puddles and the shouts of male voices. Brilliant white flags with pictures of red dragons fluttered from staffs, and I caught the smells of horse and a rain-soaked breeze. I remembered a history lesson on medieval times—was that King Arthur's standard?

Jazz did say Merlyn was taken to a Sanctuary where his powers could be appreciated, so it could have been the time of King Arthur.

Whoa.

My skin flared silver as Shadows started to creep closer. They skittered away, and I sealed the peephole. I'd have to keep my eye on the Shadows as I searched for the doorway that would take me to L.O.S.T.

The next doorway opened up to a place where the air was so clear and clean that it had to have been a time thousands, if not millions, of years ago. It was beautiful, filled with massive trees and a sparkling stream. Definitely not modern-day Earth. Wait—it was that prehistoric place where I'd rescued Jazz, wasn't it? Except this time it was dawn, the sun just rising over the distant mountains.

Doorway after doorway I opened and closed. No sign of Nire or any dank, evil-looking place, but Jazz said Nire's entrance to the Path was hidden from us. Finally, when I'd about given up, I found it.

I found L.O.S.T.

The minute I opened the Path, I smelled roses and fresh-cut grass, mixed with modern-day pollution. After spending the past couple weeks in Shallym, I was surprised how dirty the air was in my own time. It was starting to get dark, but I could make out the convenience store, the restaurant on the hill, the yellow California poppies.

I could go home. It didn't seem real.

Home.

Back to my awesome mom, my dorky brother, and my hardass dad. Back to my life in Yuma, getting ready for my senior year, playing ball with the guys . . . checking out the babes as I cruised the park with my friends in my mom's tru— Shit.

With a scowl I clenched my sword hilt. Okay, so I'd likely be grounded until college, but at least I'd be home. Where I chose to be. Not where I was trapped and forced to do something I didn't want to do.

I started to step through the opening—but something deep inside stopped me. What about Jazz? The image of her beautiful golden eyes came to me. Eyes that sparkled in those rare moments when she was happy. Eyes that watched me sometimes, like maybe she cared more about me than she let on. But most of the time, eyes that held all the concerns of the Queen of Witches . . . for her family, for her people.

Could I just walk away and leave her to battle Nire on her own?

After what she's done to me, sure I can.

The words sounded forced even as I thought them. Inside, I knew Jazz was only doing what she needed to do in order to save her people. In order to save humans and witches alike, in all times and all places.

Could I really walk away?

I sighed and relaxed my grip on my sword.

No.

I couldn't do it. I couldn't leave Jazz to fight Nire by herself. Despite everything Jazz had done to me, despite our differences, and despite the fact she probably hated me, I cared about her. I cared what happened to her, and I cared what happened to Rol. I couldn't leave.

I would stay, and this time by my choice, my free will.

It took everything I had to turn away from the Sanctuary and my chance to go home.

I sealed the opening and headed back through the Path to Jazz.

When I got back to Shadowbridge, I said nothing to Rol or Jazz about my new abilities. I just couldn't. Every time I thought about it, I felt compelled to slam my mouth shut. Sometimes I even felt as if the statue in my pocket was talking to me, telling me to be quiet. Other times, I felt like it wanted me to go back to the Path and stand at the barrier. It was stupid.

That night I climbed into bed, guilt heavy on my chest. My eyes felt heavy, too. I squeezed them shut, but a soft tapping noise caught my attention.

I sat back up, moving in slow motion, surrounded by a thick, cold mist.

I'm dreaming. Have to be dreaming.

But that tapping noise . . . that's got to be the Shadowmaster.

Face shadowed by the hood of a purple robe, Nire sat in a viewing chamber on a coarse granite dais. The Shadowmaster tapped fingernails against stone.

Tap. Tap.

The sound echoed in my head. I could tell the bastard was watching something—and then I saw caged witches who cringed and looked away from their Shadow guards.

My blood pumped through my body, adrenaline giving me an incredible rush. I reached for my sword—but nothing. I grabbed only air, unable to take on the monster.

I wasn't even there. All I could do was watch. I ground my teeth.

Nire smiled, full lips broadening beneath the hood, and the smile made me think of death. Yet that smile was familiar—and not terrible. Not terrible at all. Comforting even.

What was wrong with me?

"Come Summer Solstice, I will be at my full power," Nire said aloud. "I have bled enough witches and oldeFolke of their magic—the time has come to take Shadowbridge."

Jaw clenched, I tried to step back, but I couldn't move.

The Shadowmaster nodded beneath the hood. "Soon it will be time to draw Jasmina Corey into our trap, my son," Nire said to a man I hadn't seen standing in darkness beside the cage. "Soon the Queen of the Witch's power will belong to me and nothing will be able to hold back the Shadows. Nothing and no one will be strong enough to prevent me from cleansing this burdened earth of witches and humans who do nothing but drain the air."

"It will be as you have predicted." The man's hoarse chuckle grated on my nerves. "The bitch will be yours."

"Yes, I will have Jasmina." The Shadowmaster sighed with obvious pleasure. "And the Shadowalker will return to me."

No!

I tried to imagine my sword into my hand, to use a summoning spell to snatch it up from the world outside of dreams.

Instead, I woke up in a hurry, choking and swearing.

chapter twenty

For the next four days, Bren failed at opening the Path. His mind seemed to be on hundreds of other things. Namely, anything to annoy me.

Sometimes he would start to say something, but then his lips would slam shut and he would fidget—rubbing his hand over his pocket or tugging at his shirt.

Meanwhile, with Rol's firm guidance, Bren excelled at swordplay and hand-fighting. At least if we found Nire's Sanctuary, Bren should well understand how to use his damnable blade to free the Path. If we lived that long.

He also excelled at dirt, foul smells, and sounds only boys and men find amusing. Both Rol and Bren apparently thought it fine to bring such things to the dinner table, too, and on more than one occasion, I was sorely tempted to make wall art out of the pair of them.

They were becoming like father and son before my very eyes.

As for me, I was increasingly ignored. I performed my usual patrols to monitor Nire's incursions, saw to Shallym's needs and the other Sanctuaries, and worked with Rol and Bren on spells a few hours a day.

But never alone, just Bren and I. After the disaster at the shore with the cluster serpent, I instructed Rol to attend every training session. Bren performed far better in his swordplay lessons with my training master, and I had hoped Rol's presence would help Bren focus on his spell-work. Of course, it hadn't—not that I could tell.

Otherwise, I kept to myself. But for the first time in my life, solitude was bothering me. Bren's aloofness was also displeasing. I found myself cleaning stones to the point of polishing them, and my fingers were growing stiff from searching out and destroying cobwebs. No sooner did I put my panic at bay than it came right back, doubly forceful. Soon, I would be sweeping the very clouds from the sky to feel a small measure of relief.

And Bren—did he care?

Sometimes, I saw him watching me from his window when I took my morning walks. I swore I could almost feel the caress of his strong fingers along my forearm or his warm breath upon my cheek—almost as though he were reaching out to me, as if he were using magic to touch my heart. Maybe explore it just a little, to see what I felt.

That caused me to think he might want to spend time with me, yet it seemed he went out of his way to avoid any such possibility.

Following our fruitless daily practice sessions, Bren would spar with Rol in the training yard. Then, Bren would simply disappear. Several times I had to struggle with myself to keep from spying on him as I did when he had first arrived. I could easily have turned into my falcon form, and he would never have known the difference.

But I couldn't do it. That would be a violation. His privacy—didn't I have to allow him some time to himself? Still, I wondered what he did when he was alone. Did he think about his family? Did he think about how we might defeat Nire?

Did he think about me?

Often I thought about what Bren had said after his lesson with the klatchKeeper. "Sooner or later, we have to be our own sanctuary. You and me. Safe together—or we'll never beat Nire."

Did he mean that? And his eyes often held a certain gentleness . . .

But, no. That gentleness came and went, like rainbows and storms.

It was late afternoon, and the drawing room was quiet when I entered. Acaw had done a fine job of mending the hole I had so foolishly blasted in the wall, and my space felt whole and safe.

"Light," I commanded, and candles in the wall sconces filled the room with a gentle glow. The lone bench still rested beneath my favorite window, and I sat down, put my feet up on the bench and wrapped my arms tight around my knees. No doubt when dawn came, I would still be in the same position. Waiting and watching. I felt a sense of impending doom, something beyond the usual, as if a storm had gathered above Shadowbridge—a storm I couldn't yet see.

Lately, sleep had been a luxury.

A few minutes after I took up my vigil, hinges creaked. I glanced over my shoulder to see Bren entering—without Rol. My heart began an uncomfortably fast patter as he approached me and eased himself to the floor a few feet away.

With his polished-oak eyes and scruffy hint of a beard, Bren looked more rugged and handsome—and piratelike—than ever. His golden brown hair had grown long enough that it now brushed his shoulders. It amazed me, too, how much larger and more defined his muscles were after almost three weeks of continual training with Rol.

Why was he here? To talk about the weather again? Or maybe something even more scintillating, like sword fighting. Oh, joy.

I ground my teeth.

He took a deep breath, and I ground my teeth again, dreading the new round of inane small talk we would both have to survive. Instead, Bren flicked his fingers against the stone floor. "Do you have a plan to defeat the Shadowmaster?"

I tensed even more. What could I say to such a direct inquiry? Truth. Tell the truth. I had agreed to be honest. No more lies and half-truths, Jasmina. If my life and heart was in his hands, I had to tell him everything. If he rejected me, there was nothing to do but begin again.

Bren's dark eyes burned into me, and I cleared my throat. "Yes . . . and no. I have a plan to lure Nire out of hiding—to find Nire's Sanctuary. On the upcoming Summer Solstice, two days from now. My powers will be at an apex—as will yours—and I think it'll be our best chance."

"Why now?" Bren's tone was even, and his gaze never faltered even though he crammed his hand in his pocket. "Why this Solstice instead of the next?"

I tore my eyes away from the tiny bits of food on Bren's tunic. "Nire has always known how to find our Sanctuaries, but my magic has made it difficult. Of late, Nire's power and cunning have increased. I sense the Shadows are only days away from penetrating this stronghold. Into the original Shallym itself. If the Shadowmaster destroys us here, in our oldest and most powerful keep, we're lost."

I ran one finger along the spotless windowsill and then glanced back to Bren. "My time—the time of all witches—is running out. I have to act—with or without the Shadowalker's aid."

Bren shifted on the floor and chewed the inside of his cheek. After a few seconds, he said, "Where do you plan to take Nire on?"

"In Middle Salem." My hands grew cold. "Where we first encountered Nire and the Shadow minions. It seems the logical location. Rol and I suspect that Nire's unnatural stronghold is somewhere in that time."

"And when you lure the Shadowmaster out, when you confront Nire in Middle Salem, then what?" Bren's voice was quiet, with no hint of his typical anger or sarcasm.

"I— I don't know." The crumbs on his vest seemed huge now. Filling my eyes. "I'm hoping you can use your training and your strength and magic to break Nire's hold on the Path. Rol has taught you well, and you'll know what to do."

"If we get that far," he murmured.

Feeling a mild shock from his unexpected insight, I shifted my gaze from Bren's vest to the floor. "If I can trap Nire into one remote Sanctuary and cut it from the Path . . . It's never been done, severing a Sanctuary, but I think it's possible." I returned my gaze to his. "All I'd have to do is cut through Father's spells, sever the energy and push it away from the ribbon. I believe the Shadowmaster would be helpless then. Nire would have to live in that timeline. So, if the Sanctuary were old enough—"

"—it might be thousands of years before Nire could cause trouble again." Bren's expression was earnest as he finished my sentence.

"Yes." I leaned forward, relieved that he didn't think my ideas were stupid. "Nire's Shadows would have no organizing force, and I think they would dissipate. The hostages would be freed."

He rubbed his chin, as if thinking the deepest of thoughts. "Can Nire be killed outright?"

"I don't know." Misery coiled inside me. Surely Bren would think I was hiding things from him again. "Death might not be the best option. If Nire suffers an unnatural demise—well, I'm not certain what would happen to such an ancient creature. Nire could wind up in Talamadden instead of moving on."

Bren didn't seem concerned about Nire any longer, though. "Listen," he said. "There's one more thing I need to know." He paused for a moment, his gaze so intent that it was as if he could see deep inside my soul. "Why do you hate me so much?"

"Pardon?" I gaped at him. "You're the one who's always so angry you barely speak to me. Except to be sarcastic."

"No." Bren shook his head. "You can't stand me, and you've been avoiding me."

My cheeks burned. "Only after you ridiculed me repeatedly and told me I was like your father, which I assume is unflattering."

Bren's smile was almost triumphant. "See? I told you— you don't like me."

I looked back to the window, battling tears. Everything about this boy confused me. I didn't know what to say.

"Look, I'm sorry. About the dad thing, I mean." I heard rustling noises, and imagined Bren fidgeting with his tunic. He had a habit of unraveling his clothes, thread by thread. "It's just that all your cleaning and the way you always see the— the wrong in everything I do. It bugs the snot out of me. It makes me nervous."

The laugh was reflexive. It squeezed from my throat like a cough, and tears immediately coursed down my face. I wiped them away with angry jerks of my hand. "*I* make *you* nervous?"

"Well, yeah." More shuffling sounds issued from behind me. "Because I know I'll never measure up. I can't ever be perfect like Dad wants, or like you want. There'll always be some dirt or screw-up somewhere, because I can't help it. I'm a big zero, except in baseball."

I turned quickly this time, so shocked I almost slipped from my seat. Bren was standing near me. Close enough to touch. I gazed up into his handsome face and shook my head, still unable to believe what I had just heard. "Is that what you think? That there's something wrong with you because I'm— I'm obsessed with— with cleaning?"

Bren nodded as he reached down and gently brushed a stray tear from my cheek. "And I know we won't be winning this fight with Nire, because I'm not good enough. I can't even do simple spells and stuff around you and Rol." He drew his hand away from my face and thumped the side of his head. "Too stupid, I guess."

I swung my feet off the bench and stood so quickly I barely kept myself from stumbling into him. "No! Why can't you see that *I'm* the one too weak for battle?" I wrapped my arms around my waist. "What I do with cleaning, I can't help myself. I feel like if I don't clean, the dirt will take over and contaminate me. That something terrible will happen.

"You—your imperfections are normal and healthy. Wonderful, even." I searched his eyes for understanding. "But my mind won't let me rest until I've polished everything around me. So nothing bad will happen. If I don't clean, and disaster occurs—it'll feel like my fault. Like I've failed to do everything I could to prevent it."

Bren's hands were suddenly on my arms, just above the elbows. I looked up into his endless brown eyes. "Did you say I'm wonderful?"

My throat closed. Warmth spread across me, starting at his hands and spreading upward, toward my neck and face.

"I— well, yes. You are. The problem in this quest isn't you, as I said. It's me."

He pulled me closer to him. I braced my palms against his muscled chest as my heart started a frightful banging against my ribs. "I don't think you're a problem at all, Jazz. A pain in the ass sometimes, but not a problem." He rubbed his thumbs over the insides of my elbows. "You try your best to manage things no one person—no one witch— should ever have to deal with. And I understand about the dirt thing, now that you've explained it. It's like my attention problems. Something you can't help. So, zap it off me any time you want, okay?"

I gripped his shirt in my fists, needing to hang on to something as I absorbed what he was saying.

He slipped one hand into my hair, cupping the back of my head, and he smiled. This time, it was a warm expression. Inviting. My heart beat even faster as his face came closer to mine. "I've wanted to kiss you since the day I met you," he murmured, his warm breath feathering across my lips. "And so many times since."

The truth was out. He knew everything about me, even that I brought him onto the Path of Shadows, perhaps to die—and he still wanted to kiss me.

I could scarcely believe it.

Bren's mouth met mine gently. Just a brush. I tasted salt and ale on his lips, and breathed deeply of his pungent boy's odor as he pulled back to gaze into my eyes. At the moment, his smell seemed much less unpleasant, and the crumbs had vanished from my field of attention.

"There," he said softly as he settled his free hand at the curve of my waist. "Did that feel dirty?"

Shivers traveled my spine. I shook my head, his fingertips sliding through my hair and caressing my scalp.

"Trust me." He drew me close to him again, one hand firmly at my waist, the other clenched in my hair. His heat radiated through me, and I could hardly think, much less speak. "Not everything is as black and white as you want it to be," he continued. "I'm not perfect, but I'll try my best not to let you down. Maybe we can beat this psychowitch. Together."

"Together," I whispered and reached up to him.

This time, Bren's mouth pressed harder against mine, and the sudden feeling of oneness, of rightness, caused my knees to buckle. If he hadn't been holding me so tight, I would have dropped to the drawing room's stone floor. Instead, he held me closer. Tighter. Protecting me. Holding me up, supporting me with his strength.

Yes, I did trust him—totally and completely. With the quest. With the lives of my people.

With my heart.

I didn't understand why. Perhaps it was something soul-deep. Perhaps it was his innate goodness that couldn't be disguised. Whatever it was, I trusted him.

When he drew back from our kiss, I gazed into his warm brown eyes, intent on telling him what I felt. What I really felt.

"Bren." I swallowed hard as I looked up into his handsome face. "I—"

And then I screamed as Shadowbridge Manor rocked on its very foundation.

A resonant knocking sound made me cover my ears. Images of Trier leaped into my mind—the burned buildings, the burned bodies.

"No. No! Gods!"

The floors beneath us bucked and convulsed as the soul-slamming knock came again and again.

"What the hell?" Bren kept a tight grip on me as I tried to battle back my shock and horror. My insides felt like a boiling pit, already burning me alive.

Then came the sound Trier's survivors described—wood splintering, tearing like paper, even. I felt it in the pit of my stomach, and my heart twisted.

Once more, the floors shifted, this time much more violently. Bren and I fell to the floor, holding onto each other as the fortress pitched like a ship on angry seas.

"What's going on?" Bren shouted as darkness bled from the walls like oozing tar—foul darkness with fangs and claws.

Hammering sounds exploded around us. From the roof—dozens of hard, loud pounding noises, like meteors striking home again and again.

Bren crouched over me, pressing me to the floor, protecting me with his body. "What is it?" He bellowed over the roaring and groaning as Shadows crept toward us.

The foul odor of rotten dirt and sour milk filled the room. The smell of death and decay.

Shadows.

Shadows streaming in from everywhere, as if they knew right where I would be!

"Nire has broken into Shallym!" I squirmed loose from Bren and leaped to my feet. Before I even drew breath, I zapped the nearest Shadow with a pure beam of light, then mustered my power and shouted, "Cease!"

Everything kept moving, as if I had made no effort at all. As if my magic were almost completely drained—or blocked. What was happening? I was obviously limited to small protection blasts, but why did I have so little power?

Bren was up now, sword drawn, his skin pulsing silver. He sliced at the closest Shadow, causing it to vanish in so many silver sparks.

The door to the drawing room burst open, and Acaw came tumbling in. His crow-brother flew over his shoulder. Without hesitation, the bird screeched and dove toward the dark expanses that were attempting to drive us toward the wall. The elfling wielded a kitchen fork and a small dagger, and each shone with the eerie glow of oldeFolke magic. He fought with detached precision, slicing through the blank spaces before him, letting in light wherever his little hands jabbed.

I fired again, blasting apart the closest dark shape. Bren hacked at one and then another, working side-by-side with me.

Dear Goddess, please don't let them be good souls. The lost souls. Please don't let those Shadows be anyone I love.

Rol. Where was Rol? I didn't even see his energy arrows piercing the gloom outside the window.

Even through the uproar, I heard the wailing cry of Shallym's witches as they rose from their homes and kovens and burrows, flying like harpies to defend Shadowbridge.

At Bren's side, I fired on two Shadows clawing toward his head. He ducked under the dying sparkles and sliced his sword at even more Shadows. He was so close to me, as if I had used a sticky spell, yet I almost felt as if a part of him were repelling me.

From outside the windows came the screeching of hags and hag-spirits, and the answering snarl of Shadow minions. The keening of dozens of Keepers, the singing of klatches—I barely had time to begin a protective shield around Bren to block the klatch hypnosis. And then I realized he was resisting the sounds himself.

Bren was battling the klatch song without my help.

I was stunned, but I didn't have time to dwell on it.

More rumbles joined the fray, along with hisses of fire and smoke. Something broke the nearest window, and I retreated. Bren scrambled to me, then crouched, holding his blade toward the thing flopping through the broken window.

A scaled wing.

Slithers.

Dear Goddess, the slithers had been called from their day lairs by the chaos.

"What drew the Shadows here?" I pulled Bren back another step. "They're breaking in! Hurry, Bren!"

A hag burst through the broken window, leering at us. Her hag-spirit was large and dark, like a bear, swinging paws at us.

"For this day, I have waited," she growled and hurled a black ball of death-spells directly at me. I blocked them, taking care not to let them hit Bren or Acaw.

"Rol!" I cried for my training master as a maddened klatchKeeper tumbled into the room through widening holes. Outside, a slither hissed a jet of fire, burning Shadows and witches alike.

Acaw turned on the Keeper, assailing her with his small knife and fork. His crow-brother pelted and pecked—and another Keeper appeared, purple, wide-mouthed, and horrible. Without hesitation, she attacked and ate the first Keeper, then screeched at me before flying away.

Two hags swept in and struck down their errant sister, a hag who had been rushing toward me. It was a terrible thing to see her hag-spirit strangled, even as the Shadows tried to free it.

The two rescuing hags glared at me, but struck at the Shadows before flying back out of Shadowbridge.

My head was spinning.

"Who am I supposed to fight?" Bren yelled even as he hacked at another Shadow. "Witches, hags—who's good and who's bad?"

"I don't know!" I yelled back. "Fight any being who fights us. And keep slaying the Shadows!"

Bren readied his sword as an amorphous cloud of darkness slid toward him.

"We must fight or flee," I shouted. "Or we'll die right here. Right now!"

chapter twenty-one

Flee? No way.

Another surge of power rushed through my body.
The sensation filled me from head to toe, making
me feel like I was as big as Rol and twice as strong.
My arms and legs burned. I was on fire!

Blood pounded in my ears. My sword flashed silver as I
sliced through the black cloud approaching me. Like a puff
of smoke, the cloud faded away to nothing.

Snarling Shadows, like the ones I had seen on the Path
and in the prehistoric world, crept toward us. The stench in
the room smelled like rotting garbage.

The whole building shuddered and rocked as Shadow
things oozed through the walls, like black blood seeping
from the stones. Shrieks and cackles came from outside
the manor and on the roof, and I wondered if there were

more creatures trying to get in. Dark forms whipped by the windows.

More witches on brooms!

And some of them were singing, too, but it wasn't bothering me. I knew how to shut them out now. It was just a matter of knowing I should shut them out, and my brain took over and did the rest. A trick of concentration, like ignoring crowd noise during a big at bat.

One thing I couldn't ignore, though. The witches from Shallym had come to fight. But for us or against us?

My entire body glowed silver, more than ever before. But these Shadows were different—they weren't afraid of my glow like the ones on the Path. A Shadow reached for me. I swung my weapon at the thing, and silver light burst from my sword. My blade sliced through the Shadow and it vanished, clearing a place in the darkness and releasing a stream of light.

"Take that, you freak!" I yelled.

"By the Goddess!" Jazz cried out. "The Shadows. All those souls. What if—"

From the corner of my eye, I saw gold pulsating from her in eerie waves as she zapped another black spot with a bolt of pure white light from her finger. Even as she fought, she sobbed, as if it was hurting her to kill the Shadows.

While I battled, something kept drawing me to Jazz. As if my sword wanted to connect with her neck.

Horror filled me at the thought, and I poured everything I had into fighting the shadows. I grunted and shouted with every Shadow I slayed.

Acaw zipped through countless Shadows with his knife and fork, and his crow familiar attacked even more of the things than the elf did.

Rol's endless training sessions with me had instantly kicked into gear the moment I'd wielded my sword. One Shadow after another evaporated as I hacked at them. I was hyper-focused, my concentration totally on what I was doing. I barely noticed the snarling noises of the Shadows anymore.

But when my sword sliced into them, the sounds they made caused my stomach to churn. Whimpering. Almost human sounds. And then they were silenced—by my blade.

My muscles burned and sweat poured down my face as we battled. The room continued to buck and rock, making it hard to keep my balance while I fought.

"How many more?" I shouted to Jazz, barely able to hear myself over all the noise.

"I don't know." She whirled and shot light at another Shadow.

An enormous black creature sprung from the wall behind Jazz. Before I could reach it, the Shadow pounced on Jazz and ripped into her arm with its claws.

Jazz shrieked, and fury filled me.

My vision changed to hazy red. I swung my sword at the Shadow that had clawed Jazz and sent the thing into oblivion.

With a loud, grating pop, all the Shadows vanished.

Light filled the room.

The manor stopped rocking. I stumbled forward, like I'd just gotten off a boat after a wicked storm. Jazz swayed beside me, but kept to her feet.

Everything around us became quiet. Too quiet. All I could hear in the room was blood rushing in my ears and the sound of our breathing. Even that rotten stink had gone away.

The screaming, cackling, and singing outside grew fainter and fainter, and then that noise was gone, too.

For a minute.

I could sense them. That weird connected thing I had noticed before, coming and going, like my sharper hearing.

It was as if the witches of Shallym had retreated, and then the angry ones regrouped. A dull roar started at the bottom of the hill, followed by screaming. I felt witches dying. Like knives in my chest, my back. Images flooded my mind. Some dropping in battle. Some being murdered.

The room was trashed, and I could imagine how that must be driving Jazz nuts. I kept my sword at the ready, my heart still thundering, prepared to strike any black thing that moved, or any traitorous witch with funny ideas.

The crow screeched and landed on the elf's shoulder, and I jumped, almost taking out the damned bird with my sword. "The villagers are agitated," Acaw murmured. "Some are in rebellion. This is not good. No doubt they are angry." His eyes fixed on me. "No doubt they believe this attack to be your fault." And he vanished.

Before I could swear about what he said as loudly as I wanted to, Jazz collapsed to her knees, her face pale. Her golden glow was so faint that for a second, I thought it had disappeared. "The Shadows have gone," she whispered. "For now." She crumpled onto the floor.

"Jazz!" I rushed over, dropped my sword and knelt beside her. A giant rubber band squeezed at my chest as I pulled her into my arms.

Her eyes rolled back. Her face sagged, and she felt weightless.

Blood poured from her arm, more blood than there should have been, I was sure.

"Rol!" I shouted. "Jazz is hurt. Help me, somebody!"

Acaw reappeared out of nowhere with a jar and a cloth in his gnarled fingers. His crow-brother flapped down and landed beside Jazz.

"What's wrong with her?" My fear for her nearly choked me.

The elf held up the jar. "Salve for the queen's wounds. It will slow the spread of Shadow in her blood."

"What?" My arms started to tremble. "One of those dark things is inside her? In her blood?"

"No time for talk." Acaw set the jar on the floor. "You must dress her wound. Only you can touch the queen."

"But I— I don't know what to do." Total helplessness filled me, and I wanted to take my sword and hack at something. Like that evil Nire bastard. Especially Nire. "Where's Rol? Can't he do it? I might screw it up or something."

The elf's gaze held mine. "Rol cannot help you now. You must do this."

"Oh, man." I eased Jazz on the floor and wiped sweat off my forehead with the back of my hand. She looked so vulnerable lying there, and I was terrified she would die. If she did, I didn't know what I would do.

I hadn't realized until that moment how much she meant to me. And how much I . . . loved her.

The thought shocked me so badly it nearly knocked me on my ass. Acaw's words drew me back to reality—that I had to do whatever it took to help Jazz.

"Cleanse the wound first." Acaw moved behind me and gave me a wet cloth. "This has a binding agent that will help to decrease the flow of darkness."

"Jeez." My hand shook as I took the rag and wiped away the blood. God, there was so much, and I didn't think it would stop pouring out of her body and onto the floor. "She'd hate all this mess," I murmured as I looked at her pale face.

The crow screeched just as I finally got the bleeding to stop, and I nearly jumped out of my skin.

Three claw marks ran along her forearm. But they weren't red—they were black, like road tar. And bubbling.

"Quickly now." Acaw handed me the jar, and I lifted off the lid and set it on the floor. It smelled intense—like peppermint on steroids.

He pointed to Jazz's scratches. "Use your fingers to dip out the salve and spread it on the queen's wounds."

I jammed my hand into the slimy stuff and put the clear glob on Jazz's arm. My fingers tingled as I wiped salve over the scratches. That weird silvery glow surrounded my hand, and then the black wounds shimmered silver and stopped bubbling. I held my breath—was the salve helping Jazz?

Acaw's crow-brother hopped onto his shoulder as the elf moved to the other side of Jazz. "You master even the Shadows in her blood. Rol has trained you well."

"Huh?" I glanced at him as I smoothed more salve over Jazz's arm. "Rol didn't teach me any first-aid."

Acaw just smiled. Or at least on him I thought it was a smile. On most people it would have been considered a grimace.

"Do we need to wrap her arm or something?" I asked as I wiped my fingers on a cloth the elf handed me.

"Nay." Acaw shook his head and retrieved the dirty cloth from my hand. "'Twould only make it worse."

I tucked a strand of Jazz's black hair behind her ear, my fingers brushing her cheek. She felt cold to my touch. What had it been, all of twenty minutes ago that she had been so warm in my arms when I kissed her?

With my heart in my throat, I asked, "Is she going to be okay?"

"Only the Goddess knows." Acaw shrugged, and I wanted to pound him. I wanted to pound anything or anyone I could get my hands on.

"Carry her to her room where she can rest," the elf instructed. "If 'tis not already too late."

Before I could shout at him and ask what the hell he meant, he was gone. Vanished.

The little jerk.

Where the hell was Rol? I couldn't imagine what would keep him from Jazz's side. He was never far away. Could the Shadows have hurt him, like they hurt Jazz? Or maybe a witch or hag gone bad.

Shit.

I bit the inside of my cheek, trying to keep from seriously freaking out. Everything would be okay. Jazz would get better, I'd find Rol, and we'd go after Nire on the Summer Solstice, just like Jazz had planned.

Taking care not to bump her arm, I scooped Jazz up and carried her out of the drawing room and upstairs to her bedroom. Her cinnamon-and-peaches scent surrounded me, along with that sinus-clearing peppermint smell of the salve.

Just as I laid her down on her bed, she moaned and her eyelids fluttered. "Bren," she murmured. "Something . . . wrong."

"Jazz." Relief eased through me in a warm wave as I knelt beside the bed and took her hand. "You're going to be all right."

Slowly she opened her eyes, their golden color dimmer than normal. "We must find . . ." Jazz swallowed and took a deep breath, "what drew Nire's scouts here. Allowed them through— my pro— my protections."

"I don't understand." I brushed a strand of her black hair away from her face.

But she closed her eyes and her head rolled to the side.

That rubber band squeezed my chest again. "Jazz." I shook her shoulder, but she remained silent. I laid my head over her heart. To my relief, I heard it pounding, and felt the rise and fall of her breathing.

"You get some rest." I kissed her clammy forehead and stood. "I'm going to find Rol."

The moment I started walking away from the bed, my gut clenched. I felt the statue wriggle in my pocket, and I swore it told me to stay. But I had to find Rol. I had to save Jazz. It took all I had, but I broke through the bedroom door and into the hallway.

Sweat cooled my body as I jogged down the stairs and into the trashed drawing room to grab my weapon. Wind swirled through the broken windows as I knelt to pick up the sword, and I noticed Jazz's blood drying on the stone floor. It looked black and sticky, and kind of wicked. I hoped it wouldn't stain—that would drive Jazz out of her mind. Maybe I'd clean it up for her before she saw it.

Yeah. That would be the nice thing to do.

"Rol!" I shouted as I turned my back on the drawing room and hurried through the manor. Where was he? My chest got tighter and tighter as I ran through the kitchen, out the back door, and into the courtyard. "Rol!"

He wasn't anywhere outside. Not in the smithy, the training yard, nor the stables.

Screams still rolled up the hill from the village—hags, Keepers, and other witches. My hearing was getting way stronger, and they were way loud. At the moment, I didn't care.

When I finished checking everywhere I could think of, I ran into the kitchen and smacked right into Acaw.

The elf almost toppled over, and his crow-brother screeched at me from his window perch.

"Sorry," I muttered. "Where's Rol? I can't find him."

Acaw shrugged. "Nire's minions have taken him away."

"What?" I grabbed the elf's tunic and clenched the leather in my fist. "Rol was taken and you didn't bother to tell me?"

The crow shrieked and flew at me, divebombing my head. I let Acaw go and stumbled back.

Acaw straightened his tunic and gave me a snotty look. "Attending the queen was of utmost priority."

I raked my hand over my hair, about a billion thoughts going through my head, and not one of them told me what I needed to do. "You're right and I'm sorry. But Rol— God damn it. We've got to help him. Now."

"That is for the queen to decide." And the stupid elf vanished. Again.

Damn! Rage filled me, hot and furious. I ripped out my sword and waved it in the air as I roared out my frustration.

Still brandishing my weapon, I bolted from the room and hurried upstairs.

Rol, taken by the Shadowmaster? What did that mean? What would happen to him?

I rounded the corner of Jazz's room, came to a complete stop, and my sword slipped from my fingers and clattered onto the stone floor.

She stood in front of her bureau, looking as pale and as beautiful as Mom's white roses—not a hair out of place, her clothing spotless, all the blood gone. The only evidence of the battle was her arm, which she cradled to her chest.

My heart thudded and I wanted to reach for her. To make sure she was all right and to comfort her. Instead, I said, "You're up."

Brilliant observation, Bren.

Jazz nodded, but she didn't smile. "Thank you for dressing my wound." She glanced at her arm and back to me. "No one, save Rol, will touch me, and he's—" Her lips trembled and tears glittered in her eyes.

"Gone," I finished for her.

"Acaw informed me." She lowered her head, and I crossed the room and gathered her into my arms. I stroked her hair as she sobbed against my shoulder.

My head ached, and I fought back my own tears. Guys weren't supposed to cry, right? That's what my dad always said—be a man.

But Rol had become like a dad to me. More of a father than mine ever was. And, well, I didn't think Rol would mind if I got a little soppy over him.

I brushed at the wetness in my eyes. "We can get him back, right?"

Jazz pulled away from me. "It's possible." Rubbing at her arm, she sighed. "But we need to take time to think this through."

With a sound of frustration, I raked my hand through my hair. "We can't leave Rol in the hands of that bastard a moment longer. We need to go help Rol. Now."

She rubbed harder at the wound as she stared at me with her golden eyes. "It wouldn't be wise to go without a plan."

"We can't afford to wait." I started pacing the floor and raised my hands. "The way I see it, if we don't help him now, Rol could die." Something drove me beyond the need to find Rol. Like I needed to take Jazz somewhere and take her there now. The statue in my pocket giggled in my head, and I went stock still in front of her.

"I— well." Jazz looked away from me, scrubbing at her arm so hard I was afraid she would open the wound.

"What's wrong?" I put my hand over hers, and she jumped back.

I frowned. "Something's the matter. What is it?"

Jazz looked about ready to crawl out of her skin as she rubbed her arm harder and harder. Her skin seemed to be growing darker where the scratches were. "Something has affected this Shadow wound." She glanced at my pocket and went totally still. "You have—" She broke off and brought her gaze to mine and swallowed.

"I have *what?*" A hot flush crept over me and my ears started to buzz. She couldn't mean the figurine, could she? What difference would it make if she knew about it or not? It was mine. And she didn't need to know about it.

Her hand started rubbing the wound again, but she clenched her fists and moved her arms so that they were straight at her sides. "We agreed to be honest with each other, yes?"

"Yeah. So?" I folded my arms across my chest. "What has that got to do with going after Rol?"

"Possibly everything." Jazz motioned to my pocket. "What do you have that you aren't telling me?"

"None of your business." I scowled and started bouncing my knee.

She lifted her chin. "We can't go after Rol until I know what you are hiding from me."

"I'm not hiding anything!"

"Show me."

"No."

Clenching her fists, she advanced toward me. "For the safety of my people, I'll be forced to break my promise to myself and spell your breeches into oblivion."

I blinked. "Huh?"

"I'll make your pants disappear so that I can see what you've hidden."

My face was so hot I was sure it had to be bright red. I just stood there for a moment.

Her fingers twitched.

"Oh, hell." I dug into my pocket and wrapped my fingers around the statue. I tried to draw it out, but I couldn't. My arms shook and my entire body trembled.

Jazz frowned.

Why couldn't I just take it out of my pocket? I gritted my teeth, and with everything I had, I yanked the thing out.

The figurine flew from my hand and landed at Jazz's feet.

chapter twenty-two

Oh my sweet Goddess. No wonder my stronger magic wouldn't work during the fight with the Shadows! Something had been blocking me!

I stared at the Shadowmaster's leering golem. The hateful creature wriggled and thrashed on the floor. The room seemed to spin, and a dank water-and-mud odor invaded the air like slow-acting poison.

Using what little motion I had left in my aching arm, I raised my hands and bound the treacherous abomination. Mud and thatch, carved into human form, painted and fixed—given life by Nire's own foul breath. It would die now, but its wicked purpose had been served. Nire's strength against me had been solidified by a seed of evil planted in my own home. And the Shadows—the golem had been their beacon and their passkey, admitting them straight into my stronghold once Nire broke the bonds protecting Shallym.

Bren brought this to me. Upon the fates of all witches, I had no idea that he hated me so much. That kiss—his words of trust—lies, all of it.

Pain dug into my arm and into my heart, and I could scarcely tell which wound was deeper. Tears clouded my vision as I tore my gaze away from the golem and studied Bren's angry face. His once-handsome features were twisted, and he looked like he wanted to snatch his prize back from the floor and clutch it to his heart until he doomed us both.

"How could you have done this?" My voice trembled as I fought a wave of sobs. "How could you have brought death into my one place of safety? Into our one place of respite? I thought— I thought you had come to care about this quest. Of your own accord. I thought you had come to care . . . for me."

Bren said nothing. His brown eyes, harder than ever and half-shielded by his mussed hair, darted from the golem to me, and back to the golem.

My insides began to shake. The throb in my arm was almost too much to bear, and the ache of Rol's absence nearly brought me to my knees. I doubled my fist and pressed it against the wound, as if to hold down the Shadows even as they took root. There was little I could do to stop their relentless progress, but Bren—he was another story.

"Will you say nothing?" I swallowed, dizzy from the sudden loss of—of everything. "All of this feigned ignorance of our world, our ways. Bravo. You're a master tricksman. I was completely fooled."

Still, Bren kept silent. His lips—lips that had pressed against mine even as he betrayed me—formed a tight line.

"You must have known I would have to banish you from the Path. Or did you hope to win my heart and persuade me otherwise? Perhaps you planned to take me to Nire yourself?" I jammed my fist farther into my wound, trying to keep the Shadows still. "Why did you have to sacrifice Rol? Why not just kill me and have done with it? Answer me!"

Bren's eyes flashed. He seemed oddly frozen, and as I glared at him, snatches of his thoughts flew forward and hammered at my brain.

Damn you . . .

Can't . . .

Love . . .

Damn, damn . . .

Door basement . . .

HELP . . .

I blinked. The intensity of Bren's gaze doubled.

HELP . . .

HELP M . . .

Donkey . . .

Ah God . . .

His eyes fluttered down, then up, and the light silver haze of his power flickered over his skin.

HELPMEDAMMIT!

The force of Bren's focused thought was so great I stumbled back and shook my head. The fog of my emotion split open, and truth barged through.

Bren didn't just look frozen. He *was* frozen.

The golem had him enthralled.

Even now, the hideous little doll was giggling and thrashing, gasping for breath, and—no! Dread seized me with cold fingers. If it died before I could cut its ties to Bren, Bren would pass into Talamadden before I could so much as lift a finger. A new shiver rippled up my spine, this one clammy and sly, almost daring me to back away. If I allowed this to happen, we could find each other, free of all this stress, this responsibility—no. No!

How could I even think such a horrid, irresponsible thought?

Weakness . . . mind and blood . . .

I shook off my growing chill for a moment and tried to begin a spell, but the pain! Already, the Shadows had claimed my arm. It wouldn't obey my commands to move.

My hand. Sweet Goddess. I couldn't even lift my hand to conjure—and the Shadows would pollute any magic I offered.

"Listen to me, Bren." My tone echoed through Shadowbridge, and no doubt all the way to the rebelling Shallym witches, but it was necessary.

Bren flinched as if I had slapped him.

Good. My heart thundered. At least I still had that much sway. At least he could hear me. "Close your eyes."

Bren's lids fluttered again, and silver sparkles pulsed across his skin—but he didn't close his eyes.

At the sight of his inability to act, I forced myself to plunge full into his soul, made myself reach to the deepest parts of his mind and heart. It was a horrible violation, but what choice did I have? If I didn't reach him, he would be dead in minutes.

"Don't fight me," I insisted as I moved farther toward the base of his life essence. "I'm not ordering you about for my own pleasure. You have to close your eyes."

Bren's gaze seemed to catch fire, and the fury in it burned me, deep inside my own base. It was as if our souls were engaged in mortal conflict. I ground my teeth but held my concentration, urging him, fighting the golem's presence.

Bren's eyelids drifted down. Slowly.

The golem let out a long, dying breath.

"Now!" I yelled.

Bren hesitated, but his eyes closed.

I muttered the spell for release as forcefully as I could, hoping it would work without the action of my fingers. Hoping Bren's own will would fight the possession.

My entire body was shaking as I attempted to break the golem's hold on Bren, and bit by bit, I felt the golem's possession recede—and slip away. My consciousness dropped like a stone, down, fully into Bren's essence.

Into his core of power.

So strong. Unimaginably strong and blinding.

I lurched back, stunned. No one is that powerful! No one except . . .

I had always imagined Nire's magic to be so old and intense as what I found within Bren. So incredibly strong. My breath caught deep in my chest, and the connection between us ripped in two.

What is Bren? By all of the witches on the Path, what is he?

For a moment, Bren seemed impossibly tall. Imposing. And possessed of more raw power than even an insane witch might desire.

And then he was Bren again.

Angry. Hurt. Holding himself and no doubt feeling like I had stripped him bare out of malice and spite—but he was Bren.

"What the hell did you do to me?" He was shaking. "And what the hell is that—that weird doll thing?"

"A golem," I answered reflexively, and realized I was afraid not to. My arm ached so much I feared I might faint, but I forced myself to keep standing. Showing weakness in front of Bren was no longer an option. "A tool of the Shadowmaster. He used it to find my stronghold. I thought at first you had brought it on purpose, but clearly, someone gave it to you. It had you enthralled."

Bren's stubborn glower told me that he did not understand.

"The golem has a life of sorts, given by Nire. It cast a spell on you so that you were bound to it, and yet barely aware of it." I clutched my arm tighter to me as the full realization filled my mind. "The golem made you wish to hide it, to refuse to part with it."

Understanding rippled across Bren's handsome face, and my heart started to ache again. So much was beginning to fit into place—so much I didn't want to see or to know.

"The freak in the bathroom." Bren rubbed his hands up and down his arms and his skin was pebbled like gooseflesh. "The greasy guy. He gave the golem to me."

"Alderon." More pieces clicked into place. "My father's mistake. And the man who took your mother's truck. At my suggestion."

Bren was still hugging himself and shaking, and I wished I could go to him. I wished I could wrap my arms around him and soothe him. He was looking at me like I had betrayed him in the worst way possible, like I was betraying him again by failing to offer my comfort.

"I'm sorry for what I had to do to break the golem's spell," I murmured, fighting the impulse to kiss him. "Touching you that deeply, that intimately without your permission or consent. I know what that must have felt like."

"Don't do it again," he said in a flat voice. "Next time, let me die. Understand?"

I winced, but I nodded. These things were a matter of personal choice. For most beings, there were things in the universe worse than death, and Bren had made himself clear. From now on, he would be responsible for saving himself.

Which I now had no doubt he could do.

Shadowalker.

Whatever I had sensed inside him, it was far more than I was prepared to deal with. And far more than I understood, but one thing was clear. My earlier instincts had been correct.

Bren was definitely not human. Not fully, anyway. What was inside him was of the oldeFolke. And ancient. As if a piece of him had existed since time began.

Like Nire.

I rubbed my wounded arm. The flesh had grown as cold as night and almost as dark. The Shadows inside me were working to drain my life's energy.

Images of Alderon pushed into my mind. Things my father had said. Some of Alderon's fighting skill. The way the silver had sometimes played on Alderon's skin, though never as much as Bren's.

There was some connection between Bren and that bastard, too, but what was it? Bren was not the Shadowmaster. That much I believed. But he was also connected to the Shadowmaster in some way I could not comprehend.

Sweet Fates. Had I found a savior for my people, or a false god? Had I doomed the witches of the Path?

My vision swam, distorting the room of the place where I had thought to live until the Shadowmaster was finally defeated. But my home, like so many other things, was lost to me now. Violated and unsafe.

There was precious little time left, for Shallym or the other Sanctuaries, or for me. I couldn't battle the Shadows inside me for much longer. Bren was right. We had to go after Nire right away.

But Bren's distant frown did nothing to reassure me, on any point.

He would have to learn his magic and learn quickly, because I wouldn't be able to help him much past the next day.

"Why won't you come near me?" he asked, catching me off guard so badly I almost screamed.

Honesty. We were supposed to be honest, and I wanted to cry again. That was a vow I could no longer keep with Bren. Not now, and perhaps not ever again.

"My— my wound," I said, hedging. "The Shadows are still active. They will move faster if you touch the site."

Bren regarded me with a measure of concern and seemed to accept this half-truth. "So, as soon as we get you patched up, we're going after Rol?"

Patched up. I laughed in spite of myself. More tears threatened, but I held them back with a touch of my old coolness and grace under pressure. Bren had opened my heart so much that to close it against him felt like slashing off a part of my soul. But as always, what choice did I have? All that mattered now was saving Rol and helping Bren to his destiny.

"Yes." I fished a smile out of the depths of my pain. "As soon as we lay our plans."

No sooner did the words leave my mouth than Acaw entered, carrying a live oak branch. His crow-brother hopped and fluttered on his shoulder. Immediately, the elfling's eyes traveled to my arm, and I saw his instant understanding— and the grief-stricken expression he quickly buried.

"Your Majesty," he said with his typical even cadence. "Shallym is in complete mutiny. The oldeFolke have taken to spelling each other, and the klatchKovens are in open revolt. The witches are demanding the Shadowalker's blood for this attack, and if you do not take him away from here, I fear they will have it."

The elfling took a long, rattling breath, and with unchar-acteristic emotion, he added, "It has been a pleasure to be in your service. Most of the time."

With that, he held out the branch.

I accepted it, and using the broom to support myself, I offered the elfling a proper bow. "You have been most kind. Be released with a free heart, and farewell."

"I will do what I can to steady Shallym." Once more, Acaw bowed. His crow-brother squawked, and the two of them turned and vanished, as was elfling practice.

Bren scooped up his sword from where he had dropped it. He straightened, eyeing me with something between suspicion and fear. "Um, what just happened?"

"I released Acaw from my service." I struggled to mount the broom, leaving room for Bren to climb on behind.

"Why would you do that?" Bren sheathed his sword as he edged up beside me, trying to look into my eyes, which I kept averted.

"Because I won't be returning to Shadowbridge. Come. It's no longer safe here." I scooted forward to be sure he had enough space to climb on. "You get your wish to fetch Rol immediately, for Middle Salem is the only logical place to go."

Typical to his jackass-stubborn nature, Bren held back and gave me a wary frown that made me love him twice as much, and broke my heart twice as badly. "I'm not sure about this, Jazz. Something doesn't feel right."

"Rol's absence is acute and painful for us all." I nodded, and wondered if Bren could sense all that I was hiding from him now. About how the Shadows were eating into me, deeper and deeper. "Get on. We have no time to rest. No doubt Shallym's forces will return shortly, and we should be away before they attack us."

"But your arm." Bren pointed.

I clenched my teeth. "I can handle flying with my good hand. Don't worry about that."

Still, Bren hesitated.

"You're the one who said we have to be safe with each other. Just this once, trust me. Get on. Don't touch my wounded arm again, though. Under any circumstances."

Bren stood for a moment, then mounted the broom. He let his hands rest lightly on my waist. Even that small touch nearly made me break into pieces, because I wanted him to hold me. I wanted to see him as the innocent boy he was when I brought him onto the Path. I wanted to wrap my arms around him and feel comfort, and know everything would be okay.

Weakness . . . mind and blood . . .

My mother's voice rose and died in my mind, once and for all. If I could resist my wish to turn to Bren at this most delicate moment, there was nothing at all weak about me.

Nothing.

Whatever errors I had made in life, whatever mistakes I had committed, I was atoning for them all.

"Open," I commanded my bedroom window, and the breeze hit me full in the face as the shutters sprung wide. From down Shadowbridge Hill came the roar of the masses, killing each other. I scarcely had the strength to fly, thus a ceasing spell was out of the question, even though the golem had been destroyed. I would likely need all my strength to somehow get Bren through the Path's barrier.

If I could do it at all.

As we flew through the window, heading for Middle Salem, a tear did escape. It felt cold against my cheek. Was I riding with Bren for the last time? Would I ever feel his touch again after this ride? I sighed, knowing the answers to those questions as we lifted high over Shallym. Even at such heights, we could hear the pandemonium below.

"It's pretty wild down there," Bren yelled.

"The Shadowmaster's darkest dreams are being realized." I shifted on the broom, keeping my good hand on its wooden neck. "We are turning on each other."

Bren's grip on my waist was more confident. Less desperate than it had been on previous rides. And as I requested, he didn't touch my wounded arm. Already, the Shadowcold was spreading up toward my neck and down into my chest and hip.

"Is it a long way to Middle Salem?" he asked, yet somehow I sensed he already knew.

"Middling-fair." I could only hope I would maintain consciousness that long. "We have to find entrance to the Path and soon."

"Jazz, I have something to tell—" Bren stopped, his body tensing behind mine. "Watch out!"

chapter twenty-three

The slither flew at us, just yards away and closing in. Its cavernous mouth widened, teeth glinting in the sunlight. A witch rode the beast's back, her mad cackle driving it on.

"By the Goddess!" Jazz cried.

I knew what I had to do. I knew she didn't have the strength to guide us away from the slither fast enough. All the hours of practice in my hideout allowed me to take control of the broom at the same time I withdrew my sword.

The broom dropped fast and sudden. Jazz gasped, and I could feel her trying to regain her command of the branch. "What's happening?"

"I'll explain later," I shouted over the roar of the enraged slither and the witch's screech. "Don't fight it. Let me handle this."

Holding onto Jazz with one hand, my sword in the other, I used the power of my thought to force the broom down. I circled behind Shadowbridge Manor, the heat of the slither's breath practically on our necks. The powerful flap of the dragon's wings rumbled as loud as thunder while the beast chased us. I had learned from Rol that slithers couldn't breathe fire while flying, so at least we had that on our side.

Where is it? There!

Jazz sucked in her breath as I guided the branch through the grove of trees behind the manor, everything a blur around us. The ground rumbled as the slither landed and smashed through the trees. By the time we reached my hideout the broom was flaming, and I could hear the slither's claws pounding the earth as it charged toward us. I touched down on the opposite side of the stream, next to the Path. Jazz stumbled off, and I tossed the burning branch into the stream. Smoke filled the air.

The dragon crashed through the trees. It was almost on top of us.

"Don't harm the slither," Jazz cried as I raised my sword.

I whirled around, took the sword point and sliced into the Path. Jazz gasped, but before she could say a word, I yanked her by her good arm through the opening.

The slither tore into the clearing of my hideout and released a blast of fire just as I closed the Path behind us. The smell of burnt leaves and hair mixed with the mold and dirt odor of the Path, and I realized the slither had singed the hair on my arm.

"Come." Jazz's voice was a ghostly whisper as she took my hand and pulled me through the Path. I could tell her strength was fading, but she was pushing herself forward.

Shadows whined and shrieked as they reached for us from the walls. I clenched my sword hilt and the silver glow of my skin intensified—and as usual, the things shrank away from us. I had been on the Path so many times in the past week that the moving floor no longer bothered me. I'd gotten used to the Shadows, too. They weren't like Nire's Shadows that had attacked the manor. These were lost souls, not yet drawn into Nire's clutches. That much I finally understood.

As we hurried along the Path, that rubber band feeling around my chest kept getting tighter and tighter. What the hell had I done, bringing that stupid golem into Shadowbridge? The nasty thing had possessed me, making me feel gross and disgusting inside. It had made me lie to Jazz, and I had promised to be honest with her.

I should have been stronger. I should have thrown the thing as far as I could the second that bastard gave it to me. It was all my fault Shadowbridge was no longer a safe place for Jazz. And it was my fault she was hurt and that Rol had been taken.

What kind of champion was I turning out to be?

Ha. I was a joke. I was nobody's champion.

I almost stopped walking the Path, I was so disgusted with myself. Jazz pushed on ahead, but I knew she was weak. How could I help her?

Yeah, some champion I was.

But, still. When we fought those Shadow minions, for the first time I really felt like I was the Shadowalker. I had felt strong, powerful. All the training that I had gone through with Rol had clicked, and I knew exactly what to do. And on the broom I was able to take over and save us from the slither. I had even opened the Path with Jazz right there.

The golem had been holding me back, keeping me from telling Jazz and Rol that I had learned to use my magic; I just knew it. Without that thing in my pocket, I felt a sense of freedom, like a weight had been lifted from me. But still I felt that somehow I should have been strong enough to resist it.

Rol. What if Nire killed him? I would never forgive myself if anything happened to Rol or Jazz. Never.

"Here." Jazz's voice was weak and her breathing sounded harsh, echoing in eerie waves. "Open the Path—I don't have the strength."

Again I used my sword to slice the Path, and sealed it once we had stepped out. We were in a clearing in the middle of a thick forest. I'd been to this Sanctuary during my practice sessions. I'd been to them all. In the distance, ocean waves crashed against the shore, and I smelled a briny odor mixed with the rich loam and pine of the forest.

When I turned back to Jazz, she was staring at me with hurt in her golden eyes. "That was what you were doing all those afternoons when you were alone. You practiced in secret. And you hid your progress from Rol . . . and from me." She blinked, and a tear slipped down her cheek. "You've hidden so much, even after you swore to be honest."

With a sigh, I slid my sword into its sheath. I wanted to go to her and wrap her in my arms, but the fact that she thought I had betrayed her was apparent in the rigid way she held herself. I didn't think she would welcome my touch.

"Look, Jazz. I'm really sorry." Frustration filled me and I wanted to pound something—anything. Instead, I picked up a rock and flung it through the trees. It crashed through pine boughs, and my now-sensitive hearing heard a soft thud as it landed. I turned back to Jazz, my gaze locking with hers. "I wanted to share everything with you. That first day we were at the ocean, I tried to. But I think that golem thing kept me from saying anything."

"Ah." Jazz nodded, her stance relaxing as understanding came into her expression. And her eyes widened. She looked at the glittering wall beside us, and back to me. "You could have left at any time once you learned to open the Path. You knew that, didn't you?"

"Yeah, and I've explored all of the Path." I shrugged. "I figured out how to do it the first day you showed me. I was so mad at you I thought about going home. I almost did. But I realized I couldn't leave you to face Nire alone." I pulled at a thread on my tunic as I met her eyes.

Her lower lip trembled, and I thought she was going to start crying harder. She turned her gaze to the sky. "We have to go to Middle Salem—it isn't far now. Perhaps five miles to the north. Will you call a branch to us?"

"Wind!" I raised my hand and caught the live oak branch that came hurtling from the trees. I had practiced that, too, this past week.

This time Jazz climbed on behind, holding tight with her good arm. She buried her face against my back and all but melted against me. Her exhaustion was obvious, and my fear for her intensified.

"Are you sure there's nothing we can do for your arm before we go after Nire?" I asked as I guided the broom upward.

"No." She sighed and said, "Since we are likely flying to our doom, let me know more about you. This time without secrets. Everything—especially your family. Tell me about your parents."

Likely flying to our doom? I didn't like the sound of that. Was she giving up on herself? On me?

Wind whipped my hair around my face and my sword bounced against my thigh as Jazz and I flew toward Middle Salem. My hair had grown over the past three weeks, and I knew my dad would hate it even more than he already had.

I figured I would let it grow even longer.

"Bren?" Jazz's soft voice brought me out of my thoughts and back to flying on a broomstick with a witch.

On a broomstick with a witch.

Hell, I was the one flying the damn broom. I was a witch, too.

Maybe none of this was real. Maybe I was really in a white padded room and laced up tight in a straightjacket— that actually made more sense. But the girl behind me felt real. I didn't have to pinch myself to know it wasn't a dream and I wasn't going to wake up.

"Will you tell me about your family?" she said again.

I thought about her question, but I didn't know what to tell her. After all this time at Shadowbridge, my family seemed so far away. Which I guess they were. But it felt like an eon since I'd seen Mom, Dad, and Todd, and their faces were becoming kind of fuzzy in my mind. I felt a twinge of homesickness and realized how much I missed them. Even my hardass dad.

"You really want to know about my parents?" I finally asked.

"Yes." Jazz moved her head against my back as we rose far above the treetops. "What are they like?"

I laughed, the sound bitter even to me. "Dad thinks I'm a screw-up and he probably believes I'm a total loser for vanishing with the truck." A lump lodged in my throat, and I swallowed hard. "I wonder if he's even worried. If he even misses me."

"I'm certain he does," Jazz said so soft I could barely hear her, even with my sensitive hearing. "What does he look like? What's his occupation?"

"He's pretty normal looking, I guess." I shrugged and gripped the rough wood of the branch tighter as we flew beyond the forest. "He has brown hair and eyes like me. He was sort of a jock in high school, but after he went on some kind of exchange-student program, he decided to major in history. So now he's a professor at the community college. I guess that's why he expects me to do so well in school."

"History?" Her voice sounded odd, like it was a big deal or something. "What kind?"

"American, especially the colonial stuff." I glanced down and saw that we were passing over farmlands with barns, pastures, and little brown animals that I figured must have been cows. "He has a real thing for the seventeenth century. He has this whole collection of crap, but Todd and I have never been allowed to go near it, 'cause he thinks we'll break it or something. He keeps all the junk locked in his den."

Jazz tensed behind me, and she felt colder. What was wrong with her?

Before I could open my mouth to ask, she said, "Tell me about your mother."

Mom's face flashed in my mind, and I had this weird ache behind my eyes. I could see her sitting in the stands at one of my baseball games, wearing her dark sunglasses. "Mom's usually pretty cool. Always after me to try new things—expand my horizons and all that stuff."

I shook my head and mimicked my mother's voice, "'Get out of the concrete. Try the abstract, Bren. Consider the impossible, Bren.' She's always telling me 'respond, don't react,' and she's always on my case about my language."

I tried to see what we were passing over as I talked, but the clouds below us had become too thick. "Mom and I have this special relationship. Nobody means more to me than her. And I think she feels the same way. She got Dad to let me go on this trip to see my friend. She's probably totally freaking out and has my face on a bunch of milk cartons by now."

"Milk cartons?"

"Uh, never mind."

"What does your mother look like?"

"She's average, like Dad. Blonde hair and blue eyes. Pretty, for a mom, I guess. Except she's always wearing purple, which is too stupid for words, but she loves it." I shifted on the broom and it wobbled a bit. A broomstick's definitely not the most comfortable way for a guy to travel.

"What's her occupation?"

"Mom's old-fashioned. She always stayed at home with me and my brother." I pictured her in our backyard, where she spent a lot of her time every evening. "She's got this huge garden and raises plants and herbs, and this room where she grows mushrooms and stuff. Her horticulture club says she's amazing."

"Oh." She was quiet for a moment, and then asked, "How old are your parents?"

I shrugged. "In their early forties. Dad's starting to go gray above his ears, but I think mom looks the same as she did when I was little."

"And what about your brother?"

I grinned. "Todd's fourteen and a pain in the ass." I pictured his blue eyes and blond hair, which looked so much like Mom's. "He used to follow me around when he was younger, and it drove me nuts. Most of the time now, he's hanging around with his friends or messing with all his pets. He's practically raising a zoo in his room. He'll be a freshman this fall when I'm a senior." I grinned. "Can't wait for initiation." That was, if we survived Nire.

"Where are your parents?"

"They would be home by now." My soul twisted at the thought of how worried they must be. "When I left, they flew to the East Coast with Todd for vacation. To Massachusetts, I think. That's where Mom and Dad first met."

Jazz went very still. "I see."

I wondered what she was thinking, but I was sure she wasn't going to be honest. Something in my gut told me she had started lying to me about lots of things after that goddamn golem.

Everything had changed between us since she had gone inside me with her magic. Since she touched me . . . like that. I couldn't explain it, but having someone that close was almost like, well, sex. And she hadn't asked my permission or anything.

It was humiliating. Even the memory of it made my face burn. And she'd been weird with me since she did it. Like she regretted being that close to me. That made me ten times madder.

What did she find out about me that freaked her out? I wanted to force her to tell me, but just thinking about what she had done made my skin crawl like there were centipedes inside my flesh.

It was like Jazz had probed every part of me, and I felt . . . violated. Even though I knew she did it to save my life, a part of me hated her for it. She had also heard in my thoughts that I was in love with her. That wasn't something I was ready to share.

For a moment I was quiet, feeling the wind on my face. The smell of fish and brine was strong, with Jazz's sweet scent blended in.

But there was something different in the air, too. Something rotten and evil. A stink like sour milk and rotting meat. The clouds grew darker and churned, like a big thunderstorm was building up. But worse. Much, much worse.

Jazz hunched closer as if she was in pain.

I turned and spoke over my shoulder. "Hey, are you okay?"

"I'm fine." I heard the lie in her voice and anger coursed through me like hot lava.

"What's wrong?" I shouted. "Why are you shutting me out? Why are you lying to me?"

She froze, not moving a muscle, but I heard her sob.

Aw, man. I had gone and made her cry again. What the hell was I supposed to do?

"All right, Jazz. We'll do this your way. But I'm going to trust you to tell me what I need to know to help us defeat Nire." Maybe I couldn't trust her with telling me the truth about anything else, but I knew she would do whatever she could for the witches.

"Of course." Her voice came out in a choked whisper. "We're almost there."

I figured I might as well change the subject. "So, are we at the place where they held all those witch hunts?"

"Yes. Middle Salem." She nodded against my back. "The year in this Sanctuary is now 1696, four years after the witch disasters." Her words were tight and matter-of-fact.

"That's wild that we're going to the late seventeenth century. My dad would—" I stopped, strange thoughts churning in my brain. My father had been unusually fascinated by the Salem witch hunts. Why hadn't I remembered that before? It was almost like it had been blocked from my thoughts, and all of a sudden it was there. No, there couldn't be a connection. Or could there be? It didn't make any sense. My dad was a jerk, but—

As I guided the broom into the churning clouds, everything around us grew black and colder still. A gust of wind blasted us. Jazz screamed as the wind knocked us sideways.

I lost control.

The broom spun around and around. Everything whirled. My heart pounded. I was sure I was going to wet my pants. Round and round we flipped. I had no idea which direction was up or down, and it was all I could do to hold on. We were going to fall off and splatter all over the streets of Middle Salem.

No. I wouldn't let that happen. That feeling of being hyper-focused overcame me, even as we spun through the clouds. I realized in that instant that I had always performed best under pressure—always able to block out distractions when it counted the most.

I could do this. For her. For me.

Concentrating like I had practiced over and over and over, I reached deep inside. I searched for my source of magic. Raging warmth surged through me as I grabbed hold of it. The magic burned within me, building and building as I focused on the broom. I focused on stopping the rolling motion. At first, nothing happened, and we kept spinning. Then, gradually, we turned more slowly, until we finally leveled out. Slumping back against Jazz, I breathed a huge sigh of relief. And realized our hair was standing straight up.

No, we were hanging upside down. And we were approaching a church steeple dead-on.

I jerked hard to the left, and we rolled upright. But we were still going too fast. Smoke filled my nose. The live oak branch was on fire!

We shot over a road and some houses—the outer part of a village. It was dawn in this Sanctuary, and people were out tilling the land and feeding animals. They screamed and ducked as we zoomed over their heads. Lower and lower we dropped. Our feet almost dragged on the ground.

My muscles were taut, my jaw clenched as I struggled to bring us to a halt. I reached for my source of magic and with all my might, commanded the broom to stop.

The broom stopped.

We kept going.

Jazz lost her hold on me, and I cried out as I flipped through the air. In the next instant, I slammed into water. It gushed up my nose, filling my mouth and eyes and ears. Deeper and deeper I was propelled underwater, until I finally slowed.

Above me I could see faint green light and I struggled to swim toward it. My sword hit my leg as I fought to reach the surface.

My lungs burned. Air. I had to get air. My chest ached. My lungs were going to explode. The sword tangled in my legs, dragging me down. Hot knives stabbed my lungs and chest. I felt lightheaded. Dizzy. I had to get to Jazz. I couldn't leave her alone to face Nire. Murky green light grew brighter above. Almost there.

Cold water was replaced by even colder air as I burst above the surface. I gulped all the air my lungs could handle as I trod water. My whole body ached, and I felt like I could sleep for a week. But I looked to the shore and saw Jazz sprawled on the grass.

Not moving.

"Jazz!" A burst of energy returned, and I forgot everything but getting to her. I swam to the shore, crawled out, rushed to Jazz, and dropped to her side.

Relief flooded me as her eyelids fluttered. She coughed and clutched her stomach with her good arm.

I leaned over her, water dripping from my hair and face onto hers. "Are you okay?" I brushed moisture from her cheek with the back of my hand as she nodded. Taking care not to touch her wounded arm, I helped her as she struggled to sit up.

"I'm fine. Thank you." She was a mess, covered in dirt and leaves, and on top of it, I was dripping water all over her. If she could have seen herself, she would probably have freaked.

I pulled her to me and pressed her to my chest, because I needed to feel her close to me. I needed her. She shivered, and I wished I wasn't wet, so that I could warm her with my own body heat. "Sorry about that stop," I said as I pushed my soaked hair out of my face.

Her teeth chattered so loud I could hear them. "F-f-far better to land here, than t-to have smashed into that h-house."

Glancing in the direction she was pointing, goose bumps popped over my arms. She was right. It was a big house, too. The base was gray rock, and the rest was white boards. A few more yards and someone would have been scraping us off the wall.

A man stood beside the house—and I knew him. Blood rushed in my ears, and I started to shake. It was the bastard who caused all the horrible things that had happened to Jazz and Rol.

"Jazz!" I got to my feet so fast I yanked her up with me. "That guy. He's the one who gave me the golem thing."

"Alderon?" She blinked and stared past me. "Where?"

My stomach dropped when I looked back toward the house. Alderon was gone. "He was there. By the porch. It was him! I know it was."

Leaving Jazz behind, I raced toward the house. But when I got there, no one was in sight. I turned back to Jazz and saw her limping toward me. And behind her, a mob of people moving from the street toward the pond. A very angry-looking mob, carrying burning torches and wooden crosses and things like pitchforks.

I charged across the distance between us, grabbed Jazz's hand, and ran, pulling her along with me. "There's a whole bunch of really pissed-off people coming at us," I shouted. "Can you freeze them?"

Jazz looked miserable and shook her head. "I can't. Not now."

I raised my hand like I had seen Jazz do so many times. "Cease!" I commanded.

Nothing happened.

Obviously, that was a spell I needed to practice. The crowd roared as we ran for our lives.

"By the Goddess!" Jazz seemed to find the strength to run faster, and I didn't feel like I was dragging her anymore. Cold air plastered my wet clothes to my skin, and my boots squished as we ran. My sword banged my leg. I didn't dare let go of Jazz's hand to pull my weapon out.

Just as we passed the house, I glanced down a small alley-way and saw the freak with the weird blue eyes. "This way!"

I could hear the crowd shouting, coming closer, as I yanked Jazz's arm and headed after the bastard. He ran down a set of steps that looked like they led into the cellar of the house.

When we reached the steps, the door below was closed and there was no sign of Alderon. I dropped Jazz's hand and withdrew my sword, holding it at the ready. Slowly, I walked down the stairs. "He went in here." Clenching my sword in one hand, I grabbed the handle with my other, and started to open the door. The freak's words went through my mind. The words he had said when he gave me the golem.

"In the cellar. You will find the door in the cellar, brother. Remember that, or you will be sorry."

chapter twenty-four

I was finally back on the ground in Middle Salem.

Even now, fours years later—after they crushed my father, Giles Corey, to death for refusing to stand trial, for trying to expose the human corruption behind the witch hunts—the citizens of Salem Village were coming to kill me. They would likely overtake us on the threshold of Samuel Parris's house. How fitting. I would die here, where the whole nightmare began. The prejudice and land-grabbing. Thievery and murder in the name of religion, blamed on witches.

If only we had landed east, back toward the ocean—toward town. We might have had a chance to call Nire out and at least enter the more important battle.

My breath was ragged, and my mind was spinning. My wounded arm was completely useless. It felt dead, like my soul. The Shadows had gone deep, and soon, Bren would realize the truth about what was happening to me.

Dear Goddess. He'd realize the truth about himself.

I ran my fingers through my matted hair, and dismissed an urge to clean myself. Wasted time, wasted magic. Finally, for once, I was fine as I was.

But Bren—when he found out about his true origins, whatever they were—he would have nothing but his own courage to comfort him.

How I hoped I would be there with him when the moment came, because in truth, I did love him. As the prophecies foretold, I had given the Shadowalker my heart.

Shouts of the approaching mob hurt my sensitive ears, but I noticed an odd dulling in the roar.

"Open the cellar door," I urged Bren, who for some reason was hesitating.

"I— I don't want to." There was a darkness in his voice, and I moved my eyes toward him. He gripped the handle, and everywhere his skin met the metal, a cold silvery glow seeped across his flesh.

The mob's roar grew louder still.

"You have to do it." I touched his shoulder with my spared hand, but I knew I should limit my physical contact with him. "Whatever we find inside, we'll face it together."

Bren's fingers tightened on the handle. "When Alderon gave me that— that thing, he said the door was in the cellar. And now, Alderon's here. Do you think he meant Nire's Sanctuary is here?"

The Shadowcold in my breast deepened, stabbing against the remnants of my soul. I nodded. "Likely, yes. If that's what he told you."

A sigh escaped Bren, but I saw the muscles in his arms bunch. He leaned back, putting his weight into the pull, and the Reverend Samuel Parris's cellar doors swung open.

No doubt if I had tried to release the doors, Nire's magical protections would have killed me. The fact that he was able to do it and survive spoke much about Bren's power—or possibly about his identity. Dark suspicions had joined the Shadows inside me, fighting to get out. Still, I didn't share those thoughts with Bren. Instead, I used what few powers I had left to make candlelight in my uninjured palm.

We stepped inside, into a darkness so deep and cold that the flame offered us little but a bubble of brightness—only a few inches in any direction.

Bren slammed the doors closed. For a moment, he cast about, looking for something to bar them from the mob, and then he shook his head. I watched as he grew still, reaching within himself for his boundless energy.

Thumps and rattles told me the doors had been barred, inside and out. Bren paused. With a determined scowl, he raised his hands and touched the wood.

Outside, I heard a terrible roar, followed by screaming.

"What did you do?" I murmured, edging close to him in the dank, sour-smelling space.

"I created the illusion of a slither in front of the doors." He lowered his hand and gave me a quick grin. "Figured it would freak out those superstitious idiots."

All I could say was, "Well done." And to myself, thank the Goddess. Perhaps he needs me very little now, after all.

He ran his hand through his damp hair, his wet tunic clinging to his chest. "What should we do now, Jazz?" Bren's eyes were full of the old innocence, and again, my heart ached. I had to betray him one more time.

If I had known, if I had only known, before it was too late . . .

For my family and my people, I closed my eyes and summoned my own courage. "I believe you should lead us. You may find that you have—well—an instinct for Nire. For where Nire is hiding. And Alderon appears to have an affinity for you."

"I don't want anything to do with that son of a bitch," Bren growled, and I opened my eyes. Silver flashed across his skin, and I flinched.

"Yes. I understand." My palm warmed as I held the light before us. "I've hated him for many years as well, but people are not always what they seem."

"Whatever." Fabric rustled as Bren shrugged.

Desperation pooled in my cold stomach. "People, or witches, even Nire—they may not be as black and white as you think. Just as you have often told me. They might have hidden motives. Reasons we don't understand."

Bren wasn't listening.

I raised my voice. "They might have families."

"There's Alderon!" Bren cried.

He grabbed my good wrist and jerked me forward, into the darkness, his sword flashing silver as we went. We quickly ran ahead of the range of my light, and I realized Bren could see without it. I couldn't. But I could hear. My witch's ears detected Alderon's heavy footfalls ahead, echoing. We were in a passageway of sorts. Not very wide, not very long, judging by how sound moved.

And other, more horrifying noises rose to my ears. The wails and whimpers of Shadows, and their scrabbling and oozing and clawing. For some reason, these were the only sounds I could hear. My gut tightened as the Shadow wound twisted. It was blocking out my senses, letting in only the foul darkness of Nire's evil.

Down we ran, farther and farther below the ground. The dirt walls around us oozed water and black slime. Here and there, a rat scuttled across our path.

Bren kept a firm grip on my good arm, and though I stumbled, I never fell.

Finally, the ground leveled, and I sensed we had reached a series of chambers. The walls seemed dry now. Packed. As if someone had worked to make them more presentable. Somewhere in the distance, a silvery light played against a small opening.

A doorway? A portal?

Bren changed course for it in a flash. He was holding me up now, almost completely, but he didn't seem to notice my increasing weakness. I was so cold my teeth were chattering—from the molded chill of the air and from the Shadows encircling my innards like fingers of doom.

We blundered through several rooms, each more finished than the one before, and at last, we passed into a lighted room. I blinked as the bright glow pierced my glazed sight.

This room had stone walls and a marble floor. It was broad and long—and furnished. Not unlike Shadowbridge.

"Well, well." Alderon's voice was thick with sarcasm as he walked into the light. "The Queen of the Bitches has arrived, along with her trained seal."

"Shut up," Bren commanded, easing me down until I was standing on my own power. I swayed.

Alderon chuckled. "Come now, brother. Surely you have no real interest in this maggot. She is nothing to us."

Light blazed as Bren wielded his sword, squaring off with Alderon.

"Don't do this," I croaked, forcing each syllable from my throat. It, too, was beginning to refuse my commands. "Don't kill him."

"Why the hell not?" Bren leaned forward and stomped, swinging the blade near Alderon's chest.

"You don't know." Alderon's smug expression made my good fingers twitch. "Gods be hanged. Amazing. The wench knows—I can tell. But she didn't let you in on our little secret."

"What secret?" Bren glared from me to Alderon, his hands gripping his sword even tighter.

I dropped my gaze from his.

"Tell him, Jasmina. Go on." Alderon laughed again. "This will be worth watching."

My throat was almost completely still. I worked the muscles, battling tears. My words were failing.

"Tell me what?" Bren asked in a deadly quiet tone. "What damn secret, Jazz?"

"I didn't know until—when the golem . . . —and then when we got here . . ." I choked. Talking was too difficult. I raised my good hand, and with trembling fingers, I wrote it in shimmering gold, even though I knew it could be seen by anyone watching.

Don't kill Alderon without due thought. He is your brother.

For a moment, Bren said nothing.

"You think it impossible," Alderon said. "But look at me, boy. Look deep in my eyes, and join with me for a moment. You will feel the truth."

"Joining? Been there, done that," Bren said through clenched teeth. "I'd rather die. How can you be my brother? You look almost as old as my dad."

"I am." Alderon's smile was unbearable to me. I curled my weak fingers, and wracked my feeble brain for a spell. "Your human father is but ten years older than I am," Alderon added. "In truth, you and I are half-brothers."

Before Bren could respond, Alderon lunged toward me.

He must have sensed my impotence.

In seconds, his filthy arms pinned me to the cold marble floor, and his meaty hands closed around my neck.

Bren shouted.

Alderon lurched, fell away, and was still.

Hands lifted me gently from the ground. Bren's face was suddenly inches from mine, and I struggled to think, to put information together. My consciousness was becoming a stage, and the curtains were opening, then closing. Opening, then closing.

"I didn't kill him." Bren gestured with his sword. "I bashed him with the hilt. Come on. We're going after Nire. Together. This Alderon stuff—we'll deal with that later."

I nodded, too numb to protest.

No minions. My chill grew deeper still. Just Alderon. This was wrong. So wrong. Had Nire grown so arrogant as to believe in victory with no fight at all?

Once more, we moved forward, toward the darkened reaches of the large chamber. Once more, Bren had wrapped one arm around my waist, fairly carrying me, with no comment or complaint.

He still hadn't realized. He still didn't know the whole truth. Should I tell him?

The buzz in my head was unbearable. The Shadows that were eating me alive, turning me into one of their ranks, had reached my thoughts, whispering and chattering.

Other whispers, too. More familiar. From far below where we walked.

The prisoners.

My mother?

Bren was pulsing silver as we walked, keeping the Shadows at a fair distance. I flinched from him, too, but he didn't notice. With each step we took toward the back of the chamber, the sour smells and air of doom grew heavier. And heavier.

Dungeon, I thought, projecting as best I could toward Bren's mind.

He barely hesitated at the sound of my voice in his head, accepting it without question. "What about it?" He pulled me faster. Harder.

My mother. I hear her below. There must be a dungeon. Promise me, no matter what, you'll set her free.

Bren took a deep breath. "Do you think Rol's there?"

Likely so.

"Okay. I promise." He forged ahead, then paused. "That was rotten. Wait a minute. First off, you'll be with me, so you can set her free. Second, I'd set her free because she's your mom, even if Rol wasn't there."

The urge to throw myself into his arms was nearly more than I could fight.

"Listen, before we do this, before this all gets way crazier—you already know, but I'm going to tell you anyway." Bren stopped walking, and before I realized what he was going to do, he pulled me to him, ever careful of my injured arm. His damp clothing chilled my skin, but then the warmth of his body burned away the cold, if only for a moment. Bren's grip tightened on my waist and he pressed his lips to my forehead before drawing back only slightly. "I love you, Jazz. I'm really pissed with you over a few things, but I love you. Just know that."

The light from his skin made a bright shine around us, and when I looked into Bren's eyes, I could see truth in those brown depths.

He did love me. He truly did care.

At that moment, in the very mouth of Nire's lair, I felt safer than I had ever felt. No longer lost. Found. At home in Bren's arms.

I love you, too, I thought as forcefully as I could.

Bren frowned. "Say it. I want to hear you say it out loud. I need that."

I can't. I looked away from him again. *The Shadows—my voice. I'm sorry. It's already gone.*

Bren's embrace loosened. "What do you mean—like gone, forever?"

A tear found my cheek, but I forced myself to nod.

"What else will they take?" His voice was suddenly urgent. "How do I stop them?"

Everything, I thought. *And you can't stop them. But if you stop Nire, I won't be trapped in the Shadows.*

Relief surged through Bren's muscles. "If I kill Nire, you'll be okay?"

I groaned inside. How was I supposed to answer that? In a fashion that would take his hope when he needed it most? With an outright lie?

Thinking of the promise of Talamadden, I chose a compromise. *In a manner of speaking, yes. I'll be okay.*

Bren's eyes narrowed. He sensed something. I was sure of it. But his heart blinded him to the truth.

"Fine. Good." He let me go, then looped his arm under mine, lifting me up and sharing his strength as he marched me toward yet another chamber. "Let's take care of this and get out of here."

The chill in the air deepened, and the Shadows creeping through my body began to wriggle and itch. The original site in my arm writhed, and if I could have spoken, I would have screamed. As it was, I pulled back.

My strength was not enough to stop Bren.

"What?" he mumbled as we neared the next open doorway.

I have a suspicion. I tried to slow Bren down again, to no avail. *Something I think you should know about Nire before you face the Shadowmaster in battle.*

"All I want to know is how to kill the bastard." Bren lumbered forward, jerking me into the darkness, and into an even larger and danker marble room. The floor seemed to glow and slither—with magic, not creatures.

This was it. We had entered the heart of Nire's unnatural stronghold.

And in that chamber was a presence, a foul energy I more than recognized. I had been fighting it, in one form or another, for the last four years.

The light from the floor was dim, and the air fairly crawled with Shadows. They snapped and hissed, closing in on us but falling back when Bren let his silver glow to flare. His eyes blazed with purpose. "I think we're in the right place, Jazz. Just tell me how to finish the job, and I'll get it done."

"You were never one for thinking," said a voice from deep within the Shadows. Woman or man—I could not tell.

"Action, action, action. You need to expand your mind. Consider the impossible. That is one reason I allowed you to travel unsupervised."

I was too late.

Bren had come to a complete halt. His chin was forward, and his free hand clenched the hilt of his sword. "Is that Nire?" he asked.

I don't know, I thought. But I was fairly certain it was.

"Of course, of course." Nire's voice rang in the silence. "Welcome, Brenden."

My arm was still intertwined with Bren's, and I felt him freeze as he realized what I had been suspecting.

A strangled cry escaped his throat. He dropped me and fell to his knees. The last thing I heard before I fainted was his agonized cry.

"No!"

chapter twenty-five

A force drove me down. Pain stabbed my legs when my knees slammed into the glowing stone floor, yet I barely felt it. My sword clattered beside me, the sound echoing through the chamber.

I couldn't think, couldn't grasp what was happening.

No way—it wasn't possible . . . was it?

"Mom?" I whispered.

"Of course." She stepped into the dim light and smiled, a purple glow surrounding her.

It was my mother, looking about the same as always, but wearing a purple robe instead of a purple dress like she usually wore. I could even smell the sandalwood incense she burned at home, mixing with the rotten-meat and spoiled-milk stink of the Shadows.

"Get up, Brenden." She gestured with one hand. "Don't sit there with your mouth hanging open. We have much to do."

It was unreal.

As if I was home and my mother was lecturing me about trying new things and keeping my room clean. A part of me wanted to run to Mom and hug her, because I was so happy to see her. I wanted her to tell me that everything would be okay, that it was all just a nightmare.

But I knew it was all too real.

Except my mom couldn't be Nire.

I shook my head, thoughts rattling inside like marbles, and I grabbed the hilt of my sword. It scraped along the slithering floor as I dragged it to me. "No. My mother is not some monster named Nire. You're just pretending to be my mom. Well, it's not going to work because I'm going to kill you, you evil bastard."

Mom snapped her lips shut, forming that same straight line, like whenever she had enough of my big mouth. "Heroism and self-sacrifice," she said after a moment. "Well. You're trying new things—finally. Considering the impossible. Just consider this, consider me—my power. *Our* power. Give it a moment to sink in."

I swallowed hard, chills rolling down my spine. "Jazz. Tell me this isn't my mother."

Blood froze in my veins when Jazz didn't reply, even in my head. I glanced down to see her lying on the floor, and my heart stopped. Was she okay? Did Nire do something to her?

"I told you to get up, Brenden," my mother—Nire—said, her voice tight with impatience.

My body automatically responded to the mother voice, just like I was at home. But as I stood, I gripped my sword. Silver flashed along its length and glittered on my skin. Mom-Nire flinched, as if the glow bothered her eyes.

Shadows skittered deeper into the darkest corners, making hissing and popping noises. My damp clothing felt sticky and heavy against my body.

She raised her chin and held my gaze. I had grown so much the past couple of years that I was a good head taller than her, and she had to look up at me.

Clenching my weapon's handle with both hands, I gritted my teeth. "What did you do to Jazz, and where's my mom?"

Mom-Nire's face softened, and she gave me the same smile that she always did when she caught me doing something good. "Search in your heart, my Brenny-boy. You know I'm your mother."

Brenny-boy. Mom hadn't called me that for so long, I had almost forgotten about it. I had made her stop when I was in third grade because I was too old for a baby nickname. Even without her calling me Brenny-boy, in my heart I did know. The person standing in front of me was my mother, the woman who had raised me, kissed my scrapes when I was little, encouraged me and told me I could do anything I put my mind to doing.

Expand your mind. Consider the impossible.

The one person on Earth I belonged with, the one person I would have done anything for—before leaving on that trip to San Diego.

But now I didn't even know who she was.

A lump crowded my throat and an ache lodged in my chest. *No, God, please no. Don't let this be happening.*

I forced myself to speak, still holding my sword at the ready. "I— I don't understand."

She smiled. "This is all part of the plan, Brenny-boy."

"Don't call me that again. Ever." Anger sparked within me, growing until it blotted out everything else, and my skin and sword glowed even brighter. Shadows screeched from their corners. "Are you telling me that my whole life has been a lie? Every goddamn bit of it?"

"Brenden!" Even as she flinched from my silver glow, her blue eyes flashed and she scowled. "Do not use that kind of language."

In that moment, I saw her resemblance to Alderon as clear as day. Why hadn't I recognized it before? And my nightmares, the vision. I had sensed something familiar about the evil being, and now I knew why. All the pieces were falling into place. That had to have been what Jazz had found inside me—that I was part oldeFolke. Not fully human.

And that I was related to Nire.

No wonder Jazz didn't trust me anymore.

Fury burned in my gut, and I gripped my sword tighter. "We're way beyond you bitching about my swearing, Mom. You have a helluva lot of explaining to do."

Her face turned a darker shade of red than I'd ever seen it get when she was pissed with me.

She opened her mouth as if to reprimand me again, then snapped it shut. As she smoothed the folds of her robe, I could tell she was trying to get a grip on her composure.

"I am your mother, and you will treat me with respect." Mom-Nire's hands twitched at her sides, and purple sparks dripped from her fingertips like in my dream of Nire, and in the vision. "I have raised you well and kindly, and I owe you no explanations. However, in order to satisfy your curiosity, so that we may proceed, I will tell you what is necessary."

I wanted to check on Jazz, but I was afraid to let my guard down. I kept my eyes trained on Mom-Nire. "First tell me where Dad and Todd are."

"At this time they are safe, in the dungeon." She gestured toward a doorway on the far side of the room, guarded by countless Shadows. "Your father proved to be so much useless baggage, and Todd has not yet grown into his own powers. He is of no use to us at this time."

No.

No, no, no!

Light blasted out of my arms, my hands, even from the tip of the sword. A few shadows fell forward, shrieking as they dissolved.

Nire seemed unaffected. She had that mom-knows-all look on her face as she insulted my dad, and my brain felt like it was twisting in on itself.

Dad was supposed to be the bad guy, not Mom. Everything was so screwed up; I didn't know what to think. My arms were aching from holding the sword. I lowered it to let the blood flow, but kept my stance ready for the slightest movement by Mom-Nire or the Shadows that were inching closer and closer.

I couldn't believe it. I was worried about protecting myself from my mother.

"What about Jazz's mother and Rol?" I asked as I tried to work it all out in my mind. "Are they in that dungeon and are they going to be okay?"

"To answer your question, yes, at this time Jasmina's mother and training master are in the dungeon." Mom-Nire narrowed her eyes. "But that's irrelevant. I have allowed them to live only to lure the Queen of the Witches here, to me. Now that she has arrived, they are of no further consequence. They must be eradicated."

Allowed them to live? Eradicated?

I blinked, trying to absorb what she was saying. "You—you really kill people?"

She returned my stare, her face as calm as if we were discussing my day at school and the C- I got on my term paper. "I do whatever is necessary to rid civilization of this blight. Of witches who don't know their own power and others who are nothing more than warts on the face of Earth."

It was too much. "You— you're a murderer?"

"Of course not." Mom-Nire sniffed. "I am merely attempting to bring this world to what it once was, and exterminate all that is unclean and unsuitable."

"Oh, God." I dragged my free hand over my face, my mind and soul wanting to refuse that last bit of information. "You really are a freakin' Hitler. Like some crazy kind of witch-Nazi."

"I am not a Nazi." Mom-Nire's face turned almost as purple as her robe. Her purple aura flared brighter, and her hands shook and twitched at her sides. "And I am certainly not a witch. I am the most ancient of the oldeFolke. I have seen Earth change over the centuries from the peace and quiet wisdom of my people, from the total joining we shared with the universe, to the weak magic and war practiced by this . . . this filth." Her face twisted into a scowl as she pointed to Jazz's still form.

Fire burned in my head. "Don't talk about Jazz that way." Power surged through my arms, chasing away the ache of holding my weapon for so long. I shifted my sword and silver pulsed from my arms and along the blade. Shadows skittered away again.

And again, Mom-Nire flinched from the silver glow.

Was it hurting her somehow?

For a moment, she said nothing, just studied me. Then she gave me that mom smile. "Perhaps you will have a better understanding of your purpose if I explain it to you. We are wasting valuable time."

My purpose? What the hell was she talking about?

She sighed and walked closer, so that she was only a few feet away. "I took up with your father, a human, in order to breed new life into the oldeFolke. To bring them back to what they once were, and save this pitiful planet. I selected him for a variety of reasons."

"You . . . bred me?" I could hardly speak. "Like you'd breed dogs or gerbils or something?"

The corner of her mouth turned up. "In a manner of speaking. But I always knew you were extraordinary. I cultivated your strength through athletics and education."

My whole life had been a lie. "That's why you got me started in Little League and stood by me. That's why you were always there. To see to my training. Not because you cared."

"Of course I care, Brenden." Her look was almost pleading, as if she wanted me to understand what she had done. "Out of my many, many sons, I knew you would finally be the one. And your father pushed you so hard because he sensed your destiny was one of greatness. How great, he had no idea."

My body went numb, and I could barely feel the sword in my hands.

Many sons—I had many brothers?

Alderon . . .

Anger flared through me. I sliced my sword through the air and silver sparks shot at the closest Shadow. It screamed and evaporated into nothingness.

I gritted my teeth. "Dad knew about all this?"

Mom-Nire's jaw tensed. "Not until now. He believed your talents to be in baseball, of all things, hoping for scholarships, I imagine. As if those pitiful dreams were enough for my son, the Shadowwalker."

"What are you talking about?" My rage was so great that more silver shot from my sword, extinguishing another Shadow.

She kept her hands down, but I saw her fingers twitch. "You are the one with enough power to rule at my side, to help cleanse the world and restore it to what it was millennia ago."

Mom-Nire smiled, looking as pretty as I remembered ever seeing her.

I flexed my hands on my sword grip as I stared, my jaw nearly hanging to the squirmy floor. She was insane. My mom—or this crazy person in her place—had lost her mind.

Jazz stirred near my feet, and I heard her low moan. I needed to help her—but how?

And then I remembered what she had said earlier—if I stopped Nire, Jazz wouldn't be trapped in the Shadows.

Oh, God.

I almost dropped my sword as the reality of my choice set in. Kill my own mother, or let Jazz be taken by the Shadows, where she would be one of those tortured souls for eternity.

Mom-Nire took a step closer. "You brought me the means to increase my own powers so that we shall be rid of the witches once and for all. Thank you, Bren."

Bren. Jazz's voice, faint in my mind. I glanced at her and saw her eyelids flutter. *Free the Path of Shadows. And don't let Nire touch you—or me.*

"For too long, Jasmina has annoyed me," Mom-Nire went on, and my gaze snapped back to her. "She is the most powerful witch queen of all time, and her energy will now be mine. Step aside. I will join with her now and have done with this."

My thoughts had been skittering all over the place, my focus nonexistent. But the second Mom-Nire implied she was going to mess with Jazz, I blocked out everything but the choice I had to make at that moment.

I raised my sword and stepped in front of Jazz. "Don't you touch her." My blade and my skin glowed such a brilliant silver that Mom-Nire recoiled, flinching from the light. "I love Jazz, and you're not going to hurt her."

"You would kill me, your mother?" she asked, her voice—my mom's voice—filled with pain, as if I had betrayed her.

My gut twisted. No. She had betrayed me.

But could I kill my own mother? How could anyone be forced to make that choice?

"Don't come near Jazz or me," I said, grasping for straws and time. I had to make a decision—had to figure out what to do next. What kind of choice did I have? I loved Jazz. I loved my mom. Jazz represented the good in the world. And I had just learned that my mom was a mass murderer.

My mind raced, searching for a solution. A class discussion on Adolf Hitler popped into my mind. Our history teacher had asked the question: If we knew what Hitler was going to do, but had the chance to kill him before he brutally exterminated all those people, would we do it? Would we kill him?

Most of the class, including me, said hell yes!

Yet, here I faced the same question, only it applied to my mother and not some dictator from a history book. My mom, who was really an ancient being who had killed thousands of witches and humans, and planned to kill more.

And planned to have me help her do it.

Mom-Nire's robes flared around her form as she stepped closer and held out her hand. "Come, Brenden. It is time to help me, as you have now fully come into your powers. When I take Jasmina's energy, you and I together will be invincible."

I narrowed my gaze. My skin pulsed silver, and Mom-Nire stopped moving toward me. But purple sparks continued to drip from her fingertips, as if she was prepared to battle me if she had to.

"Do you have any idea how powerful you can be?" She tilted her head, and it reminded me of all the times she told me I could be the best player on my baseball team as long as I believed in myself. And expanded my mind. And considered the impossible. "The magic within you often skips generation after generation after generation. You are the first in countless centuries to have powers that rival my own. At my side, you will be revered and respected, and all will bow down to you."

This time I stepped toward Mom-Nire. "You can't go on like this, killing innocent people. You've got to change."

"I think not." She raised one hand, the purple sparks dripping from her fingernails like glittering amethysts. "Move out of my way so that I may claim what is now mine."

"No." I gripped my sword tighter, and the silver glow around me pulsed and grew stronger. Shadows hissed and slunk farther back into the darkness. "I know there's good in you. I love you, Mom. Don't do this."

But Mom-Nire's attention fixed on something behind me. I followed her gaze and saw Jazz trying to sit up.

When I looked back to Mom-Nire, she held out her palm. Purple light shot from her fingertips and enveloped Jazz in a shining purple bubble. In the next second the purple light started to turn gold. The gold streamed from Jazz's body—

Mom-Nire was stealing Jazz's energy.

"No!" I swung my sword at the rope of purplish-gold energy linking the two people I loved.

Sparks exploded as my weapon severed the stream of light.

Shock, like electricity, slammed through my body. I stumbled back, almost tripping over Jazz.

Jazz cried out in my mind. Mom-Nire screamed. My body throbbed with adrenaline. Yet, I had never felt so clear-headed, and so highly focused as I did at that moment.

I crouched in front of Jazz, shielding her body with my own. "If you want to murder Jazz, you're going to have to kill me first, Mom."

chapter twenty-six

JAZZ The jolt from Bren breaking Nire's connection with me had shocked me back to my senses. For the moment. For the moment only.

What I had to do was painfully clear, but my strength was nearly gone. I could no longer broadcast a thought, and I could scarcely lift my good arm toward the taut muscles along Bren's back as he crouched before me. But I had to. I had to touch him. To join with him. The lives of my people depended on it.

His shoulders were squared, and his sword was drawn. Shadows hurled themselves at him, two at a time, three at a time. From his crouched position, still protecting me, he cleaved the Shadows in two without seeming to think about his actions.

"Give up," his mother commanded in a cold, detached voice. "You cannot leave this place alive without my consent."

Bren said nothing.

The two seemed locked into a battle of wills.

An endless stream of Shadows bled out of the wall, surrounding Bren. The silvery glow from his skin increased, driving them back a few paces. He lowered his sword and held it, point down, in front of him, steadying himself against the false spell-floor as Nire glared at him.

"Do not be a fool," she growled, reverting to oldeWords. For a moment, I could see the age on Nire's face, and the pain. The endless pain of a creature left behind by time, and by everyone it had ever known. It must be horrid to live forever, or long enough for it to seem like forever.

Then, the look on Nire's face shifted away like blown sand, replaced by the ready madness I had expected to find when I met the Shadowmaster.

Bren appeared to understand his mother's ancient speech, because he stiffened. His muscles flexed, and I could tell he would do whatever he could to save me. He was ready to protect me from his mother, even if it meant his own death.

No human, or half-human—no being of any sort—should be forced into such a position.

My fingers twitched with the effort of inching toward him. If I could reach him, I could end his torment—and my own, and perhaps Nire's as well.

For the Shadowmaster was in torment. No amount of insane rage could mask the tortured gleam in her blue eyes.

Nire's world had moved on without her, rejected her. It killed everything she loved until she could love nothing beyond her fantasy of restoring the past. Though I couldn't agree with her methods, I understood what she wanted—and why—at a level so deep it made my heart cry.

I ached for her, and for Bren.

"Get out of my way, Brenden." Nire's words were a snarl wrapped in growls.

"I'm not moving." Bren's voice was deadly quiet. There was no hint of his usual giddiness or energy. Only a flat power. The fine silver edge had enveloped his skin now, somehow different than before. It hummed around the Shadowalker like a shield.

Nire should have been afraid, but instead she was confident. I could tell by the deep purple shimmer in the air around her. Nire had forgotten fear, along with reason and measured concern. There was little left of a once-splendid being, and her madness was a sad thing to behold.

"Brenden," she murmured, switching back to English and her more casual human voice, trying to fool his heart. "Okay, you have a crush on this girl, but she's not worth our fighting. If it will make you happy, I'll simply put her in the dungeons with the rest. Now, step aside and let me speak to her."

Every fiber in my body screamed in protest as I forced my fingers forward. My nails brushed Bren's back, and—ah!

I felt the electric snap of our connection.

So did Bren. He jerked, but thank the Goddess, he didn't speak.

My eyes drifted up and down as I let my knowledge and power pour into him, joining our hearts as surely as any wedding bond. My golden glow blended with his silvery essence like a deep and intimate kiss. He pulsed silver, then gold. Silver, then gold.

I was failing, losing everything, yet winning at the same time.

My mother could have never understood such a paradox, but I did. It was a messy, disordered, yet wonderful surrender.

I felt Bren close to me, body and spirit, and I knew it would have to be enough to sustain me in the between-time when I finished, and when I eventually passed from the world.

In seconds, Nire witnessed the change in Bren's aura.

Her scream split the air like a whistling axe, but Bren held his position. I don't believe he fully understood what was happening.

"Step away from her!" Nire shrieked, though already her voice was becoming dull to my ears. Everything was becoming dull. "Brenden, break the connection. Jasmina is trying to kill you!"

Bren shuddered, and my cold throat tightened.

Would he believe her?

His legs shifted. He leaned forward slightly, but he didn't move away from my hand. My heart flooded with a warmth that almost drove away the growing Shadows within me. He trusted me. Bren knew I wouldn't hurt him.

Nire screeched again, and her robes billowed as she swirled forward. Her Shadow minions followed like a filthy cloud.

"Stop," Bren said.

The command tone was unmistakable. I could almost hear my voice mingled with his.

Nire froze, her expression bewildered. Around her, Shadows fell to the floor like stiff refuse. I saw the Shadowmaster's teeth clench as she fought against the spell and rose above it, lurching toward us.

But it was too late.

The last of my essence drained into Bren. The powers and knowledge that were essentially me were now his forever, given freely of my love, and accepted freely because of his love for me.

My hand fell away from him, and he stood. His sword was firmly in hand, and he glanced over his shoulder, locking eyes with me.

With the last ounce of outward strength I possessed, I smiled at him.

That seemed to be all he needed.

Bren whirled on Nire, and as he had several times before, he seemed to grow. Larger and larger. Tapping into the pool of his incredible powers—and now, mine as well. The silver that once glittered around him flared. Shadows exploded or shimmered and disappeared—released from bondage, thank the Goddess.

Nire's screams of frustration filled the air.

The Shadowalker's voice was deep when he spoke, and his words echoed from the cold chamber walls. "I'll tell you one more time, Mom. Back away. I won't kill you, but I won't let you touch Jazz or me."

My blurred vision caught the purple streaks of Nire, swaying in place. She seemed to be weighing her options. Deciding. If any but her own favored son had stood between the Shadowmaster and me, such a being would have no doubt perished in some horrid fashion. But Nire cared for Bren. She had plans for him. That was obvious, even as she risked another step toward him.

Bren's gaze took in our surroundings in one sweeping glance. Understanding lit his handsome face, and I knew that everything from his countless hours of training with Rol and our discussions had fallen into place.

With a bellow that caused the remainder of the Shadows to flee or disintegrate, Bren raised his sword and brought it crashing point first into the false spell-floor in front of his mother.

Nire's Sanctuary rocked as the spell-binding cracked. Fissures snapped in every direction, the sound like gunfire.

But the spells did not break.

The Shadowmaster swayed again, this time because the unnatural floor bucked and twisted. She raised her hands, the purple sparks growing between them until a ball of energy formed. But then the floor bucked so hard the Shadowmaster lost her footing and stumbled back. The energy ball dropped to the floor and burned through it until it vanished.

The Shadowalker was steady on his feet. His stature and his glow only grew as he held his sword in both fists and hacked at the false walls, the spelled ceiling—at the very core of Nire's dark energy, her binding spells. The origin of the dark chains enslaving the Path.

He moved so quickly Nire didn't have a chance to regain her composure or her footing.

The stone hiding the essence of the walls and ceiling split and crumbled, turning to dust, revealing more and more bands of Nire's dark magic. Her containment spells shone like sparkling obsidian, woven through the glittering gold threads of the Path my father and I had established.

Bren didn't hesitate. His face reflected an intense concentration as he raised his sword, ready to slice into the fabric of the Path of Shadows.

"Stop!" Nire commanded in oldeWords, but her spell had no impact on her son. Just as my commands had never affected him when he was concentrating.

Without a flicker in his focus, Bren raised his sword higher still, and with a single mighty stroke, his blade met Nire's bonds.

The crack of thunder filled the room, and a stench like charred flesh attacked my nose.

Bren's sword was wrenched from his hands. A force flung him backward and he landed on the buckling floor.

All went still.

The spells were intact. Shaken, but intact.

Goddess save us.

He failed to free the Path of Shadows.

My eyes closed, but my heart felt strangely at peace. We had failed, but we had failed with our best effort. Who could ask more of us than that?

And Bren.

Brave Bren.

Every flaw, every fault, every imperfection—he was splendid. Bren was the truest champion I had ever known.

chapter twenty-seven

For a fraction of a second, I was too stunned to move. My muscles still vibrated from the impact of my sword slamming against the containment bonds holding Nire's hideout to Salem—and to the Path.

As the room shuddered to a stop, Mom-Nire held out her hand. She summoned my sword with a purple rope of power.

It rose from the floor and shot toward her.

"No!" At the same time I scrambled to my feet, I commanded my sword to return to me just as I had practiced with branches and rocks in my hideout. The weapon halted in midair, our magics battling for it.

Thanks to years of physical training, I had at least one thing Mom-Nire didn't—athletic ability. With the force of my magic, I mentally held the sword in place while I leapt toward it and snatched it from the air.

Mom-Nire shrieked. Purple energy grew around her, pulsing so strong that a few stray rocks falling from the ceiling simply bounced off the glow. "Very well, Brenden. I have given you many chances to prove yourself to me. I shall contain you with your father and brother until you realize your destiny." Her voice lowered, and she added, as if it pained her to say it, "If then you still fail to join me, I shall be forced to slay you."

"Mom?" My heart clenched, and a part of my soul withered and died. "You— you would kill me?" I hadn't really believed it until that moment. My own mother.

Stones rained from the ceiling as the spell-room's covering started to collapse. Mom-Nire's eyes filled with misery as she raised her hand and spoke in that ancient language I somehow understood. "I do not wish to. I love you more than I have loved any of my sons. But I cannot allow you to stand in the way of what must be done. The decision is now yours, for I have no other choice."

Gripping my sword hilt tighter, my eyes rested on Jazz's beautiful face as she lay unconscious at my feet. I knew there was never a doubt of what my choice would be. I might fail, but I wouldn't give in. And I wouldn't stop trying.

I swallowed past the pain lodged in my throat as I looked back to Mom-Nire. "I love you, Mom. But I could never do what you're asking. I can't murder innocent people. These witches and others have a right to live, just as much as you do." Begging with my heart and soul, I said, "Please. Stop this now. There's no reason why we can't all live together in peace. Join the witches, Mom. Please."

Her body visibly shuddered with the force of her sigh. "I am truly sorry, my son." She splayed the fingers of her hand and shouted, "Cease!"

Everything around us went still. Rocks stopped falling from the ceiling. The room stopped shuddering. All was completely silent. Only I remained untouched by her spell.

When Nire saw that I was unaffected, her eyes widened and her lips parted in surprise. Like with Jazz, her commands had no power over me when I was focused. But I knew she could use her magic to hurt me in other ways if I wasn't careful.

Mom-Nire's face darkened as she screamed, "Bind!"

Purple ropes of her power streamed from her just like they had in my nightmares, and then they began to swirl around me. In a reflexive movement, I swept my blade through the cords. They dropped away, writhing on the floor like jeweled snakes.

"It can't be. Your powers—" Nire straightened, her face hardening, no longer the soft features of my mother. For the first time, I glimpsed the ancient being that lived inside the youthful shell—the creature who truly belonged nowhere in the modern world.

Mom-Nire lifted both arms and held her palms outward.

Purple bled from her fingertips, hovering before her hands. My heart pounded, and I readied my sword as dark light condensed and grew into a glittering fireball. This one grew much bigger than the one she had dropped before.

With a flick of her finger, the ball raced toward me.

I swung my blade. Sparks exploded and bits of the fire-ball landed on my skin. It burned like acid, and I shouted from the pain.

I didn't have time to dwell on it. Mom-Nire flung another fireball at me, and another. They sizzled through the air, the sound like frying bacon, the smell like burning electronics.

Years of baseball training and weeks of swordplay with Rol made my actions automatic. My magic intensified as I batted away one fireball after another, sending them careening around the room. Power filled me, and my focus magnified. But the fireballs were coming faster and faster.

A fireball slipped past my blade. It caught me on my right cheek. Intense pain rocked me, searing my skin. My eyes watered, and I could smell my own burnt flesh.

I barely managed to deflect the next fireball. This time I swung the broadside of my sword and knocked the ball straight back at Mom-Nire. Her robes caught fire. The room filled with the acrid odor of burning cloth.

"Damn the fates!" she shrieked.

My face was in so much pain that it was almost enough to drive me to my knees. I forced myself to ignore it as I watched my mother use magic to put out the fire on her robes. I never lowered my sword, no matter how much my arms ached.

It was then that I noticed the Shadows. They had crept so close they were within just a few inches of me. Hadn't Mom-Nire's order to cease worked on them? Or were these new Shadows, come to replace the ones she had commanded and I had destroyed?

I pushed all thoughts away and swung my sword in a disciplined arc. Silver burst from my weapon and seared every Shadow I could see. Screams filled the room and their stink intensified.

I didn't take time to think about anything. I squared off with the Shadowmaster, ready to take on whatever she threw at me.

Smoke swirled within Mom-Nire's purple glow. She clenched her fists and stared at me, no doubt thinking of what else she could do to contain me.

Or kill me.

Nire's blue eyes turned to ice, and I was sure she was going to hurl some kind of death spell. "Your father has been right all along," she said after a moment of silence, sounding very much like my human mom, the one from my memories. The one who wasn't real. "You're irresponsible, Brenden. You'll never change."

My gut twisted to hear my mom say those words, and my father's voice echoed in my head, "Brenden, you're too impulsive. Brenden, do you always have to be so irresponsible?"

"You always react." She took a step forward. "You've never learned how to respond."

I sucked in my breath and clenched my sword hilt until my knuckles ached. My cheek burned from the fireball wound, but I blocked out the pain until I felt nothing but my power humming through my veins.

"Look around you." Nire swept her arm before her, waving to the shattered remains of the room. The bands of her containment spell still glinted through the brown of Salem's dirt and the gold of the Path. It was all woven together in a big twisted knot. "You've caused all this destruction."

I gritted my teeth as she stepped within several feet of me, but I forced myself to remain quiet as she continued.

"How could you possibly think you could be anyone's savior?" Her voice had grown cold and cruel, her face twisted. A stranger was approaching me. A person—a being—that I didn't know. "You do not belong in today's world, any more than I do."

Nire, the Shadowmaster, finally came close enough. My blade flashed as I raised the point and put it to her chest. Over her heart.

She gasped as I gently pressed the tip of the cold metal into her robes.

I kept my eyes locked with hers. "If you take one step closer, if you try anything, I'm prepared to defend myself and all witches."

Nire shuddered and flinched as my silver glow brightened at the conviction in my words. I wouldn't actually kill her, but she didn't know that.

No matter how much I loved my mom—or rather the person I had known as my mother—I couldn't let her murder anyone else. I wouldn't let her force me to follow in her footsteps.

"You're a failure, Brenden," Nire croaked, her voice harsh and bitter.

"I used to believe it when people told me I was a failure." My self-confidence grew as I fully understood who I was inside. I had been that person all along, too. Just trapped and twisted by doubt. "Now I understand that no matter how many times I might fail at something, I will never give in. That's what makes me alive—and what makes me belong anywhere I choose to be."

"But you have failed me, my son." Nire's fingers trembled at her sides, as if she intended to raise them.

"Don't even twitch." My voice was calm as I pressed my sword point deeper into her robes. "The choice is yours. Do as I say, or this ends now."

Nire winced as I moved the tip tighter against her flesh. My senses were so attuned I could feel the pounding of her ancient heart through my sword.

Before I could react, Nire spun away from me and shot a purple fireball at Jazz.

The fireball slammed into her neck. Jazz cried out, and I smelled her burned flesh and clothing. And then she went limp again.

Rage powered my magic as I swung my sword and flung bolts of silver power at the Shadowmaster.

The magic struck her like a fist to her gut. It threw her from her feet against the far wall. Her head smashed against cracked rock. The Shadowmaster dropped. She landed face-first on the squirming floor. Nire went completely still.

I wanted to run to Jazz to see if she was all right, but I knew what I had to do.

Before it was too late.

Kneeling beside Nire, I laid my sword beside me. My soul twisted as the Shadowmaster moaned. I yanked her arms behind her back and bound them with her own spell ropes that still littered the floor. I used my own magic to keep them tied.

She moaned and flexed her fingers and tried to move. I pushed her head back down to the floor. "Don't move."

When the Shadowmaster's hands were secure, I grabbed my sword from where it lay beside me. I strode toward the center of the Path of Shadows. Where I could see the containment bonds squirming.

Nire struggled to her knees as I raised my weapon. "No!" she screamed.

I had no doubts left in my heart. No fear of failure. I could almost hear Jazz's voice, telling me she believed in me. Saying that she loved me.

Power within my core bubbled up, hot and molten. My skin and my sword flamed brilliant silver.

Nire shrieked and fought against her bonds as she staggered to her feet.

With confidence I didn't have the first time I tried, I swept my blade downward with all my strength, all my magic, all my belief. My sword connected with Nire's containment spells. An electrical charge swept through me as I hacked into Salem's dirt, Nire's dark bonds, and through the Path itself—slicing it all in two.

chapter twenty-eight

Flashing light pierced my eyes, once more rousing me from my stupor. I felt so very weak, and yet I knew what had happened.

Praise the Goddess. Bren freed the Path of Shadows.

Nire's false Sanctuary had been cut from Salem and the Path like a foul tumor. Smells of dirt and mold spilled throughout Nire's chamber, which started to pitch and buck once again. My neck burned, no doubt a wound from Nire's magic, taking yet more of my strength.

"Fool." Nire gnashed her teeth as she straightened, her hands still bound behind her. "We have no choice but to flee into Salem. We'll be trapped here, in this time, this place, forever!"

But Bren must have already thought of this, remembering what I had discussed with him at Shadowbridge. He came to me. I saw a bleeding slash across his cheek, and my heart cried out for him. But the wound only made him more beautiful to me. More precious.

He lifted me from the trembling floor, and though his clothing was still damp, his arms felt powerful and warm against my near-frozen skin. As he held me close to his right shoulder, his sword still in his left hand, I could tell he was being careful.

"To the dungeons," he rumbled to Nire. "Now. Move!"

He held his sword point to her chest, his silver brilliance causing her to writhe in pain. She turned, stumbled forward, her hands bound behind her back, blood flowing from the wound at the back of her head.

And then we were walking. And walking. Even as the Sanctuary melted to nothing around us. Nire's purple glow lit the way like some eerie lantern.

I faded in and out of consciousness, but I was aware when Bren prodded Nire forward with his sword tip. I felt her magic struggle with his—and fail, just as mine had so many times.

Moments later, I heard the resounding screech of metal as Bren used his mind to open the dungeons. Raising the bars that held my people captive.

Rol's rumbling voice . . .

A boy's, not unlike Bren's . . .

A man, shouting Bren's name . . .

Hundreds of cries, of pleading . . .

Two eyes hovered close to my face. I could barely make out the golden outline as I lay limp against Bren's muscled shoulder. They looked . . . sad. And familiar. Fingers brushed the cold flesh of my cheek, and I knew. It was Mother.

My mother was free.

Relief tapped my remaining strength, threatening to steal my breath. Mother would help Bren. Thank the Goddess. Someone would be there to help him.

"What mess have you made, daughter?" Mother's voice was as stark and judgmental as ever, but for once, it needled me only a bit, not even forcing a frown. Some things would never change, after all. Some things, like my mother and her never-failing negative opinion, remained as constant as the sea.

"He destroyed Nire's spells," someone yelled. "The walls are dissolving. And the floor—look! Torn as if an earthquake split the ground in two."

"It's all falling away. We're in Salem now. Free! We are free!"

"Which way to the door to the Path?"

"Which way to Shallym?"

"Which way to Camelot?"

Mother's sigh undercut the chaos. "This is a terrible wreck of a rescue, Jasmina."

"Silence!" Bren thundered into the night. His masterful voice rang clear in the now-natural air of Salem. Nire's Sanctuary had completely vanished, leaving only scarred earth around us, and the gaping entrance to the Path. "Salem's beginning to break off the Path, and when it pulls loose, the whole Path will collapse. There's no time to argue. Jasmina created a place where we'll all be safe. Everyone, follow me!"

Bren turned, holding me tight to him, and led everyone onto the failing Path. He ran, forcing Nire forward. I bounced against him, helpless as a rag doll. At times, I could see the Path's energy wane, then surge, like power tripping along a broken wire.

Once more, Nire's poisonous words went to battle with Bren's. Shadowmaster versus Shadowalker. Nire's hissing questions stabbed my mind, as if she were speaking with me.

"How long do you think you can do this, son? How long can you keep your mind on the task at hand? What happened to responding? You're reacting now. Just reacting . . ."

A flicker of fear made me even colder than cold. Nire was pricking the center of Bren's soul. I felt each piercing pain.

He was listening, but resisting her magic. He kept moving, not allowing his former self-doubt to take over. Not allowing the hurtful words to shatter his confidence.

Bren had changed. He believed in his own power. He believed in himself.

People were starting to shout, and I felt Bren's stride grow broader. He was walking the shadows, leading my people—our people—out of danger.

If only he could get them off the Path before it was too late.

I tried to muster the strength for a thought, a word, a whisper—anything that might help him, but once more, darkness consumed me.

chapter twenty-nine

Jazz went limp against my shoulder, and I knew she had passed out again.

BREN →

The Path shook and blinked, and from behind us came awful ripping and tearing noises. It sounded like a thousand car wrecks.

We had to get to L.O.S.T.—had to get there before Jazz got worse. Had to get there before Salem tore loose, and we were all trapped on the Path forever.

Countless witches trailed behind us as I strode along the dying energy ribbon, prodding Nire forward with my sword point. She continued to hurl words at my mind, words designed to make me doubt myself. But those words no longer mattered.

Because that was all they were. Words. Words have only as much power over us as we allow them to have, I realized.

The Path shuddered, and my breath caught in my throat. We had to hurry if we were going to make it.

The moment I knew we were at L.O.S.T., I slid my sword through the Sanctuary's door. I blinked as light flooded the entrance. Nire shrieked and turned her face away. Without her sunglasses, she couldn't handle the brightness.

Witches, both human and oldeFolke, spilled through the opening and into L.O.S.T.

"We are saved!"

"The Shadowalker has delivered us to Sanctuary!"

Their cries echoed through the clear day. Clean scents of wind and roses blended with the mold and dirt smell of the Path. Modern pollution even smelled sweet in comparison to the Shadow stench.

"Are you coming, Brenden?" Dad asked as he came up beside me, his eyes avoiding Mom-Nire's.

"Right behind you," I replied, but I didn't dare leave the Path. I had to keep my eye and my sword point on Nire.

Rol was the last to leave. "I will care for Jasmina while you do what you must." He held out his arms, and with reluctance I allowed him to ease Jazz's limp body from my shoulder, while I pressed my sword point deeper into Nire's robes. Letting Jazz go was like letting a piece of my heart go.

"What's Brenden doing?" I heard my dad say as I sealed the Path behind Rol. After that, I heard nothing but the moaning of the failing Path.

With my sword in one hand, I grabbed Nire's arm with my other and started pushing her down the failing, fizzling energy-ribbon. Thank goodness it wasn't far to the Sanctuary I needed to take her to.

"Brenden, it's just you and I now." Her voice became my mother's again. Gentle and loving. "Together we have tremendous power. Such incredible power."

God, I wanted to listen to her, especially now that Jazz was safe. I wanted to believe my mom, but not because I was evil. Because I was losing her, forever. And that hurt so much. Almost too much to stand

My steps slowed as her voice wrapped around me. "Imagine how powerful we could be together. Nothing—no one— would be able to stop us."

Even as I reached the place I had intended to leave her, my decision wavered. Why was I fighting her? This was my mother. Maybe she did know what was right for me. For us.

"Oh, Brenden." Mom smiled and gazed up at me. "I love you, son."

I stopped and looked at the doorway to the Sanctuary where I had planned to open the Path and shove her through. How could I do this?

"Release me, Brenny-boy." Her voice flowed over me, as sweet and pleasant as the song of the klatchKoven—

What had happened with those beautiful and carnivorous witches flashed through my mind. And the flower-headed beast in the ocean.

Jazz's words of warning rang through my mind: "Don't drop your guard. Not until you've heard the oath sworn by their hearts, even as other words spill from their lips."

I shook my head, breaking the bonds of Mom's magical voice.

Mom frowned.

No—wait. This creature wasn't the mom I knew and loved. She was the Shadowmaster.

With the last shreds of my resolve, I slit open the shuddering Path. Nire screamed as I pushed her through the opening and followed her. It was evening in this Sanctuary, so the light wasn't bright enough to hurt her eyes.

The place where I brought Nire was the prehistoric Sanctuary where I had helped Jazz fight off the Shadows. During my practice sessions with the Path, I had explored it, and even though there were dinosaurs, it was green and beautiful, filled with enough food and water to allow her to survive for the balance of her lifetime. Nearby was a cave, suitable shelter from bad weather, and where she could stay when the light was too bright.

And there wouldn't be people in this timeline for millions of years. Maybe by then she would be dead. Maybe no one else would die because of her.

I struggled against the ache in my heart to do what I had to do. Cold air spilled from the opening in the Path behind me. The moldy smell mixed with the unbelievable crystal air of that ancient time in Earth's history, reminding me that I would be trapped there, too, if I didn't hurry.

"You cannot leave me here." Nire's panicked gaze darted around us, taking in her new reality.

I clenched my teeth, trying to hold back emotions that threatened to take over. "Turn around. I need to cut your bonds."

Eagerness lit her eyes before she spun to offer me her tied hands. I backed up until my feet were on the Path.

Reaching out my sword, I sliced through her bonds with the very tip.

"I love you, Mom," I said at the same time I began sealing the Path.

As the opening closed forever, I saw Nire whirl and fling a fireball. The Path closed before it reached me. A sad smile touched the corner of my mouth as I imagined the fireball bouncing off the wall and returning to her. I hoped she hadn't just hurt herself.

Using my mind, I imagined Mom's Sanctuary like a big golden bubble on the ribbon that was the Path, just like Jazz told me she was planning to do.

My heart started hurting again, right in that place it always hurt when I felt like I had let my parents down. But I did what I had to do. And I hadn't hurt my mom. I had spared her life, and countless others.

Plunging my sword into the floor of the Path, I cut the Sanctuary free, just like snipping a ball off a string with scissors. Then I used the pictures in my mind, the pictures Jazz had drawn for me, to shove the Sanctuary far away from the Path.

That was it. Mom was gone. Forever.

In my grief, I barely heard a rumbling. Low and harsh and jerky. Like an escalator getting jammed. The mystical ground beneath me started to shake big-time, and my gut clenched.

The Path was collapsing—not a moment to lose.

With my heart in my throat, I ran as fast as I could, back through the draining strand of energy.

I had to get to Jazz.

chapter thirty

There was sun on my face. And the faint smell of freshly cut grass, and roses. A ch-ch-ch-ch-ch sound filled the air, and I knew.

L.O.S.T.

Bren had brought me back to L.O.S.T.

My body . . . so, so cold. But someone was holding me. Someone was clinging to me as if he could grip my life's essence and force it to stay.

Bren.

A boy spoke. He sounded like Bren, but younger. A man, like Bren but older, told him to stay back.

"Do something," Bren whispered. His words were filled with pain.

"There is . . . nothing to be done," Rol replied. I felt a hand close over my ankle, and I knew that it was my loyal training master. "Once the Shadows invade flesh, the body is lost."

Another hand brushed my hair. "She has always been so beautiful," my mother whispered. Her voice was choked with tears. "Even though she failed to tend to her appearance. No matter. She's terribly young to have paid such a price."

Bren held me closer. "Leave her alone. This is your fault! She was trying to be perfect, for you. Because it was what you wanted!"

I heard my mother cough, a clear indication of shock or confusion. I wished for the strength to open my eyes, to speak and comfort her.

"She could never be perfect," Mother whispered. "Her training, her father—she did the best she could, but—"

"Shut up!" Bren yelled. He pressed his face into my hair, and he, too, sobbed. His familiar scent of dirt and boy surrounded me, comforting me.

The moment was coming. It was almost upon me, and I was determined to use the last breath of the Goddess to grant Bren's earlier request.

He seemed to sense it, to feel the approach of the second when my body would surrender its energy and free my mind for a last few seconds of lucidity.

When I opened my eyes, he was gazing into them. Tears spilled down his injured cheek and onto my face, warming my cold flesh.

"They're safe," he said. "All of the witches, your family—mine. I trapped the Shadowmaster in a Sanctuary and cut it loose. It worked—just like you thought it would. And the Path, I'll build it back, okay? We'll help the witches together."

I smiled, and with Bren's help, I raised my numb fingers to brush his wet cheek, tracing the wicked wound that would surely leave a scar.

He held my hand against his face. "Sorry. It's messy, I know."

As my fingers lingered on the gash, I let my eyes speak. I let my gaze tell Bren that I didn't care anymore about messes or perfection, until at last I saw his nod of understanding.

What might it have been like to kiss him again, and again . . . Bren would have made a splendid husband. And I wouldn't have been my mother, criticizing, holding him back.

I wasn't my mother. I had given up my very self to make sure Bren succeeded. Followed the higher purpose, just like Father. And I was very proud of that.

As I finished that pleasant thought, the blessed rush of strength I had been waiting for arrived.

Immediately, I opened my mouth and struggled to speak.

Bren bent closer, until his lips touched mine ever so gently. A soft, sweet kiss that nearly brought tears to my eyes.

When he pulled back, I forced my throat to give life to the single emotion swelling within me. "I love you, Bren."

And even as he smiled, Bren's face began to fade from my vision.

L.O.S.T. faded away as well. My eyes closed of their own accord, and I was finished. Like a bird rising toward sunrise, my soul broke away from the Shadows and lifted upward.

For a moment, I hovered above the crowd, and stared down at my body. And at the boy I loved. There was sadness, and then a releasing.

I moved on toward Talamadden, lighter than a whisper in the morning wind.

chapter thirty-one

Five months later.

The girl was cringing on the Georgia ground, even though the mob that attacked her had long since taken off to find new people to torture. She was dressed in black jeans and a black sweater, and she had her head covered as she sobbed. Even through the paint and makeup, I could see the soft glitters of golden witch-light escaping.

We landed without a sound.

I kept the veil of invisibility around the slither as Todd slipped to the ground. He was so damned cocky for four-teen, swaggering like he was a big man. *The* man. I cleared my throat loud enough to make him jump and glare back at me. After that, he slowed down and approached her more carefully.

"Hi," he said, sinking down on his haunches beside her.

The girl looked up, and I heard her gasp as she recognized the silvery witch-light shining from my kid brother.

Todd grinned. "So, what do you say, beautiful? Want to get L.O.S.T.?"

I groaned and rolled my eyes. Did I ever need to teach that little freak a better line.

But it worked. Already, the girl had taken Todd's hand, and they were headed back toward me. I flicked a finger, and the veil fell away from the slither.

The girl gave a yelp of surprise, but Todd patted her on the shoulder. "Don't sweat it. It's just our ride. Brooms aren't my style."

When we landed in L.O.S.T., my father was waiting outside the shop where I had first met Jazz. Thank the Goddess she'd had the foresight to build that freaky store so the oldeFolke would have spell and potion ingredients. Otherwise, there might have been riots. Dad still didn't like the shop much, said he wasn't crazy about animal eyeballs and bins full of teeth—but like everyone else, he treated it like a community center.

My dad, at Witch Central. It still amazed me. He looked so different outside the display window showing off a box of rotted eggplants surrounded by stacks of snake skins. No suit, no tie. Nope, not anymore. Dad had a beard. And sideburns. As usual, he was dressed in his jeans and Live Oaks Springs Township sweatshirt—but as we touched ground, I could see the tension on his face.

Todd helped the girl toward a welcoming committee of young witches, and my father strode toward me, holding out a paper. "There's another one. This one oldeFolke, in England." Dad cleared his throat. "One of the hags sensed it and told me. You'd better get there fast; he'll be killed within the hour."

"I'll do it!" Todd shouted and snatched the paper from Dad. Todd whistled, and I heard the flap of wings. Big wings.

My slither snorted as Todd's yearling swept over the store and settled in the parking lot. I shook my head, staring at the two-hearted dragon nuzzling my kid brother's dark hair. This one was red, and twice the size of the one he raised for me.

Todd's breeding program was a huge success. The punk had always been good in biology, and the oldeFolke loved him. Even the hags fought over who got to make him dinner most nights, and if Dad had allowed it, he could have had his pick of klatchKoven beauties—until Todd saw what they really looked like and damn near got his finger nibbled off, that is.

"Okay, okay." I shrugged, gripping my slither's reins. "But remember. Be polite. And take one of the elves, why don't you?"

"Awesome." Todd smiled broadly, and for a moment he reminded me of our mom, with his vivid blue eyes and blond hair. He stuffed the paper into his pocket and jumped onto his own slither's back. "I'll go find Acaw. I think I saw him back near the highway, tending some holly bushes."

Dad frowned as he watched my brother and the slither take to the sky. I could tell it had taken everything Dad had not to counter me and tell Todd he couldn't go.

"Your brother's too young to be off on his own like that," he said, still watching the sky. "He's impulsive and—"

I cut in. "Irresponsible?"

Dad's gaze snapped to mine, and he saw my amused smile.

"Yes. Well." He stroked his beard. "I suppose you heard that a time or two while you were growing up."

"Try a few million times, Dad." I clapped him on the shoulder. "Todd'll be fine. He's a sharp guy. Besides, he's taking Acaw, and there's no one I trust more, except you and Rol. Todd needs something to keep his mind off Mom. He still misses her. I can tell."

Dad studied me for a moment, and his brown eyes became serious. "Have I ever told you how proud I am of you, Brenden?"

My throat tightened and my smile faltered. "You didn't have to."

His gaze avoided mine. "I should have. I sure hate to think how much I must have sounded like our sweet Dame Corey," he said, referring to Jazz's mom and I almost snickered. Sweet. Yeah right. About as sweet as burned sugar. "Never letting up, always carping about every little thing," he added.

Hot breath slid across my neck as my slither snorted behind me. "It's all right, Dad."

He sighed and met my eyes. "I never said it, but like your mom frequently said, I've always thought you were destined for something great." The corner of his mouth curved beneath his beard. "Of course, I was thinking right field for the Red Sox. I never quite figured you would grow up to be the King of the Witches. Don't know if I'll ever get used to that."

"Me either." I grinned but pitched forward, yanking my slither's reins, when a massive hand slapped my back.

Rol steadied me by grabbing my arm. "May I have a word with you, Your Highness?"

My slither growled a warning, obviously feeling protective toward me. "Jeez, Rol. Think you could take it easy on the hale-and-hearty greetings?" I rolled my shoulders to lessen the new ache. "And can't you just call me Bren?" At least he wasn't calling me "boy" any longer.

Dad nodded to Rol and said he had to get back to work. I was glad they got along—it was like having two dads around.

Rol explained that mediation was needed between some hags and a klatchKeeper, and I shook my head. I wondered if there would ever be a quiet day in L.O.S.T.

After I signaled an elf to stable my slither, Rol and I walked into the village. I couldn't help but remember the first time Jazz brought me here, and I hadn't known what the hell was going on. I glanced at Rol. I'd grown about an inch in the past few months but I doubted I would ever be as tall as him, or as buff as he was.

"It's been about five months now since . . . Jazz." My voice caught as I spoke. "I miss her so much. I don't think I'll ever get over losing her."

Rol sighed, loud and deep. I knew it came from the bottom of his soul. "I, too, miss Jasmina."

I stopped walking, the familiar ache growing deeper. Rol pulled up beside me and waited for me to speak.

"When she first got that Shadow wound, I said I'd never forgive myself if she died because of me." I looked away from him and fought to talk past the gigantic lump in my throat. "It was my fault the golem led the Shadows to Shadowbridge. I should have been stronger."

"Jasmina's passing to death's haven—it was no fault of yours." Rol placed his hand on my shoulder and squeezed, drawing my gaze back to his. "You must release this guilt and some of your anger, or you will be unable to meet the queen again."

A tingle crawled down my spine, and I shrugged off his hand. "What are you talking about?"

He stared at his battered boots and looked back to me. "I . . . thought you knew. I was impressed, even, that you had made no impulsive attempt to find what cannot be found."

The tingle on my spine developed rabies. I jerked from the painful sensation, my fists clenching and unclenching. "Quit talking in riddles, Rol. You're making it sound like Jazz didn't die."

"She died," he said flatly. "Too young, from evil intent."

Almost as Rol spoke, Jazz's voice echoed in my mind, from way back before the battle at Nire's nightmare Sanctuary from hell. "But Father was killed by humans in a frenzy of fear—a natural death in the order of the universe. Such a death barred him from Talamadden, the special haven within Summerland, and a possible second chance . . ."

I staggered back from Rol, stunned and furious. "This death's haven, this Talamadden, it's an actual place, like a Sanctuary on the Path, isn't it?"

Rol's sigh made me want to break his neck. "Yes—and no."

Now I did get in his face, fists doubled and ready for action. All thoughts of magic fled my mind. I'd beat him to death. Much more satisfying that way. "Start making sense before I kill you," I warned through clenched teeth.

For once, Rol looked a little rattled. "She would not wish me to tell you—ah, well. She is not here to chastise me."

His calm face tensed, and his dark eyes pierced mine as I came to a stop right in front of him. When he started talking again, his voice was low, like he was scared somebody might hear him. "As a witch killed too young and by evil intent, no doubt Jasmina went to Talamadden, and so, according to legend, may win a second chance at life. But you must understand this, Bren. No living person has ever been to death's haven, and none of the dead has secured a return to our knowledge. It may be only legend at best. At worst, a cruel and evil fancy to torture wounded souls like you."

"I'm not a wounded soul, damn it." The lie sounded good in the bright sunlight. How would it feel at midnight, when I couldn't sleep, thinking about where Talamadden might be and how I could get there.

Rol seemed to relax. "Then we're agreed. You won't attempt some foolhardy search for Talamadden?"

Warmth crept through me, but I struggled not to show it. "Of course not. I'm King of Witches, now. I have responsibility—and Dad and Todd and everything."

The look I got from Rol communicated the teeniest amount of belief in the whopper I'd just told. He seemed to be deciding about something, then went into his walking-statue routine and remained mute.

I was tempted to turn him into a real boulder just for kicks.

———————————

By the time sunset approached, I'd worked myself into an almost complete freak-out. I wasn't sure where to try the first time, but if Jazz was still alive, or her soul was, in whatever way, maybe I could talk to her.

I had to believe we meant that much to each other.

After checking for Rol and Jazz's thoroughly annoying mother, I escaped to the glen behind the mom-and-pop restaurant, which was now the province of a dozen elf chefs.

After Jazz died, Rol had showed me the glen, and told me how much Jazz loved it. How she thought it represented the best of her favorite place—L.O.S.T. It was a pretty cool spot, full of trees and a small pond. When the wind blew, little ripples broke the blue surface, and the sun on the water looked like the gold in Jazz's eyes.

Sometimes, when I missed her too much to bear, I had come to the glen to talk to her, and I pretended she could hear me. I had no idea that she might, of course.

Rol. I'd kill him later.

I sat in the dry grass beside the pond beneath the live oaks. Autumn leaves fell in lazy spirals, settling around me, and the chill fall breeze caught my hair.

I thought about what Rol said earlier, about releasing my guilt and anger.

Was that the key? Could I do it?

I'd have to forgive myself first, and I didn't know if that was even possible.

With a frown, I looked into the water as if I might see her there, but my own reflection stared back. I rubbed my fingers along the wicked scar across my right cheek and remembered Jazz touching it just before she died. Just before she told me she loved me.

For a moment I thought I could almost smell Jazz's cinnamon-and-peaches scent, and my heart thumped.

Just wishful thinking, Bren. I turned my attention to the pond and acted like Jazz was beside me.

"Mom—I mean Nire—I still can't get past that," I told the tiny waves on the water's surface, deciding just talking like I always did might be the best approach. "I've written down everything I know about her and given copies to the oldeFolke, so if she ever shows back up again, maybe they can keep her contained." I sighed. "Dad divorced her not long after I—uh—cut her loose. What else could he do?

"I— I miss her, though." I picked up a flat rock and skipped it across the pond. "Not Nire. I miss the mom I loved when I was growing up, like Todd does. It's like she died, too, you know?"

The wind blew, and the waves picked up. A few of them splashed against the grassy shore. I pretended the sound was Jazz's murmur of support.

I bit the inside of my cheek and found another rock. It felt flat and cool between my fingers before I flung it toward the pond.

As my thoughts turned to my half-brothers, I frowned. "Todd and I still haven't found Alderon. It's too bad he got away before we had a chance to capture him. But we will." I scooped up another rock, this time flinging it to the other side of the pond and into the grove of live oaks. "Finding all of our half-brothers will be a hell of a job. It's been a challenge figuring out if those we come across are loyal to Nire or actually good people, but it has to be done."

More waves splashed against the ground.

"Your mom's a real pain in the ass." I started to pull at the drawstring on my shirt, and then dropped my hand. "She's helping me a lot with this King of the Witches business, though. She and Dad argue all the time, but I'm afraid that deep down, he really likes her. Kind of like us. Opposites attracting, and all that garbage."

The fall breeze tickled the scar on my cheek, and I imagined I heard Jazz's laughter.

I shook my head. "My dad—I never would have believed he'd take all this in stride. But he said if Todd and I belonged here, he belonged with us. And then he made that computer program to help us keep track of witches we rescue, and where we take them.

"The new Path's doing well. I've been able to attach two Sanctuaries." I smiled at the thought of all the good work we'd done in the past five months. "Dad's computer program helps with that, too, since he's loaded in so much history information, and he gives me a hand picking the best places."

I scrubbed my hand over my stubbled cheeks. "Oh, hell, Jazz. I can't do this. Rol told me about Summerland. About

Talamadden—death's haven—and the fact your soul might still be hanging around somewhere."

My voice sounded desperate, and I hated it. Couldn't stop though, not for anything. "I can't believe all this time, I could have been looking for you. That maybe you could have been talking to me or sending me dreams or something."

The stillness in the clearing grew absolute, and I couldn't bite back about ten curse words.

"Are you out there?" I yelled. "Don't leave me hanging like this, you arrogant witch from hell! I—"

My words got all choked up, but I coughed just like Jazz's stupid mother and made myself finish. "I love you! I won't ever love anyone else, and I'm coming to find you no matter what, so— so, you might as well just talk, if you can."

The clearing remained as quiet as a tomb.

Another string of curses swelled in my head, but just then, a puff of breeze grew stronger and lifted my hair from my shoulders. Jazz's scent was so strong that I looked around, as if she might be somewhere near me. Was she there, trying to tell me something?

Forgive yourself.

The word was a whisper in my mind. Was it Jazz, or wishful thinking?

What Rol said—I knew I needed to. But if only I had been stronger! If only I had thrown that damn golem far, far away, Jazz would have lived.

Forgive yourself.

I closed my eyes tight and searched my heart. What would Jazz want me to do?

Forgive yourself.

Yes. I had to let go of the blame. I would never have hurt Jazz intentionally. Nire's spell had been too powerful for me to overcome, especially since I had been completely unaware.

It wasn't my fault Jazz had died. I loved her and would have done anything in my power to change history. To save her.

My eyes still closed, I lifted my face to the heavens. "I love you, Jazz," I said again, this time gently, with all the feeling in my heart.

I love you, too, Bren.

My heart pounded as the whisper caressed my ear and Jazz's cinnamon-and-peaches scent filled the air. I slowly opened my eyes, praying that she would be sitting on the grass beside me.

I was alone.

Yet not. I felt her presence, strong and vibrant.

"Jazz?" I held my hand up, willing her to touch me.

On another path, another day, we'll be together again, Bren. A feather-soft caress brushed my fingertips, and her words floated on the wind. *Don't come looking for me in Talamadden, please. You'll only get yourself killed.*

"I miss you so much." I swallowed, choking back the emotion welling up inside me. "I want to be with you now."

Another path. Another day. Her words grew fainter. *Don't do anything foolish. Just know I love you.*

"Don't leave me." I jumped to my feet, but I knew she was already gone. "Come back!"

For a long time I waited, hoping I would hear her voice again, feel her close to me. Long after the sunset had melted into darkness, I stood at the shore, listening with my ears and my heart.

Nothing spoke to me. Not even the breeze. Anger and frustration stirred within me, mingling with the pain in my heart.

I was going after her. Of course I was going. Talamadden, wherever it was, whatever it was—no way in hell I wouldn't find it, and Jazz, and I'd bring her home, and that was that.

The simple thought of searching for her, even without a plan or a clue about where to start, gave me energy and purpose I hadn't felt in five months.

Her words echoed in my mind.

We'll be together again.

Whether she meant to or not, Jazz had given me another precious gift.

Hope.

To Write to the Authors

If you wish to contact the authors, please write to them in care of Llewellyn Worldwide, and we will forward your letter. Both the authors and publisher appreciate hearing from you and learning of your enjoyment of this book. Llewellyn Worldwide cannot guarantee that every letter written to the authors can be answered, but all will be forwarded. Please write to:

Debbie Federici and Susand Vaught
% Llewellyn Worldwide
P.O. Box 64383, Dept. 0-7387-0561-6
St. Paul, MN 55164-0383, U.S.A.

Please enclose a self-addressed stamped envelope or one dollar to cover costs. If outside the U.S.A., please enclose an international postal reply coupon.

Many of Llewellyn's authors have Web sites with additional information and resources. For more information, please visit our Web site at:

www.llewellyn.com

Llewellyn Worldwide does not participate in, endorse, or have any authority or responsibility concerning private business transactions between our authors and the public.

Stay on the Path!

Llewellyn would love to know what kinds of books you are looking for but just can't seem to find. Witchy, occult, paranormal, metaphysical, or just plain scary—what do *you* want to read? What types of books speak specifically to you? If you have ideas, suggestions, or comments, write Megan at:

megana@llewellyn.com

Llewellyn Publications
Attn: Megan, Acquisitions
PO Box 64383
St. Paul, MN 55164-0383 USA
1-800-THE MOON (1-800-843-6666)

And be sure to check out Llewellyn's Web site for updates on new books from your favorite authors.

www.llewellyn.com

The **Desire Code**
7 Keys to fulfill your wishes for success, wealth and happiness

Pierre Franckh
Munich • London
Copyright © 2015 Pierre Franckh

German Copyright © 2009 by KOHA-Verlag GmbH Burgrain
Originally published in Germany under the title:
Erfolgreich Wünschen, 7 Regeln wie Träume wahr werden
by KOHA-Verlag

The **Desire Code**
7 Keys to fulfill your wishes for success, wealth and happiness

Project Management by Michaela Merten
Translated by Katerina Tepla
Edited by Lorna Smeadman and Paul Parry
Cover Design by Renaud Defrancesco

First U.S: edition published by
Pierre Franckh & Michaela Merten,
81545 Munich, Germany

ISBN 978-3-946547-33-4

Also available as an

e book

www.pierre-franckh.com
www.happiness-house.de
www.michaela-merten.com
www.paulparry.com
www.thedesirecodebook.com

The Desire Code

7 Keys to fulfill your wishes for success, wealth and happiness